THEM LANEY BOYS

PaPa Sab

Introduction

This is a story that deals with the questions of manhood. We as a community have yet to truly define manhood so many of our young black boys take to the street to define it for their selves. This story takes place in the mid 1980s during the crack epidemic in the city of Compton, California. Mama Jo is a single mother that has the arduous task of raising five boys and one girl by herself. Hopefully you will enjoy this brutal story about life, love, pain and tragedy. I'm dedicating this novel to my homeboy James Dunn who told me to write about both sides of the streets.

I also would like to thank my family and friends that have supported my writing. I would like to thank the Etched N Stone staff and people backing my literature. I also would like to thank Shay Fresh for keen eye and skill as a photographer. Last but not least is that great graphic designer Rafael Rodriguez.

Sincerely
PaPa Sak
The Kingpin of the Inkpen!!!!

SOLDIERS OF MISFORTUNE

The stench of poverty lurks in the air
For that little crumb of cheese people refuse to share
Awakened by the screams of the lifeless living
The soul yearns for peace but that dream is not given
So they strap up their boots to hit the pavement running
Vented anger released through trigger fingers gunning
Mamas pray for another day
To only watch theirs sons become prey in another way
The asphalt is deadly untold stories leak blood
Comrades become united under a flag of peculiar love
Where rules and regulations are established within
And boys are taught to be soldiers before they're taught to be men
Their nature says war because something's not right
Warriors ban together teaching each other how to fight
Suffering is normal and pain is a religion
And shame on the one whose tears are not hidden
Despair is common in this insecure world
Where they'll probably pull a train on a teenage girl
Raping her innocence making her hope grim
Stripping her compassion till she becomes one of them
The abused co-dependants finding solace in their plight
While corpse find the cement during dangers in the night
Misfortune is attached to the debris of total chaos
And law enforcement is the foe that citizens want to waste off
Where arguments with allies are settled with a fist
And faith is not real because God is just a myth
So if you are not a ghetto star they'll say they never heard of ya
Then you might come face to face with your own murderer
Believing in a cause of a never ending war
Soldiers misdirected in what they fighting for

3

The Table of Contents

Boys are taught to be soldiers before they are taught to be men!!!

1

MAMA JO'S BURDEN

She had a good deck but she picked the wrong card!
Scarface

Josephine impatiently sighed as the correctional officer slowly opened the gate. He pointed towards the direction of the assigned seat and she nodded. She was craving a cigarette when she realized she wasn't able to smoke. That heightened her irritation as she sat her plus sized frame in the uncomfortable seat. She was at Folsom state prison visiting her husband after another appeal had been denied. Growing tired of the long trips made her contemplate on the relationship she had with him. They both grew up hard on the East Side of South Central Los Angeles. They hardly got along and would fight constantly when he was out. She cordially bonded with her husband now that he was incarcerated but it was really just a façade. She admitted to herself that she loved the man. But love didn't keep everything together.

She looked around as though she was paranoid since he hadn't arrived at the window yet. She was a pretty woman that had allowed life to harden her features. She was only thirty years of age but lines in her face made her appear older. She looked down at her body reminiscing when she was much shapelier. Her beauty attracted men far and wide during her prime. Her voluptuous frame and sexy disposition was the talk of the East Side. But it was Michael Laney who caught her eye.

"What's up Jo?" Michael startled her from her thoughts.

"What's up Mike, are you doing good?"

"The best I could be doing; being a man looking at thirty-five years." He replied.

"You seem like you in a good mood?" She said sarcastically.

"I actually am in a good mood. I'm starting to look at things a little different. Maybe I can handle things better than I did in the past."

"Well you wouldn't be in this muthafucka if you could."

"Why you got to talk like that? Every time I deal with you, you treat me like you resent me or something. I'm your husband." Michael firmly replied.

"Nigga Please, that's by common law. You ain't bit more taken me to the alter. The government decided we were man and wife, not you." She replied. The cynicism was evident in her tone.

"Whatever way it happened, we are still man and wife. We had some good times together Jo. Come on now, it wasn't all bad?"

She ignored his question. She refused to make eye contact and began looking around at other visitors.

"Damn I need a cigarette." She sighed.

Realizing that he wasn't getting anywhere he decided to change the subject.

"How are the kids? Were you able to get that house in Compton through section eight?" He asked enthusiastically.

"Mike we been moved into that house. I was able to get new furniture and everything. Shit, it's been over a year now." She dismissed his enthusiasm.

"How are all the kids? I know Joseph is taking charge of everything and stepping up to be the man since I'm gone?"

"I guess, but I think Jordan is more of a leader than Joseph. Don't get me wrong, they both growing up to be two tough little niggas but I see more heart in Jordan." She grinned.

"How is my little girl Janelle? She's growing up too huh? I remember when she was born and she's eleven years old now."

"Yeah she is growing too fast. She already got ass and titties so I got to make sure she ain't fucking yet. She got her period and everything." Jo laughed. She always liked talking about her kids.

"What about Jason and the twins?"

"Jason is going to be a lover boy type of nigga. I can tell that shit already. But he got some hustle in him though. If any of my kids gone make money it will be Jason but he will probably blow that shit on some silly ass girl. The twins are tough than a muthafucka. I seen Joseph and Jordan roughing them up the other day and they showed much heart."

"It would have been good Jo if one of them would have had my first name." Mike playfully complained.

"Nigga, why are you tripping? They have yo last name. Damn, Mike they can't have anything related to me?"

"But they supposed to have my last name." Mike protested.

"That's why they got yo last name." She fired back.

The tension was in the air. He wondered if she would be this sassy if glass wasn't between the two. When he thought about it the second time he realized that she probably would. He slightly chuckled.

"What's so funny?"

"I'm just laughing because I picked a tough ass woman to have babies with. But you know Jo, I've been reading a lot lately and we should raise our babies better than how we came up."

"What you mean by that?" She glanced up at him.

"I just think that we should have a better way of thinking for them than Crippin. I'm seeing that these little young niggas coming up is taking it way out of hand. It ain't like it was when we were coming up. These young fools today done taken it a step further." He shook his head.

"Damn nigga you act like you scared." She replied.

"I ain't ever been scared of a muthafuckin thing." He snarled.

"Then what the fuck you talking about our sons shouldn't be Crippin? We was there in the beginning now everybody Crippin and you want to turn away from it."

"I can't turn away from it. This is what I got to roll with until I die but that don't mean I want the same for my babies. If

8

they can do better than I did that would be cool." He firmly replied.

"Oh they gone do better than you did, best believe that. As far as them Crippin, I'm gone raise them to be down for they family. But if they become Crips I won't knock them for it."

"Bitch you tripping." Mike blurted out.

"Naw nigga you tripping. The pen done made you sorry for being what you are. I ain't gone ever let my babies feel sorry for what they are. You chose this life so why in the fuck you punkin out now?" She fired back.

"Punkin out? You better watch who the fuck you talking to." He stood up.

She stood up when he did, challenging him through the glass. Her eyes narrowed as she looked him directly in the face.

"What the fuck you gone do to me? I'm gone raise them how fuck I want to raise them. They my burden not yours. You guaranteed three hots and a cot nigga. So what the fuck you gone do to me?"

He stood there wanting to lash out in anger. He knew that it was a lost cause so he stood staring at her vehemently. His six foot one inch frame stood glaring at her while his muscles bulged through his penitentiary issued buttoned down. Jo felt a hot flash all over her body as she was suddenly aroused by the potential violence. She reminisced for a brief moment about the angry sex they once had. That was the relationship they had. Fighting and angry sex brought about the six Laney children.

"Laney, take a seat or your visit will be over." The familiar correctional officer yelled.

Mike slowly sat down and Jo followed. They never broke eye contact. Mike decided to lighten up the situation.

"That's us huh? Fighting then fucking."

She blushed. It was so true that she began to regret not getting a conjugal visit. Then it dawned on her why she had come in the first place.

"Look Mike, I can't keep coming up here way from Compton. It's hard on me and I definitely can't bring all six of the

9

kids. So this might be the last time I'm coming up here and you know I ain't good with writing letters." She lowered her head.

She didn't understand why she felt so guilty but she did. He wasn't as disappointed as she thought he would be. In fact he saw it coming. He allowed himself time to take it all in. He slowly breathed out as if a monkey was off his back.

"You know what Jo, I understand. You shouldn't have to deal with this shit if you ain't up in here. Just do me the favor of letting my kids know that I love them?" He gently asked.

She nodded. She tried to give a lighthearted smile but it wouldn't appear on her face. She appreciated him understanding her position.

"You know I got love for you too Jo. You Mama Jo, the mother of my babies and we will always have that bond." He smiled.

"Really though!" She agreed.

She stood up to end the visit and he stood up with her. He put his hand to the glass and she did the same. As many times they had fought they were leaving this situation on good terms. He paused for awhile as if to take in her spirit then he walked away. His penitentiary walk displayed the heart of a soldier. His entire disposition was that of respect and courage. Her eyes followed him as he went to the end of the hall waiting for the Correctional Officer to open the door. He glanced back at her and that was her cue to leave the visiting room.

She grabbed her purse that was on the floor next to her feet. She felt somewhat exhausted. She knew that she had to come up there to face him before cutting him off. He deserved that much she felt. The visits had been growing further and further apart. But she wouldn't have been able to live with her self not telling him face to face that the visits would stop. Now that she had addressed that issue she could concentrate on other things in her life. The first thing she was dreading was the greyhound bus trip that took more than eight hours. If her money were better she would have taken an airplane back to Los Angeles. Being stuck in Northern California for a period of time wasn't so bad she thought.

When she reached the final gate outside the prison she was relieved. She went into her purse and grabbed her Kool menthol cigarette box to snatch up a square to puff on. Her black dress she wore blew against her body from the strong wind. The sun was outside bright as could be but the wind pretended not to care. Her five foot five frame struggled towards the bus stop while she was getting some relief from her cigarette. The wind wasn't easy but she was glad that she didn't have six babies in tow walking through the wind. The hotel room away from the kids was a small vacation for her. That was the only thing she could look forward to in these long trips up to Sacramento. She smiled at the thought of being away from the kids for a short spell. By that time she had made it to the bus stop. As she sat on the bench she realized that she was just in time. The bus was one stop away from her stop. She quickly dragged on the remains of her cigarette, flicked it to the curb then hopped on the bus.

While Mama Jo was making her journey back from Sacramento Joseph her oldest son was making another journey. His mother was about six hours in her trip back when he decided to roll with the homies. They had given him some Old English Beer and a thirty-eight, six shot pistol. They had already gave him the run down about putting in work for the hood. He wasn't as nervous as he should have been. He was outside later than he should have been as well. His sister Janelle warned him before he left that if mama got home and found out he was still outside she was going to whip his ass. That didn't scare Joseph necessarily because it had been a long time since Mama Jo gave him a whipping that hurt. He would pretend to be in pain out of respect but they both knew he was faking. Besides that was the last thing on his mind.

"Look here cuz, when you blast on a nigga its way different than fighting a nigga. You got to know that you ain't ever gone see that nigga again." Do-Dirty explained.

"This is Crip for life, cuz." Joseph firmly replied.

"Foe Life!" Snake reiterated.

They hopped into the stolen Chevy Caprice and rolled out. Joseph sat in the back seat feeling the surge of power run through his veins. Somebody was gone die tonight. His eyes narrowed on his dark handsome face. He had grown to be a young man with strong African features like his father. They were both of dark complexions with sharp features that were common among most east African peoples. He had the promise of growing just as tall as or even taller than his father. For the past two years he had grown tremendously. He was now looking down at his mother when they stood side by side. He was the man of the house and he had to go out into the world and face all of its harsh realities. Besides, he was going to be a Crip like his father was. The only way to prove he was worthy was to be willing to put in work against the enemies of Crips.

They crept through the enemy's neighborhood patiently stalking their prey. They were trying to follow the noise. Do-Dirty's eyes narrowed when he spotted people hanging out.

"We gone catch these muthafuckas slippin big time." Do-Dirty whispered.

Joseph frowned as they approached the crowd. Do-Dirty had turned off his lights by now. He slowly cruised up on the pack. He nodded to Joseph and Snake and they both poked out of the passenger side window and began shooting into the crowd. It was about six enemies hanging out but Joseph was surprised how good he was with his aim. He saw one fall then another. He didn't know what they had done to him or his hood. All he knew was that they weren't Crips so they needed to die.

"We don't die we multiply!" He remembered Do-Dirty saying.

His body felt a sensation that he had never felt before. Without mercy or warning he seen his bullets pierce the bodies of those referred to as Slobs. This was a feeling he wanted to feel again. The power was overwhelming for the young thirteen year old.

Do-Dirty had driven off by the time Joseph had shaken out of his trance. His thoughts had wondered back to the here and now to find Do-Dirty and Snake celebrating.

"You a down ass little nigga cuz. I swear I ain't seen a young nigga do dirt like that. From now on we are calling you J-Ridah."

Joseph smiled without saying a word. He appreciated the compliment but appreciated the power even more. He tightly gripped his weapon practically vowing to never let go of such power. They dumped the stolen car about three or four blocks from the kick it spot. All three of them were ready to get drunk and brag about the deed they just committed. Some of the homies were hanging out in different spots so they decided it was just the three of them tonight that would hang together.

"Cuz, you gone have to get rid of that strap. More than likely the police can trace that shit. So make sure you get rid of it quick." Do-Dirty explained.

"Where can I get another?" Joseph's voice cracked.

Snake realized at that moment that Joseph was still a kid. But he had the kind of heart that some grown men didn't carry. He stared at the young soldier for a moment and decided to answer the question.

"We gone find you a strap that don't have any bodies on it tomorrow. But what time Mama Jo expecting you to be in the house?"

"I ain't worried about that shit right now." Joseph replied.

"But I'm worried about that shit young comrade. It's probably good you go inside early tonight since we put in work and everything." Snake replied.

"He's probably right J-Ridah. We know you a down ass nigga but Mama Jo likes trippin sometimes. She is liable to come out here with a belt hunting yo ass down or something." Do-Dirty added.

"Naw, it's cool cuz. Mama went to go visit my pops up in Folsom. It takes her a gang of time to get back from out there. I got time to hang out with the homies. You still got that weed?"

13

Snake smiled and nodded his head. He had been hoping that the young soldier would stick around but his mama was a little crazy. Since she was way up North he didn't have much to worry about.

"So yo pops was an OG Crip that ran with Raymond Washington?" Do-Dirty asked.

"My mama says he knew him before he got killed in 79'. He also knew Tookie. But that nigga was West Side while my pops was from the East Side like Raymond Washington." Joseph proudly explained.

"So this shit runs through your veins. But we not from L.A., we claim Compton Crips. And since you live in Compton and you putting in work with us, you are a Compton Crip too." Snake explained.

"Yeah, I ain't from the same hood as my pops so I'm down with this hood." Joseph replied.

Do-Dirty smiled. It was time to blaze up the weed and hang out. They were laughing out there for hours when it dawned on Joseph that his mother might be home by now.

"Ay cuz, I'm heading to the house to get some sleep. This weed make you sleepy than a muthafucka." Joseph said.

"Yeah it's getting late so we all probably should go home and crash. Ya'll niggas C' up." Do-Dirty replied.

Joseph slowly walked to his house lost in thoughts. He just started smoking weed so he had to take his time getting to the house. He never really was a scary young man so he didn't have much worry. He was probably more afraid of his moms than he was of any nigga off the street. His mama was different than a lot of mamas because she was once down in the streets. He thought about his household and his five siblings. He was the oldest of the bunch and probably knew his father the best. He remembered pops sporadically in and out of his life. He was a soldier running the streets claiming his cause. Now Joseph was now a part of the same cause. A grim smile went across his face after the thought. The only way he knew. His thoughts were interrupted when he reached his front yard. He saw the light on in his mother's room and the light on in the living room. That was clear indication that his mother was home. He walked into his yard filled with patches of grass here and there. The house was a light tan with brown trimming. In the drive-way was his pops' old school thunderbird that had been broken down for years now. He took slow steps towards his front porch then paused when he reached the top step. He slowly sighed bracing himself for whatever his mama had in store for him. He unlocked the door with his latchkey then slid the door open. The squeaky noise from the door hinges more than likely alerted his moms. Nevertheless he walked in with his head up. His posture was that of confidence. When Mama Jo walked into the living room from the kitchen she saw it. She leaned on the door frame of the kitchen staring at him. The kitchen didn't have a door just the frame of one at the entrance.

"At this very moment you look just like yo daddy." Mama Jo commented then took a couple of drags from her cigarette.

Joseph smiled, clearly taking it as a compliment. She wanted to ask him where he had been but chose not to. He would have to be a man much earlier than he was supposed to be. She opted to talk to him at the dining room table.

"You want a beer?" She calmly asked.

He surprisingly nodded as he walked towards the table. After grabbing both of them a beer from the refrigerator she sat down at the table. She could smell the marijuana all over him once she sat down. At least it isn't Sherm she pondered. Sherm was a cigarette dipped in the drug called PCP. He opened the beer without saying anything and began to drink from the bottle. She stared at her oldest baby with a mama's love.

"You gone have to be a man now I see. Yo daddy told me to tell you he loved ya'll."

"What is he going to do now that his appeal got denied?" Joseph inquired.

"Shit, what can he do but stay in jail? I got his address if you want to sit down and write him."

"That's cool. Mama tonight I went out and put in work with the homies. It was some shit we had to take care of." Joseph admitted.

"Don't ever speak up on what you did in the streets. Not even to yo own mama. Ya hear me? That's some shit that you keep to yo self."

"Yeah, but I didn't even tell you what I did." Joseph replied.

"And you shouldn't. Just finish drinking yo beer then try to get some rest because you still getting yo ass up for school in the morning." She replied.

"You tell everybody else what daddy said?"

"Not yet. I was going to wait until they got out of school to tell them. Everybody was asleep when I got home except for you." She glared at him.

He was just a child but she could tell that he had entered into grown man's business and would have to man up. If she were a woman that cried much she probably would have shed a tear. Joseph seen the sympathy in her eyes and understood his mother's undying love. He was content with that and she didn't need to say them. He finished the last of his beer then stood up to walk in the bedroom. He reached over suddenly and kissed his mama on the cheek. She was pleasantly surprised.

"Now go in there and get you some sleep."

He went into the room he was sharing with his brother Jordan. He climbed over the junk scattered over the floor and laid into his twin bed. It was only a box spring and a mattress but that was all they could afford. His other three brothers slept in a room together. While his sister Janelle slept in the room with Mama Jo.

It was late for Mama Jo but she decided to clean up the living room and the kitchen. She knew she would have to get on Janelle about cleaning up. She sure wasn't about to clean up after all these boys by herself. She didn't really expect the boys to clean up so she would have Janelle help her from time to time. She could tell at times that Janelle resented having to clean up after her

16

brothers. Joseph and Jordan usually cleaned up their own mess but Janelle was responsible for cleaning up for Jason and the twins.

She kept cleaning until her eyes got heavy. She took a seat on her worn couch to catch her breath. She thought about the world she was introducing her babies to. They would have to be tough or they would be ran over. That was her biggest burden. Raising young black boys in a world that didn't care if they live or die would be rough. She was determined to teach them how to be soldiers. Soldiers she thought. Her eyes slightly closed as her weariness began to catch up with her. Joseph was well on his way to being just that if he continued to hang with Do-Dirty and Snake. He had brought them around his mother a few times and she seen what they were right away. While Joseph went to use the restroom she made both gangsters promise that they would never let Joseph mess with Sherm. They had never met a mother like that. They both solemnly promised with sincere admiration and respect for Mama Jo. She slightly smiled when remembering the incident. She started snoring lightly at this point. It had been a long day and now that her house was in order she could rest. Suddenly she began to shake violently. Her eyes widened as she awoke from her slumber. She blinked her eyes incoherently trying to get focus when she heard…

"Mama wake up." Janelle said.

"Huh, what did you say?" Mama Jo replied.

"I got up to use the restroom and seen that you were asleep on the couch. You want to be in your bed don't you?" Janelle replied.

Mama Jo got up from the couch and followed her daughter into the master bedroom. Her bed sounded good at this point. The long day was finally over.

2

THE HOOD TOOK ME UNDER

I'm rolling real slow with the lights out!
Ice Cube

"Ay Pookie, tell that nigga J-Ridah to come down here quick. I think these niggas is trying to ride on us." Do-Dirty yelled.

A car was rolling up with its lights out and it appeared as though they were creeping. Do-Dirty had the homies ready to serve whoever was coming. Before they could get half way down the block J-Ridah came running from Snake's backyard. He had his arm extended out fully with a six-shot thirty-eight revolver in his hand. He seen the car coming up and he went right towards it with his pistol drawn. Before the culprits in the car could climb out the window J-Ridah began dumping into their car. A few bullets went through the windshield, which startled the driver. He suddenly put the car in reverse and sped off backwards. When the driver reached the end of the block he spun around trying to go down a side street. J-Ridah followed close behind him loading his six-shooter while running down the street. After he emptied out his second round of bullets the enemies had driven away.

He came back to the where all the homies was hanging. Including his younger brother Jordan who they now called Gangster Jay. Two years had passed since Joseph had first put in work with the homies. Now he was well respected as a true Ridah at the age of fifteen.

"Damn, J-Ridah you too muthafuckin trigger happy for me. If you would have waited for them niggas to get all the way down here we could have ambushed them." Do-Dirty complained.

"We can't let niggas even think they can ride on the set. If they get caught rolling down the street then they gone get got. And that's on the set." J-Ridah replied.

He had already reloaded his thirty-eight still walking towards the backyard. Do-Dirty shook his head and chuckled as his eyes followed J-Ridah into the backyard. J-Ridah was talking to this little hoodrat female that had liked him for some time. He liked her too but he wasn't going to let that distract him from protecting the set. Snake was pushing up on her homegirl Tasha.

Once J-Ridah had made it in the backyard the girls looked at him with complete admiration. He sat down next to Sheila sitting his pistol on his leg. He started sipping on the bottle of Cisco he had left on the picnic table.

"Damn J-Ridah you don't want to share none of your Cisco?" Sheila asked.

"Ay Snake cuz, go get a glass from out yo house so that I can give some to Sheila."

"Naw, I can take it to the head just like you doing." She replied.

J-Ridah handed her the bottle. She smiled as she began gulping down his alcohol. She was the same age as him but his name was starting to ring out. He was in the backyard spending time with her waiting until later to go to a party. It was a house party in a neighboring set. They were allies with this other neighborhood of Crips. At fifteen years of age J-Ridah had people from other sets worried about him. He had gotten a reputation fast as a shooter for his set. He was beginning to get curious about having sex but he was more interested in banging. He wasn't quite a virgin because him and Do-Dirty had pulled a train on this shapely crackhead Do-Dirty knew. But he had yet to have a girlfriend even though he had a few prospects in mind. Sheila was the one he liked the most and that was why she was able to hang in his homeboy's backyard.

"So when are we gone be alone J-Ridah?" She openly flirted.

"I'll set something up so we can make that happen."

"You be sure to do that baby." She replied.

She wrapped her arm around his neck as they began to tongue kiss. The homeboys were a couple of houses down getting drunk and talking loud. They were both caught in the moment and could only hear the moans they made between one another. They stood up so that their bodies could touch. J-Ridah slowly pushed Sheila's body against the wall of the backyard garage so that he could grind on her. She moaned while they participated in dry sex. The time was now and Sheila was ready for him to do her right there in the backyard.

"Come on Snake and J-Ridah, leave them bitches alone so we can mob to this party." Do-Dirty yelled above the wooden fence.

This broke everyone's trance as they slowly regained their composure. J-Ridah tried to straighten out the wrinkles in his khaki suit. He had on an all blue Khaki suit with blue Chuck Taylor's with thick black shoelaces. He had to get it together so that the hood could roll over deep and represent. She walked over to him and helped him straighten out his clothes then gently kissed him on his lips. He smiled then picked up his pistol and walked towards Do-Dirty. Snake followed close behind him. Snake was two years older than J-Ridah but they were road dogs. Even though J-Ridah was younger it always appeared as though Snake followed him. They both were down to put in work but J-Ridah was a natural leader. But Do-Dirty was definitely the shot caller.

By the time everyone was gathered it was at least fifteen of the homies going to the party. Everyone wasn't strapped but enough were. They were the set that was right off of Alondra while they were going to a set that was right off of Greenleaf. They hopped in a few low riders and drove to the party.

It was around eleven by the time they got there but the party was already cracking. The Greenleaf homies were hanging out talking to women while you could hear 'Lets get it on' from Marvin Gaye blasting from inside the house. The homies off of Alondra were deep and they knew it. This in turn alerted the niggas from Greenleaf

Do-Dirty led the pack as they gathered to walk into the party. It startled some less brave gangsters from Greenleaf but it only provoked the Ridahs.

"Check this out here cuz, ya'll niggas can't be walking up over here and not recognize what hood you in." Slim stated.

"You need to quit set tripping nigga, you know where we from." Do-Dirty replied.

"Naw Slim, I told them niggas to come. This is my nigga Do-Dirty; I was locked up with him." Crazy K intervened.

Crazy K and Do-Dirty embraced for a brief moment. He walked in the party but threw Slim a vicious look before he got inside. Once inside the music was blasting and the party was jumping. Beer was passed out to everybody including minors. The vibe was live and everyone was celebrating. Do-Dirty watched the young ones do the C-Walk while he scoped out a female. She had hazel eyes with a light brown complexion. Her freckles gently spread out across her face. She noticed him when he walked in leading a pack of gangsters. She was intrigued and wanted to know more about him. Her bamboo earrings dangled from her ears matching her gold bracelets and small gold chain. Her tightly fitted dress was a golden color one-piece mini skirt. Her curves were in the right places and Do-Dirty was at awe. He didn't remember her from Dominguez High School so he assumed she was much younger.

She gave him eye contact for the umpteenth time, which prompted him to walk over and talk to her. His muscles bulging through his blue Pendleton shirt showed he was powerful. His creased blue Khakis showed his style with a one-inch cuff perfectly folded over his Krokasaks. His hairnet kept his hair neatly cropped under his black brim that complimented his light brown complexion. As he walked over she pretended to be shy. She gazed towards the floor but gave him one more glance with a subtle smile.

"What's up with you baby? You looking good in that dress, so I came over here to see what was up. I seen you looking at a nigga." Do-Dirty smoothly approached.

21

"Nothing, my name is Pam."

"Is that right? Well check this out here Pam, you slide me yo number and we can hook up later."

"You got a pen?"

"Ay Pookie, find me a pen." Do-Dirty caught Pookie walking back from the kitchen getting another drink.

Pookie scurried off to find his big homie a pen. Within seconds he returned with a pen in hand.

"Here you go big homie. I'm over there with Gangster Jay."

Do-Dirty glanced over against the wall to see fourteen-year-old Jordan. He was born to be a gangster, Do-Dirty pondered. He suddenly realized that he had been distracted from his agenda.

"Here's a pen."

"Where do you want me to write the number? I don't have any paper around here. How about I write it on yo hand?" Pam smiled.

She softly grabbed his hand and began writing her number in the palm of his hand.

"You need this pen?" She asked.

"Naw keep that shit." He replied.

"You want to dance or something?"

"Gangsters don't dance we boogie!"

Just as he made that statement the DJ began playing 'I Love Music' from the O-Jays. He escorted her on the floor as they grooved to the song. He was comfortable doing his gangster two step while she did the latest dance. After three or four songs they finally walked over to the side laughing and talking.

"I ain't ever seen you around here. Did you ever go to Dominguez?" Do-Dirty asked.

"Naw, I go to Long Beach Jordan because my moms didn't want me going to school out here. She said it was too much shit going on around here."

"That's why I haven't seen you before today. We gone have to kick it real soon."

"Yeah that will be cool."

Just as their conversation was winding down a prominent figure walked into the party. He was one of the founders of his hood and demanded much respect. He was a couple of inches taller than Do-Dirty who stood at an even six feet. His eyes were focused and sullen. His rank as an OG emanated around him. His younger homeboys broke their necks just to speak to him.

"What's up OG Rick Rock?" someone inadvertently yelled.

He nodded his head without looking in the direction of the person that said his name. People literally moved out of the way of the large gangster. He was light brown with a serious acne problem. His face appeared somewhat caved in as though he had been in many brawls. One of his teeth was missing whenever he wickedly smiled. His eyes were tight as though he was mixed with Asian descent. His arms were close to twenty inches wide. Right when he walked in the door someone handed him a beer. He swigged the beer and scanned the room.

"Any nigga that ain't from my set need to know that I'm a Top Dog nigga." He announced over the music.

Do-Dirty seen him walk in but ignored him and continued talking to Pam. He didn't even notice that OG Rick Rock had been scoping Pam for some time now and felt like his territory was being invaded. OG Rick Rock strolled over to where they were at while everyone else kept dancing.

"What's up with you Pam, with yo fine ass?" OG Rick Rock asked.

"What's up Rick Rock?" She replied. Do-Dirty could instantly hear the fear in her tone.

"Who is you cuz?"

"They call me Do-Dirty from Alondra Block."

"Oh yeah, I was locked up with yo homie C-Dog. But you over here on Greenleaf now so you need to watch what you doing."

"I'm always watching what I'm doing. Who are you, cuz?" Do-Dirty resented his tone.

"Nigga I'm OG Rick Rock, that's who I am cuz. One of the founders of this here neighborhood. I'm a grown muthafuckin man! How old are you anyway little young nigga?"

"I'm seventeen, but what that got to do with anything."

"Nigga you ain't even legal. I'm a twenty year old OG nigga so take yo young ass somewhere and get the fuck up out my face, cuz." He dismissed Do-Dirty.

Do-Dirty glanced over at Pam and it was obvious to him that she was scared of the man. Do-Dirty on the other hand was fuming inside. He knew he wasn't in his own hood but he wasn't about to let any nigga talk to him like that. He prepared himself for an attack and stood his ground.

"I ain't going anywhere nigga. Who the fuck are you to be giving me orders?" Do-Dirty sneered.

Rick Rock slowly turned around more surprised than angry. Pam looked over at Do-Dirty and shook her head as if to warn him.

"You better take yo young ass somewhere before you get rained on cuz. Know yo place nigga." OG Rick Rock snarled.

"I do know my place and you ain't punkin me out of shit." Do-Dirty fired back.

"What nigga, I'll…"

"Come on Rick Rock take that shit outside." The hostess who was throwing the party suggested.

"Alright Nikki, I ain't gone disrespect yo house but I need to take this young nigga outside and whup his ass." OG Rick Rock announced.

With that announcement there wasn't many gangsters left in the party. In fact every male in the party came outside to side with their homeboy. Do-Dirty represented the Alondra Block Compton Crips while OG Rick Rock represented the Greenleaf Compton Crips.

After Rick Rock came out of his shirt and Do-Dirty unbuttoned his Pendleton they squared off in the middle of the street. Everyone stood around in a loose circle as spectators. Before anyone could say a word they were in the middle of the street swinging hands. Do-Dirty had to duck a few hard blows to the head. He knew not to lock up with the stockier opponent so he danced. Rick Rock felt as though Do-Dirty was an irritating fly that just needed to be knocked away. He lifted his massive arms and threw a five punch combination coming full speed at Do-Dirty. Do-Dirty stepped to the side and countered with an uppercut to the chin. The blow suddenly made Rick Rock stumble and he was stopped cold. Do-Dirty followed with a shot to the mouth and jaw. Rick Rock fell backwards without hitting the ground. Since he was off balance this allowed Do-Dirty to continue his onslaught. Rick Rock's homeboys felt each crushing punch. They were in shock as the classic David and Goliath story was taking place right before their eyes. Do-Dirty smelled blood and continued to pounce on him until he fell hard on the street pavement. Do-Dirty stood over him looking at everyone in attendance as if say 'what'.

"Naw cuz, you can't do that shit to the OG homie. Fuck that, this nigga got get served." Tango said from Greenleaf.

He pulled his long barrel chrome thirty-eight ready to start blasting. As he started to pull it out J-Ridah had already had the drop on him before he could position himself to shoot Do-Dirty.

"Whatever way you want to handle this shit?" J-Ridah stated.

"Ah cuz, you Joseph Laney, we went to Roosevelt together. You gone draw down on me like that nigga?"

"Yeah nigga, if you trying to smoke my homeboy then I'm gone have to smoke you before you smoke him. That shit was head up and yo homeboy got his ass beat. Then you want to pull out yo gat because my homeboy handled his shit."

"Yeah nigga, that's my OG homeboy. But fuck it, we all Crips anyway so lets' squash that shit." Tango surrendered.

Tango had lowered his weapon and put it away. J-Ridah still had his strap drawn and ready to shoot.

"C'mon J-Ridah, we gone roll out anyway." Do-Dirty announced.

At that moment while everyone was walking to their cars OG Rick Rock started moving around on the pavement. He was still dizzy but everyone was coming into focus by now.

"If you ever want to handle this shit again, head up, I'll be waiting. Ya'll know where my hood is at. Let's roll." Do-Dirty said.

As they was rolling off they threw up their set and drove off into the night. When they made it back to the hood they were posted in front of the Laney house laughing and joking.

"You beat the shit out of that nigga cuz. Damn Do-Dirty I bet he won't come talking shit again." Snake said.

"I know huh, next time he better watch who the fuck he's disrespecting. I put hands on that big nigga." Do-Dirty gloated.

"You did beat the shit out of him." J-Ridah agreed.

"Those niggas ain't shit. They let us come over to they hood, fuck with they bitches and I beat up one of they OG homeboys. I bet the females in they hood look at them like they some marks." Do-Dirty laughed.

"What are all ya'll young niggas out making all this noise for? It's one in the morning and ya'll act like it's five in the afternoon." Mama Jo walked outside with a cigarette in hand.

"Mama we went over into this party off Greenleaf and Do-Dirty had to serve up one of they OG homeboys." J-Ridah replied.

"They just let ya'll come over there and beat up on a nigga from their set?" She said surprisingly.

"Yeah, that shit was crazy."

"We need to start having parties in the hood. I mean, Snake's grandparents is out of town so he can have some company but he can't throw a party in the hood." Do-Dirty complained.

"I know huh, instead of going over to them mark ass niggas hood." J-Ridah agreed.

"Mama you cook something to eat?" Gangster Jay interrupted the discussion.

"It's some hot dogs in the freezer. You better boil some water at this time of night." She replied.

"Put me on some too." J-Ridah yelled after Gangster Jay.

Gangster Jay disappeared into the house while everyone continued to hang out front. Mama Jo looked at her son interacting with his homeboys and it brought back memories. It made her think of the good ole days when she and Michael were coming up. She smiled at the thought when times were good between her and her husband.

"Yeah nigga that's how we do it over here on our side." Do-Dirty proclaimed.

"Mama what are you smiling about?" J-Ridah asked.

He was surprised because he didn't see his mother smile that much. She wasn't necessarily mean but she didn't smile that often. She was tough and smiling was an expense she chose not to pay. Flabbergasted by her smile he stood in place waiting for an answer.

"It's nothing Joseph, I was just thinking about some days of the past that's all."

"Like what?"

"I'll talk to you later about it. If ya'll got some gats, you better think about a nice place to hide them as loud as you niggas are right now." Mama Jo replied.

Everyone with a strap scurried off to different areas to hide their weapons. Do-Dirty leaned on his car having the utmost respect for Mama Jo.

"I wish my mama was down like that. My mama goes to work everyday for those white folks and comes home complaining about them crackers every night. She doesn't understand this street shit like Mama Jo does."

"Aw she ain't all that!" Gangster Jay jokingly replied.

Mama Jo glanced at him in playful anger while he reached over to hug and kiss her. He had stepped back outside just before Do-Dirty made the comment.

"I was telling everyone to put they straps up because somebody over here might call the police." She said to Gangster Jay.

"Yeah, I could hear ya'll while I was inside. You know Mrs. Laura be calling the police on us." Gangster Jay replied.

"Boy how you know she is doing that shit? Don't be speaking on shit you don't know for sure about, you hear me Jordan." Mama Jo snapped.

27

"I'm telling you mama it be her. She peeks outside the window when we start talking loud then the next thing I know the police got us jacked up." Gangster Jay replied.

"Well until you see her dialing the number to the police don't speak up on it. You gone call somebody a snitch and you don't know for sure." Mama Jo scolded him.

"Ay cuz, mama was thinking about some old times when her and pops was coming up in L.A." J-Ridah said.

"Oh for real mama? What were you thinking about?" Gangster Jay replied, happy to change the subject.

"What makes you think I want to tell any of you young niggas? All I know is that we had to do what we had to do."

Janelle came walking outside. Pookie was scoping her out on the sly and she glanced at him. She walked up to Mama Jo and leaned on her shoulder with both hands.

"Yo hot dogs are ready Jordan." Janelle said.

"Why do you got yo fast tale behind out here?" Mama Jo asked.

"I came out here to tell Jordan that his hot dogs were ready."

"Well you told him, so you can go back inside." Mama Jo fired back.

"Aw C'mon mama, you let Joseph and Jordan stay out here and it is Friday night." Janelle whined.

"It ain't nothing but boys out here so you need to carry yo ass in the house. Matter of fact, everybody needs to get to going somewhere before the police roll up on all of us. I know you are grown Dennis but everybody else can call it a night." Mama directed her last statement to Do-Dirty who she knew as Dennis.

"Yeah, I'm gone call it a night too Mama Jo. I'll holla at ya'll niggas tomorrow cuz." Do-Dirty replied.

He jumped in his low rider and everyone followed suit and went to wherever they lived.

J-Ridah and Gangster Jay rushed into the house to devour the hot dogs that were boiling on the stove. Mama Jo wondered if she had to buy some more ketchup. She dragged on her cigarette one last time then walked into the house with Janelle walking a few steps ahead of her. She looked outside one last time before she closed the front door behind her.

When she walked inside J-Ridah and Gangster Jay was already sitting at the table munching down their hot dogs.

"Ya'll better clean up every bit of that mess ya'll make too." Mama Jo warned.

"Okay Mama, but tell us what you were thinking about when you smiled earlier." J-Ridah replied.

"Mama was smiling. Yeah I got to hear this. What were you smiling about mama?" Gangster Jay asked.

"Oooh mama, I want to know what you were smiling about." Janelle added.

"Don't ya'll know it's one in the morning? Ya'll should be in there asleep with ya'll brothers." She replied.

"Aw C'mon Mama!!!" They all said simultaneously.

"Alright damn, ya'll some bad ass kids." She jokingly replied.

3

WHEN A WOMAN WANTS A MAN

Even her body language told a story!
Rakim

The first time I talked to yo daddy seriously was at the Los Angeles Palladium. We had gotten tickets to the Earth, Wind and Fire concert. So Melissa, yo Auntie Jackie and I went up there looking as good as we wanted to look. Niggas was on us real tough once we got into the parking lot. Ya'll grandma rest her soul dropped us off up there. I knew I had it going on because all the niggas up there was on me. They were on Melissa and Jackie too but it was just my night. This is before I had all you badass kids and I gained all this weight. Yo Mama was fine back in the day.

Niggas in low riders were pulling up in packs. It was all the way live and even remnants of the Black Panthers were up there. They were at the peak of there fame at this time. The 'Free Huey' slogan was big back then. That was before a movement that you would come to know as the Crips emerged. I wasn't there in the beginning and neither was yo daddy but he was one of the first ones recruited. They hung out in different areas of the East Side a few years before Raymond Washington and Tookie linked up. Times had changed for the most part. People were growing tired of fighting for causes and rights for Black people. Now we wanted to party and have a good time.

I hadn't quite seen Michael when I first got there. But the homeboy Jake had told me that he was asking about me. So I figured that he would be approaching me real soon. I didn't know when but I was hoping that it was real soon. I had to be about fourteen years old at the time and Jackie was thirteen at the time. We both had bodies like we were grown women though. I had my leather boots and my blue miniskirt on that I had to fight my mama to wear. Jackie and Melissa both had on jeans and they had it going on as well. We hung out in the parking lot watching all of the excitement. There was probably no one that was our age up there. If there was someone up there our age they were pretending to be older like we were. We already had it rehearsed. Melissa and I were both nineteen while Jackie was eighteen if anyone asked. We had our tickets to get into the concert so we knew we didn't have to show any ID.

It was so live in the parking lot that we didn't have to go inside to get our groove on. We could have listened to what people were playing in their cars and still had a good time. But we had never seen a live band play before and I had worked in the summer time just to get those tickets. There was no way I would stay outside and miss Earth, Wind and Fire. After about thirty minutes we decided it was time to go inside the Palladium and watch the show. At first we thought we were missing something live outside until we got inside. Everything was so nice and there was a nice little buzz going on at this time. This was the first time I had ever smoked reefer. Melissa was able to cop some before we went up to the palladium. After we got our refreshments we found our seats. Once we knew where we would be seated we decided to find a place to smoke the reefer. We all agreed that the best place would be the girls' room.

After laughing and smoking for about fifteen minutes we came out of the bathroom feeling good.

"It's some good looking niggas in here tonight." Melissa announced.

"You better believe it girl. I wish you had gotten two joints instead of one. I feel good." I commented.

"Don't worry there is more from where that come from. The nigga that sells the weed has liked me for a while. He cute as hell too." She replied.

"Is he here tonight?"

"Naw, I don't think so."

"Well then that won't do us any good if ain't here tonight. I want some more weed right now." I replied.

We all started laughing as we walked past the concession stand. That's when Mike walked up with four of his homeboys. Damn he was looking good. He had on a blue Pendleton, with some blue khakis and some brand new krokasaks. I had known of him all my life but today was something different. I had fell in love with his walk the moment I seen him. It was something about him that let me know that he could and would protect me. I was really intrigued by him after seeing him and knowing that he had asked about me. He was looking good but I wasn't going to let him know that. Besides, I was looking good myself so he was gone have to chase after me.

"What's Up Josephine?"

"Nothing, what's up with you Mike?"

"Let me talk to you for a minute?"

We walked over to the side away from everyone. His eyes met mine and I suddenly knew what he was to me. We gazed at each other without saying anything. I was captivated while it appeared to me he was studying me. He was studying my curves, my valleys and my mountains. I felt a shiver consume my entire body. He didn't have to say a word.

"Did Jake tell you about me?"

"Naw, what was he supposed to tell me?" I lied.

"That I wanted to meet you and see what's up."

"What's up with what?" I played dumb.

"With us hooking up. I seen you a few times over at Fremont and we grew up in the same neighborhood so I was thinking about you being my girl."

"Oh for real?"

I was so excited I could have peed in my pants. But I had to play it cool because I didn't want him thinking that I was easy. I made sure to let him do all the talking because I was afraid he might notice how eager I was for him to be my man.

"For real!" He confirmed.

32

"Look here Josephine, you slide me yo phone number then maybe we can link up. I'll come by to see you tomorrow if that's…"

Our conversation was interrupted by an altercation one of his homeboys was having with some other nigga. It sounded like they were fighting over some money that was owed. Mike's homeboy was the one that owed the money but he was with four of his homeboys. It was a bad time for the other cat to try to collect. Mike put his hand up indicating to me that he needed a moment and not to go anywhere. I had forgotten that we were there to see Earth, Wind and Fire. Jackie and Melissa must have forgotten as well because they were too busy paying attention to the fight.

Before the guy could get up in his homeboy's face Mike fired on him. The punch knocked him back at least three feet. Mike looked at the homeboy that was with him and put up his hands like he was asking him if he wanted some too. The guy with him backed up and grabbed his homeboy from off the ground. Still dazed with a mouth bleeding profusely he struggled to get up. With the help of his homeboy he was able to stumble away. When it was all said and done Mike and his homeboys started laughing aloud. I giggled a little but I felt something warm between my thighs. I guess I shouldn't be telling you kids this but it was the honest to God truth. At that moment I knew that I wanted Mike to be my man. If it were up to me he would also be the father of my children.

He slowly walked over to me as though he had lost his train of thought for a moment. I smiled to kind of ease the tension. I smiled a lot more back then. He walked over and gently touched me on the cheek as if to ask me if I was alright. Not only was I fine but I also was on fire. I wanted him right then and there. From that day forward I knew who my man was.

Janelle patiently waited for the school bell to ring at three o' clock. She kept glancing at the time hoping that somehow the clock would speed up. She looked over at her homegirl Rachelle.

"On sight, I'm gone beat that bitch's ass." She snarled.

33

"Hell Yeah." Rachelle co-signed.

"Ms. Janelle Laney, do you have something you want to share with the whole class?"

"No Mrs. Simms!"

Janelle rolled her eyes at the sharp teacher. Her left leg began to jitter a little as she impatiently waited for the class to end. She didn't understand why she had to take an Algebra class in the afternoon. Her mind was never on school after lunch. But that was the way they scheduled her classes so she went along with the program. Both of her older brothers were at Dominguez High School so she was the oldest Laney at Roosevelt Junior High. Now she was going to have to defend the honor of the Laney family. Jason had grabbed the ass of an eighth grader up at the school and she slapped him for it. Tammy Fields was her name and she had a big brother that had a reputation from Greenleaf. He was about a year older than Joseph and he had just got out of Camp Kilpatrick, a lock down camp up in Malibu. Janelle felt that Jason deserved to get slapped but when he told Tammy he would get his sister that didn't faze her.

"Fuck you and yo sister nigga. Matter of fact fuck yo whole family this Greenleaf on mine cuz." She snapped.

Jason wasn't the one that told Janelle what Tammy said. After the incident rumors spread like wildfire so Janelle had to respond. She couldn't wait to get off in Tammy's ass. Everyone in the entire school had heard something about it. All the girls wanted to see who was the baddest female at the school while all the guys was hoping to see a tittie or something pop out. It was the event of the spring. It was a fight that everyone wondered about but nothing ever provoked it. Who would have thought that in their eighth grade year the two most feared females at Roosevelt would square off?

The doorbell sounded off as if it was the beginning of round one. The crowd of eager students rushed through the door. Janelle and Rachelle were leading the pack of students through the hallways and out towards the bungalows. The crowd had already gathered by the time Janelle made it to the back of the school.

Tammy's final class period was closer to the bungalows so she waited with her neighborhood friends standing behind her. The sun was out in full fashion of a spring California afternoon. A slight breeze still was in the air. The heat was enough to make both females sweat before any blow was exchanged. Janelle quickly made her way towards the back of the bungalows. As she turned the corner she stomped hard on the dirt grass filled with holes from gophers. Tammy had her arms folded with a condescending smirk on her face.

"What's up now bitch, this Greenleaf?" Tammy snapped.

Janelle didn't take the time to respond. She walked up on Tammy and once she was in arms distance she took two blows to the mouth and nose of Tammy. Tammy didn't have any time to react. In a matter of seconds Janelle had pounced on her without giving her time to breath. Tammy's neighborhood friends stared in astonishment as Janelle merciless beat Tammy down to the dirt. When Janelle realized that Tammy was incapable of rising to retaliate she took two steps back. Tammy's limp body lay on the ground with dirt covering her from head to toe. She was half unconscious while everyone just looked with his or her eyes wide open. Janelle gave an evil eye at Tammy's friends and they all quickly lowered their heads.

"Any of you bitches want some of this let me know. This Alondra Block on mine." She announced while throwing up her gang sign.

She walked away from the crowd with Rachelle following closely behind. Once they walked out of the school gate they both started laughing aloud. They gave each other dap with their fists then jay walked across the busy Alondra Boulevard. Rachelle lived around the corner from Janelle and they had been best friends since the third grade. Rachelle had an older brother that claimed Alondra Block also who was two years older than Joseph. He had caught a gun charge and was doing time in Youth Authority. Both Janelle and Rachelle were built the same. They were both small up top but was thick in the butt and thighs. They were both Tomboys who had developed into women's bodies at a young age. Rachelle was a little darker than Janelle who had a light brown complexion. Some people called them twins because they were always together and they were built the same. Secretly people suggested that Rachelle was prettier only because Janelle had scars from fighting her rough brothers. This was a classic day for them because all the speculations about who was the baddest bitch at school had now been confirmed. They were on cloud nine walking through their neighborhood. Janelle didn't think the day could get any better until she seen Pookie hanging out sipping on a forty ounce of Old English Beer. He was leaning on a brick wall near the alleyway where many Alondra Block's sold dope. He swigged his beer then glanced up to see Janelle walking towards him.

It was obvious to Janelle that he wanted to smile. But he had to maintain his cool. He scanned her from head to toe with his eyes. The beer had taken effect so it had him mellow and relaxed. His eyes started from her blue Vans to her tight 501 Levis to her T-Shirt that had Big Nell written on it.

"Damn Janelle, how you gone just walk up on me like that? Looking all good and shit."

"You crazy Pookie, what are you doing?"

"Kicking it! I heard you beat the shit out of a young bitch from Greenleaf?" Pookie said it more as a statement instead of a question.

Janelle and Rachelle looked at each other in astonishment. They couldn't believe that he had found out so fast. It spoiled her chance to brag to him.

"Word travels fast I guess." She remarked.

"Naw, I just seen your brother Baby Gangster-Jason walking by and he told me." Pookie replied.

"That punk ass nigga wasn't even there. How does he know I whipped Tammy's ass?"

"I don't know, but what's up with us hooking up? You know I've wanted to get at you for awhile." Pookie replied.

"Why didn't you just talk to me?"

"Shit! The way Mama Jo watching over you, I ain't crazy."

They both started laughing. Janelle was digging him all the way and had been waiting for him to make a move.

"Well girl, I got to get going so I'm gone talk to you later." Rachelle said. She winked at Janelle before she walked off.

"I'll holler at you tomorrow girl." Janelle replied.

"Then after I see you we gone get suspended." Rachelle remarked.

Janelle giggled to herself then turned her full attention to Pookie. She smiled slightly trying not to show her teeth. Mama Jo always said that you shouldn't let a man know how much you like him; at least not in the beginning.

"So Pookie, what's yo real name? I've always known you as Pookie but I never knew your real name." Janelle asked while giving him total eye contact.

"You ain't supposed to know my real name. I don't tell anyone my name because I don't like it." He replied.

"Ah come on Pookie! How am I supposed to get to know the real you and I don't know yo real name. You know mine." Janelle persisted.

"If I tell you my real name you got to promise not to tell people. And you better not try to clown either." He said firmly.

"Okay, Okay I promise."

"My name is Patrick Carter."

"Oh snap nigga. I thought you were going to tell me something way out. Ain't anything wrong with Patrick. I like it." She smiled.

"So how am I going to get to spend time with you Big Nell?" He replied. It was obvious he wanted to change the subject.

"I was thinking about telling my mama that I'm doing things after school. Like I'm into sports or some shit like that. Then when I get out of school we can kick it." She grinned.

"That's cool. I'm about to buy me this Cutlass Supreme next week so we can go out and all that shit."

"Yeah but you can't let my brothers know because they might trip more than my mama." Janelle warned.

"I already talked to Gangster about it already. You know that nigga is my road dog? He told me he didn't care. I hadn't told J-Ridah yet. But I don't think that nigga gone trip either. But yo mama might trip." He explained.

"Well let's keep it from all of them as long as we can. I'll talk to my mama tonight. But let me get home before she starts talking shit."

"Alright Janelle, I'll talk to you later."

Janelle walked away gently sliding her hand across his tank top shirt. She glanced back to see if he was looking and sure enough he was. She always thought that he was cute but gangster. He had his cornrows tightly done over his dark brown complexion. He had a baby face but his dress attire suggested that he was all street. Nothing but a tank top on as a shirt with blue khakis and matching blue Chuck Taylor's with fat blue shoelaces. He creased his khakis so tight they appeared as though they could stand in a corner. Janelle pondered on the thought of being with Pookie. She was surprised to see him without her brother. He and Gangster were thick as thieves. Jordan was so respected that after a while people just called him Gangster instead of Gangster Jay. He preferred 'Gangster' because he felt that he was the epitome of Gangsterism. Janelle was proud of her new found connection with Pookie because he was definitely going to be a ghetto star. Not anyone got to hang with her brother Jordan let alone be his road dog.

She turned the corner on her block to hear yelling going on outside. As she drew closer she realized that it was coming from her own yard. She ran up to her house to find Jordan and Joseph arguing in the front yard loud enough for the entire block to hear. Jason notices her and runs out to the front of the yard to warn her of the impending fight.

"Janelle you got to stop these crazy ass niggas from squabbling. These niggas is always tripping on each other." Jason blurted out.

"Where's mama at?" Janelle asked in a temperamental tone.

She was still mad at Jason for running off at the mouth and getting her into that bullshit with Tammy in the first place. But she suddenly realized that her grudge was a lot less important at the time.

"She went down to the public assistance office and hasn't been home yet." Jason replied sensing the hostility.

"Fuck you cuz, you always trying to punk somebody. Nigga you take my shit again and we gone have problems." Gangster barked.

"Fuck you nigga, I don't want yo punk ass shirt anyway. But don't be talking that shit when you want to wear my cologne. Matter of fact nigga don't ask me for shit." J-Ridah barked.

"I don't ever ask for shit. What you trying to say nigga, you wanna get down?"

"You ain't said nothing but a word cuz." J-Ridah snapped back.

Gangster took off on J-Ridah with a two punch combination to the face. It stunned J-Ridah for a moment but then he moved forward. The yard had very little grass so the dirt rose as they began to exchange blows. Fists flew at a fever pitch as each brother tried to gain ground in the conflict. Gangster ducked one of J-Ridah's punches and landed one flush on the chin. It knocked J-Ridah to the ground. While still in a daze he tried to stumble back to his feet. Gangster gave him time to rise and then went on the full offensive. J-Ridah didn't have time to breath. At that very moment Do-Dirty rolled up in his glasshouse right in front of the Laney house. He had to do a double take as he seen Gangster having the upper hand against his older brother J-Ridah. Blood came out of a cut right above the left eye of J-Ridah. Janelle seen the blood and tried to intervene.

"Mama gone kick both ya'll ass she find out ya'll fighting like this." Janelle yelled while trying to get between the two.

"Move the fuck out the way." Gangster barked. He pushed Janelle to the side like she was a pillow.

Do-Dirty jumped out the car and ran over to the two brothers. He quickly wrapped his arms around Gangster who was trying to finish off his brother.

"Naw cuz, ya'll family. Ya'll ain't supposed to be fighting with each other like that." Do-Dirty calmly said.

Out of respect for Do-Dirty Gangster didn't try to resist. He let Do-Dirty walk him away from J-Ridah to the other side of the yard. J-Ridah was beginning to catch his breath. He looked over at Gangster with a venomous look but he had too much respect for Do-Dirty to attack. He calmly wiped the blood from his head and leaned against the garage door.

"I'll go get some band aids from out the bathroom." Janelle said while running into the house.

"What's happening Do-Dirty cuz? What you doing over here?" J-Ridah asked subtly suggesting that the fight was over.

Do-Dirty let Gangster go and walked over to J-Ridah.

"I wanted to know if you wanted to go up to the swap meet with me. I want some new blue Chucks and a few T-Shirts. I want to be fresh for that party Friday night. Pam supposed to come through and everything." He replied.

They both walked towards the front of the yard. J-Ridah glanced back at Gangster with a look in his eyes that let Gangster know that the fight would resume one day soon. J-Ridah then turned his attention to Do-Dirty who by then had jumped into his Glasshouse.

"So you rolling or what?" Do-Dirty asked.

"Yeah, I'm rolling!" J-Ridah walked over to the passenger side.

By that time Janelle came running outside with a wet rag, a band aid and some Neosporin. She stopped him before he could hop into the car. No matter what, she loved both of her brothers and she wasn't going to let him leave with that cut wide open.

"Stand still Joseph. You and Dennis can leave in a minute." She snapped.

While she was patching up J-Ridah, Gangster came walking out the yard. It was obvious to Janelle that he was carrying his thirty-eight snub nose he had bought off the street. He and Pookie were hustling around the corner in the alley where she last spotted Pookie.

"Pookie over there in the alley right off Alondra." Janelle yelled after him.

"Yeah, I'm knowing. I'm about to meet up with that nigga right now." Gangster replied.

Gangster winked at her as if they both knew something that no one else knew. He smiled subtly expressing his approval that she and Pookie date. She slightly nodded letting him know she understood then finished patching her oldest brother.

"Alright now, you good." She said as he climbed in Do-Dirty's passenger seat.

Do-Dirty sped off with quickness as Janelle stood in the middle of the street. This was a crazy day for her. She had just become the undisputed Queen of her Junior High School by brutally beating her only rival. Then she witnessed her brother Jordan getting the best of her oldest brother Joseph. But the most important thing to her was now she would get to know Pookie.

"Damn you already daydreaming about that nigga Pookie and ya'll ain't even started doing it." Jason teased.

Janelle walked over to him without saying a word. Once she was in arms reach she smacked him in the back of the head.

"You need to keep your mouth shut and your hands to yourself ole punk ass nigga."

"Owww! I'm telling mama when she gets home." Jason yelled.

"You are telling mama what? I didn't raise my children to be tattle tales, so don't coming telling me no silly shit about ya'll fighting Jason." Mama Jo came walking in the yard with the twins following close behind her.

Janelle looked over at Jason with a teasing facial expression. Jason ignored her looks and walked into the house rubbing the back of his head.

"You cook something Janelle?" Mama Jo asked.

"I was about to cook those chicken wings but I hadn't started yet." She replied.

"Why not!" Mama Jo asked.

"She just walked in just a little while ago mama." Jason remarked.

"Am I talking to you? Take yo snitching ass in the room and clean up until you learn not to talk too much." Mama Jo snapped.

She dropped down on the couch and began to take off her shoes. She firmly rubbed her own feet as though she couldn't wait to come out of the shoes she was wearing. Distracted for the moment but always sharp she glanced up at Janelle.

"Why are you just now getting home? You ain't running around here being fast are you? Because I ain't got time to be any one's grandmother. What happened, that held you up from getting here?" Mama Jo stared firmly.

"I got into a fight with Tammy from Greenleaf after school. But I also was thinking about running track for Roosevelt." Janelle quickly replied.

"You beat her ass?"

"You better believe mama. I shouldn't even be getting suspended either because it was after school." Janelle boasted.

"What were you fighting with her for? Ya'll like the same boy or something like that?" Mama Jo casually asked.

"Naw nothing like that. You might want to ask Jason about that." Janelle giggled.

"JASON!!!" Mama Jo yelled into the room.

Janelle listened in from the kitchen as Jason admitted why Janelle had a fight today at school. Janelle began cooking the food daydreaming about when she would get to cook for Pookie.

4
ROWDY

Filled to the rim like the County Jail day room!
Ice Cube

The dark night hid his intentions. He was dressed in all black with fat blue shoestrings in his black Chuck Taylor's. With his snub nose thirty-eight tucked away under his belt he walked over into enemy territory. His beanie slid barely over his head. He was the predator looking for his prey. As he crept over into unknown streets he felt the presence of someone. His blood began to boil as he drew closer. He drew his weapon and began to lower his frame to get a better focus. As the unsuspecting foe drew closer he aimed. Once the intended victim was within three yards he pulled the trigger and allowed the bullets to fly.

"Alondra Block Cuz!"

He watched the body go limp as blood came from the victim's torso and mouth. His eyes focused on the helpless soul drowning in his own blood. He stood over his supposed enemy with a rush of invigorating power. He had the ability to decide if someone lived or died. The victim's body began to go into convulsions indicating that death was near. Before his eyes went blank he glanced at his killer and with the last energy he could muster he threw up his gang sign. It enraged his killer. He died with honor when they were only supposed to die in shame. He kicked the lifeless corpse in anger frustrated that he was denied his final satisfaction. He lowered his head in disappointment then suddenly walked away with earnest speed.

"Ay cuz, you seen that nigga Gangster? That nigga crept off about thirty minutes ago and I haven't seen him since?" Pookie asked Flintstone.

"Naw cuz, he was on the block a couple of hours ago but he ain't touched down since then." Flintstone replied.

Flintstone was one of the homies from the hood that was a part of their generation. He was down to put in work but he was more of a fist fighter than a shooter. He was well respected among his peers. They called him Flintstone because someone once described him like Barney Rubble, short and stocky.

"Shit I'm done with this package and I wanted to know if the nigga wanted to ride with me to recop." Pookie said.

"I'll roll with you." Flintstone replied.

"Cool, I didn't want to roll by myself just in case a nigga get to tripping."

They hopped in Pookie's Cutlass Supreme and sped off. Pookie had put a sound system in his car so the music was loud.

"Ay cuz, can I get at you about something?"

Pookie turned down his music, slightly annoyed but was curious about what was on Flintstone's mind.

"You fucking with Janelle Laney right?"

"Yeah, we just started talking but don't speak up on that shit because we still ain't told her mama yet." Pookie warned.

"Mama Jo don't take me as one of those mamas that like to trip." Flintstone commented.

"She might trip when it comes to her only daughter. So for now we keeping that shit on the hush. You here me cuz?"

"Yeah I hear you. But what's up with her friend Rachelle. Is she fucking with one of the homeboys from the hood? Or is she fucking with one of those Greenleaf niggas?"

"I doubt it if she would fuck with a Greenleaf nigga because of her brother Tank."

"Yeah, I know but I can't holler at him because he just got five more years for a gun charge. That nigga wasn't out a good month and I was trying to catch up with him to see what was up with his sister." Flintstone replied with frustration in his tone.

"Well you know he is an OG nigga like Do-Dirty, Snake, C-Dog and all them niggas. Only nigga that's around our age that get to hang with them regularly is that nigga J-Ridah." Pookie replied.

"I wasn't trying to kick it with his crazy ass too much but I was gone still get at him about his sister. You know what I mean, out of respect?"

"I'll tell you what, I'll holla at Janelle and see if she can hook you up with her."

"That's good looking out cuz." Flintstone smiled.

When Pookie copped his dope he rushed back to the spot. Standing outside when he pulled up was Gangster leaning against the wall. He smiled when he seen them pull up.

"What that Block like nigga?" Gangster playfully greeted.

"Fo' life." Pookie replied.

"Till the day I die." Flintstone added.

"Where was you at Gangster? I was looking for you so you could roll with me to go cop some shit. You know I have to go over in Greenleaf hood to cop from the essay homeboy Ernesto. Them Greenleaf niggas like to set trip but Flintstone rode with me." Pookie said.

"I had to ride on some slobs. It was on some solo shit though. You down to go cop some Sherm?" Gangster asked.

"Hell naw cuz, is you crazy? That shit making you go crazy and shit. When did you start fucking with that shit?" Pookie said incredulously.

"Shit Mike Dog let me hit some with him the other day and that shit had me on cloud nine. My moms don't want me fucking with that shit because she says my pops used to be heavy on that shit. She said it made him crazy too but that shit just gave me a nice little high."

"That's right I heard yo pops was an OG Crip back in the day." Flintstone said.

"Yeah, he was right under Raymond Washington and them. He first got to know my moms at the Palladium where the Crips first made the news for taking some niggas jacket." Gangster proudly replied.

"Ah shit, you got some pictures of yo pops?" Flintstone asked.

"Yeah, my mama got them though. She will let us look at them but she doesn't like it if we try to take them outside." Gangster frowned.

It was silent for a moment after the last comment. Gangster lowered his head and went into his thoughts for a moment. It was the middle of the week and he knew his mother would make him get up no matter how late he got home. It was hard to sleep in the Laney house in the morning during the week. If someone came in too late they had to consider that they would have to wake up early like everyone else. He contemplated going home especially after knowing what he just did. That was the first murder he had committed by himself. He had participated in drive-bys but he hadn't walked up on a man and killed him.

"Ay Gangster, you alright cuz?" Pookie interrupted his thoughts.

"Yeah I'm good. But I'm shooting to the house to get something to eat." He replied.

Without another word he suddenly walked off. Pookie glanced over at Flintstone and shook his head.

"That nigga likes to trip anyway, so if he smoking Sherm he is really going to lose his mind." Pookie commented.

"Yeah, out of the whole Laney family he is the craziest." Flintstone agreed.

When Gangster walked into the house it was eleven o' clock and his house was rowdy as usual, as if it was three in the afternoon. His mother was sitting at the table smoking a cigarette while Jason and Janelle were watching television with the volume up loud.

"Where's J-Ridah...I mean where is Joseph at mama?" He asked her while walking towards the kitchen.

"He ain't made it home yet."

Gangster went into the kitchen to get whatever was left over from what Mama Jo cooked. Suddenly a loud thud sounded off from inside the bedroom. The twins were in the room wrestling each other. It disturbed Mama Jo from her thoughts.

"Jamil and Jalil if ya'll break something in there I'm gone whip ya'll ass, ya hear?" Mama Jo yelled.

"OKAY MAMA!!!" Both twins yelled simultaneously.

Gangster sat down across from Mama Jo. His plate hitting the table made her look up from her thoughts. They made eye contact for a brief moment. She was suddenly struck by the fact that she knew, she understood. Her son Jordan had killed a man before. She never could explain her insight but she remembered seeing it in Mike's eyes. There was an innocence lost that radiated from his being. She wanted to cry for her son but no tears would fall.

"How was your day, Jordan? What did you do…today?" She asked.

Jordan slowly lifted his head from his plate. He felt like he was given a trick question. His mother never really asked him those kinds of questions. He glanced down at the macaroni and cheese then looked at his mother with a bizarre look on his face.

"I went to school then hung out with Pookie." He replied.

"You were with Pookie all day?" Mama Jo asked with more fervor.

"Most of the day yeah. Why what's up Mama, what's wrong with you?" Gangster asked.

"Why something has to be wrong when I want to know what's going on with one of my sons?"

"You normally don't do that so I…"

"So ya'll hung out at the spot all day off of Alondra?"

"Why you asking me all these questions mama?"

"Let me look in your eyes." Mama said while rising from her chair.

By that time Janelle had managed to turn the television down to hear the discussion. She knew not to comment but was nosy enough to want to hear.

"Janelle if you don't turn that damn television back up to the level it was." Mama Jo yelled.

47

Janelle quickly pushed up the volume and attempted to listen in over the sound. By that time Mama Jo had gotten up from the chair and had a hold of Gangster's face. She stared into his eyes to see if they were hazy. He struggled to loosen her grip on his face but she held fast.

"Boy you ain't been fucking with that Sherm have you?" She asked.

"Naw Mama what makes you think that?"

"Because your eyes gave a flash that I seen before and at that very moment you reminded me of yo daddy."

Gangster struggled away from Mama Jo's grip and brushed off her accusations. She knew he had done something but she couldn't put her finger on what. Her intuition alarm went off like crazy. She tried to settle herself but her hands kept shaking. She sensed murder but wasn't for sure.

"Jason run in the bathroom and get my aspirin."

"Aw mama can't the twins…"

"Boy if I have to tell you twice." She snarled.

Jason jumped up from the couch and ran into the bathroom as quickly as he could. He came back in and handed the aspirin to Mama Jo.

"It's about time ya'll took ya'll asses to bed." She announced.

Everyone began moving toward his or her designated resting areas. Mama Jo continued to sit at the dinner table. She pulled out a cigarette then got up to get some fresh air. She walked outside and stood on the porch. There was a soft breeze in the air so she covered her lighter with her hand while her cigarette hung from her bottom lip. She took a drag on her cigarette long and hard then exhaled as she slowly walked down her steps. She walked into the driveway past the car then glanced back at the house. Just as she suspected Janelle was glancing out the window. Her stern looks made Janelle quickly close the blinds.

"What am I going to do about that boy?" She rhetorically asked.

It was quiet on her block for a change. She couldn't really understand the quiet except for the fact that any of her oldest son's friend weren't hanging out. She considered that they must have found a new spot in the neighborhood to hang. They were probably tired of having the police called on them. She had made it to the front of her yard and stood quietly on the sidewalk. She enjoyed the peace away from the kids. She wondered about Michael at that moment wondering what he would do about Jordan. She remembered how he would play rough with Joseph and Jordan when they stayed on the East Side of South Central. He really adored his daughter Janelle. He was in and out of jail too much for Jason and the twins to know him well.

She could use his help right now. Maybe he could have steered Jordan away from that dope and keep Joseph from being so wild. He had become extremely trigger-happy and that was a problem for her. She grew up where some shooting took place but most problems were handled with fists.

" This new generation." She pondered.

The world was different for her when she was a Cripette compared to today. She began rubbing her eyes, feeling the sleep creep up on her. The quiet mixed with the soft breeze felt too good for her to give in to her sleep. She sat down on the concrete in her house gown. She had it in her mind that she would stay five more minutes before she called it a night. She didn't have a watch but she figured she calculate the time in her head.

Suddenly she heard a car screeching around the corner. She quickly jumped up from the curb and backed away into the yard. She wasn't about to be a victim tonight. She waited behind her raggedy gate and when she realized it was a false alarm she went back to her curb.

Around the corner and up the block her oldest son J-Ridah was hanging out with his OG homeboys. They were sharing a couple of bottles of 'Night Train' while smoking weed. It was Do-Dirty, Snake, C-Dog, Deuce, Shawny, Mike Dog and Jay-Cee. All eight of them had been drinking all day and it was starting to catch up with them. J-Ridah was the youngest but he was taller than some of them. He had sprouted in height once he reached high school. He and Gangster were almost the same height but J-Ridah had him by an inch or two.

"I'm fucked up cuz." Do-Dirty announced

"I know I can barely walk. I know if I come staggering in this late Moms is having a fit. Especially if she sees me this drunk I won't be able to live it down." J-Ridah commented.

"You know you can crash in my ride if you need to." Do-Dirty replied.

"I was gone ask you that. Then I can come in the house that morning and moms won't trip as tough." J-Ridah replied.

"You got a cool ass moms though cuz. All she asks you to do is come in the right time but she don't trip about shit else." C-Dog commented.

"Yeah but I'm a grown muthafuckin man. So I should be able to come and go as I please cuz." J-Ridah sneered.

"Nigga why you getting raw with me? I was just saying." C-Dog protested.

"Not like that, I'm just tired of having to answer for shit." J-Ridah replied.

"I know you didn't mean anything by it but honestly though you still under eighteen so you won't be grown for another two years. Yo moms can catch a case behind some shit you in cuz." C-Dog replied.

"We drunk then a muthafucka and this nigga wants to talk all sensible and shit. Let the little young nigga have some fun cuz and quit fucking up our high." Do-Dirty laughed.

"FUCK ALL CRABS, BLOOD!!!" Someone yelled.

Shots began to go off after those words. Bullets riddled the sidewall next to Deuce's house while everyone ran for cover. Their drunken state evaporated as they ran for their lives. Running in different directions J-Ridah decided to cut through Deuce's front yard. Halfway through the yard he felt a sharp pain run through his thigh and hipbone. He collapsed on the soft grass in mid stride. Tears welled in his eyes as his predators sped off. He tried to roll over but the pain was too intense for him to move. He laid their helpless allowing tears to fall down his face. His body suddenly felt extremely hot as the pain from the bullets wounds began to sink in. He screamed loudly hoping one of his homeboys would come to his aid. The first one to make it to his aid was Do-Dirty. Following behind was C-Dog then Snake. They attempted to lift him up but he screamed in pain. Trying to regain his vision he saw everyone present except for one of his homeboys.

"Where the fuck is Shawny cuz?" J-Ridah winced.

"Is that nigga still hiding? Somebody go find out where the fuck is Shawny." Do-Dirty announced.

Deuce and Jay-Cee went in the direction they thought Shawny had run. Do-Dirty and Snake attempted again to pick up J-Ridah.

"Let's take this nigga around the corner to Mama Jo and see what she wants to do." Do-Dirty said.

"Naw cuz, we need to take him to the Killer King hospital." Snake argued.

"This nigga might die if he sitting up in Martin Luther King Hospital. Naw nigga we gone take him to his mama and she will know where she want him to go. Come on cuz we got to put him in my ride and take him to Mama Jo."

They quickly put him in the backseat of the car. He moaned the entire time he was being lifted to the car.

"Aw naw, cuz this can't be happening." Jay-Cee inadvertently blurted out.

"What cuz?" Do-Dirty yelled.

"The homie Shawny is dead as a doorknob." Deuce replied.

"Naw you bullshitting." Snake replied.

"Aw that's fucked up. We gone get them slob niggas for this shit cuz. I swear to God them niggas gone die for the shit they did." Do-Dirty vowed.

Do-Dirty closed the passenger side of his car and tapped Snake on the arm.

"Look here cuz, ya'll make sure his body is taken to his mother while Snake and I go take J-Ridah to Mama Jo." Do-Dirty firmly stated.

He didn't wait to get a response. He jumped in on the driver's seat and sped off.

Mama Jo was sitting at edge of the curb finishing the last remnants of her third cigarette. She told herself she would only sit outside for five minutes. She found herself enjoying the peace for another twenty-five minutes. Now she was about ready to go inside when she heard another car screeching around the corner. The noise of the loud screeching drew closer but for some reason Mama Jo decided to stay put. As the car came closer she realized that it was Do-Dirty's car from the headlights. He usually was too cool to speed on a residential street. She wondered if the police was after him. He pulled up on her quickly putting his heavy foot on the brakes. He jumps out the car breathing hard.

"Calm down Dennis, what's wrong with you?" Mama Jo calmly asked.

"J-Ridah, I mean Joseph got shot by some slobs and he in the backseat of the car. I didn't know if you wanted me to take him to the hospital or to you?" Do-Dirty blurted out.

"Aw shit, roll us up to Dr. King hospital, can you Dennis?" Mama Jo frantically asked.

"Yeah, just tell Snake to get in the backseat with J-Ridah, I mean Joseph." Do-Dirty replied.

"Naw, I'm getting in the backseat with my baby. Let's roll!" She yelled.

Do-Dirty sped towards the other end of the block until he got to Rosecrans Boulevard. He made a quick left and sped down Rosecrans as if there wasn't a stop light in sight. He quickly made that right turn on Wilmington Boulevard and pushed the gas harder. J-Ridah winced at every turn he made as he laid his head in Mama Jo's lap. Mama Jo didn't think to bring a jacket and she was only dressed in her nightgown.

Do-Dirty pulled up in the emergency entrance stopped the car and jumped out. Snake was already out by the time he had gotten to the passenger side. Mama Jo sat impatiently as they carried her son out of the car and into the hospital.

"We gone serve those slob niggas for this shit cuz, I swear." Do-Dirty said loud enough for only J-Ridah to hear. When they got him to the front desk a young black girl in her late twenties or early thirties was sitting behind the counter. She had a dark brown complexion with her hair in a bun. She wore a hospital uniform with a pink shirt and white pants. She stood up when she seen Do-Dirty and Snake bringing in J-Ridah. She had a complacent, nonchalant look on her face.

"Can I help you?"

"My homeboy got shot so he needs to see a doctor." Do-Dirty proclaimed.

"Does he have insurance? You have to fill out these forms in order for him to be seen by a doctor." She replied.

"Bitch, he could be dying and you talking about some forms. Is this bitch crazy or what?" Snake fired back.

"I'm sorry sir but I have to follow the rules of the hospital." She firmly stated.

"I don't give a fuck about rules. My homeboy bleeding all over the place and you want to know about forms." Do-Dirty cut in.

"If ya'll wasn't so rowdy we wouldn't have to worry about these kinds of problems. I have rules I have to follow or I'm going to lose my job." She snapped.

"Rowdy? Rowdy!?! Bitch you ain't seen rowdy…"

Mama Jo touched Do-Dirty on the shoulder and he stopped in mid-sentence. She moved closer to the counter and leaned in towards the receptionist. Her face was stern, her eyes were sullen and her lips were curled. She looked the young woman right in her eye.

"I'm the mother of this boy right here. If he has to die because of some paperwork you won't ever have to worry about a job again. Now I mean that from the bottom of my heart. Now think hard and quick on how you want to handle this." Mama Jo said.

The young woman seen the look in Mama Jo's eyes and began moving quickly.

"I'll sort out the paperwork while I call a doctor to come bring your son to the back. What is his name ma'am?" She asked.

"Joseph Michael Laney. His birthday is September 8, 1969." Mama Jo replied.

The receptionist smiled while filling out the form. She then indicated to another receptionist to get an available doctor. When the roller bed came the doctor followed closely behind. He was a middle-aged White Man with balding gray hair. Most of his face was covered with the exception of his eyes. He asked the resident nurse a few question then the roller bed was taken in the back with J-Ridah laying it.

"Everything is gone be alright Joseph, don't you worry baby." Mama Jo yelled after him.

A couple of hours later the receptionist came out to the waiting room. It had slowed down since then but the hospital was still crowded. She walked over to Mama Jo who had dozed off.

"Ma'am, you can go see your son now."

"Thank You...Joyce." Mama Jo glanced at her nametag.

Joyce escorted her towards the back. Mama Jo was peeking in every corner and every room wondering where was her son.

"Is he alright? What did the doctor say was wrong with him?" Mama Jo asked.

"He had to remove two bullets from his hip. The one in his leg went straight through. He will have to learn how to walk again but he should be fine." Joyce replied.

Once they made it to the room J-Ridah sat up nervously. He was drowsy but still functioning. Mama Jo stared at him and smiled.

"I'm glad yo crazy ass is alright. Dennis and Melvin told me Shawny was killed. You gone worry me to death, boy." Mama Jo waived her hand.

"It wasn't like this when you and Pops was coming up, huh Mama?" Joseph asked.

"We had shooters just like ya'll got shooters but yo generation is more shooters than fighters. I seen it first change

54

when East Side started having problems with West Side. Raymond Washington and Tookie brought both sides together but niggas couldn't keep the peace. Not only were we fighting Bloods but also we started fighting each other. It was the beginning of something different."

"But I was shot by some Pirus. That's not us fighting against each other." Joseph tried to make sense of her statement.

"Yeah but that was the beginning when fighting wasn't an option. Everybody wants to shoot now. So you got a whole bunch of cowards that want to hide behind a trigger."

"But we soldiers though Mama. It ain't like we scared to fight we just fighting a different type of war. Soldiers use guns so that's how it has to go down." Joseph explained.

"A soldier can fight with his fists and with a gun. He doesn't have to have a gun to be a soldier. A real soldier is able to survive without pulling out a gun every chance he gets. Yo daddy would shoot but I seen him fight a plenty of times. Nowadays it's mostly shooting or jumping someone but never one on one to settle a problem. Ya'll generation just different, that's all." She replied.

"How was daddy when he ran the streets? How did he get his name and reputation?"

"Get some rest and when you wake up I will tell you all about it." Mama Jo replied.

J-Ridah dozed off with Mama Jo sitting right next to his bed. She wanted to cry but the tears wouldn't fall. She shook her head in disbelief. Her oldest baby could have died today. She didn't know about a God but she knew if one did exist he was all right with her.

5
RIDE OR DIE

Revenge is like the sweetest joy next to getting pussy!!!
Tupac Shakur

Years had past and your father and I had just had you. I was still living with my mother at the time but I would see Michael everyday. He was one of those types of niggas that was happy to be a father. He would come over to my mother's house and just stare at you for what seem to me like hours. He was always afraid to pick you up. Mama would always have problems with him because she felt he should be trying to get a job. But Michael wasn't about to get a job. He was more into robbing people and shit like that. Only thing that bothered me was that he wasn't really good at it. He got caught a few times for strong-arm robbery but he still hadn't learned his lesson.

Things began to change around the seventies. He had finally gotten a job at the tire factory and was bringing me some money for you. He was saving up for us to get an apartment together. Plus he was trying to sell a little weed on the side but he would smoke most of it. Everything was cool and he was still able to hang out with the homeboys after work. His sister Patricia would come by to visit me before I knew I was pregnant with Jordan. So we would hang with the homegirls that was down at the time. We were all an East Side family and it was the good times. Then one of the homeboys got called out over this silly ass bitch. She wasn't even cute but some West Side Crips had met up with us so that we could handle this shit. The girl's name was Vieira Williams. She was one of those types of girls with a real big butt without a nice looking face. Of course men wanted to have sex with her but it wasn't too many cats that would make her his woman.

She had messed around with one of the homeboys from the East Side named Smokey. Smokey was one of those pretty boy niggas that knew how to fight his ass off. Out of their generations Michael was one of the few homeboys that could get him in a head up fight. Smokey was more quiet like so a lot of people mistook him as a punk. But he wasn't a punk at all. So Vieira went back and told this nigga named Turk from the West Side that Smokey kept trying to talk to her after she told him Turk was her man. The truth was, after Smokey had sex with her a few times he didn't want to be bothered but she kept calling him. He eventually cursed her out and told her not to fuck with him anymore. He even embarrassed her in front of some of the homeboys because your father was there. So word had gotten back to us that Turk wanted to settle this shit head up. It was a beef between two Crips so everyone agreed that we meet up at the park and settle the shit. When your father told me what happened I wanted to make sure he took me when it all went down. Somehow I talked your grandmother into watching you, God rest her soul, and she did.

Everyone met up at the park around three in the afternoon. It was too hot for our leather jackets but we were wearing our colors. We all agreed that Turk and Smokey handle that shit at the baseball diamond. Michael had told me before that Smokey had squabbles but I hadn't seen it for myself. They stood about the same height but Turk had a little more muscle then Smokey. They squared up right in the middle of the diamond near second base while we gathered around. For the first minute no one threw a punch and I began to think the fight was about to be a dud.

Suddenly Turk rushed Smokey releasing hard blows aiming for the head. It looked as if one of the punches must have gotten through because Smokey turned red. But Turk took it as a sign of weakness and went in for the kill. This time though, when he came in swinging Smokey met him with three clean punches to the face. It stopped Turk dead in his tracks. Now Turk is infuriated so he rushes Smokey full speed and they start locking up in the middle of the field. I don't know what it was but it was obvious that Smokey had gotten the better of the exchange. Turk's mouth was bleeding and he stumbled back a few feet. His eyes were blood shot red and he was tired. Smokey remained calm with both his hands up and his fist balled.

"You want some more of this cuz?" Smokey asked.

Turk rushed at him again but this time he tried to grab Smokey. That was a bad move. When Turk reached in to grab Smokey he was met with an upper cut right on his chin. He fell backward but before he could fall Smokey was on top of him with several more punches. That final punch was thrown while Turk was almost to the ground. It knocked him out cold. I stood there in that baseball field with my mouth wide open. I wanted Smokey to win but for some reason I thought he wasn't. He proved me wrong. Michael and everyone else hugged him like he had just won the World Series. It took about twenty minutes for them West Side niggas to wake up Turk.

A few niggas from the East Side talked with a few niggas from the West Side and the shit was supposed to be squashed. That bitch Vieira was there but she felt stupid after seeing her man get beat down like that. I later heard she broke up with him behind that fight. She knew not to run up on any of the homegirls because she wasn't that type of female. So those West Side niggas had to go back to their neighborhood with their tale between their legs. We were so happy that the homeboy Spade decided to barbecue. We called him Spade because he was black as midnight. But he was one of the coolest niggas you could know. Everybody chipped in on some chicken, ribs and some hotlinks and we had us a barbecue.

They partied until about one in the morning that day. I left a little after midnight. Smokey had gotten drunk by ten or eleven that night but he didn't leave until midnight. He stumbled out of Spade's backyard and started toward home. Turk and some West Side niggas were waiting for him to get out of the party. So they must have followed him until he was close by his mother's house then they jumped out the car and started shooting him. They shot him in the upper body about seven or eight times. One of the bullets went into his head but that wasn't the one that was fatal. I could hear the gunshots a little from your grandmother's house but I didn't think it was somebody I knew getting killed. Smokey took the shots and fell to the ground. He crawled up the walkway until he made it to the steps of his mother's porch. He made it to his mother's porch and knocked on the screen door. His mother hearing the gunshots was already rushing towards her front door. She seen her son coughing up blood on her porch and began screaming. She woke up the neighbors as she held him in her arms. He died before the ambulance arrived. I was only sixteen when Smokey was killed I remember feeling sick. Unbeknownst to me I was pregnant with Jordan at that time. But what really bothered me was the fact that this was the first time I personally knew someone who was murdered. After Michael came by to tell me the bad news I stayed in the house with you for the rest of the day.

A few days later, all of the homeboys got together to discuss what happened to Smokey. Since we were all Crips we didn't know how to handle it. It was finally decided that if they take out one of ours then we have to take out one of theirs. It only took a few days for the homeboys to catch up with Turk. Later that week he was found dead at the same park he had fought Smokey. From that day forward our relationship with the West Side was never the same. And claiming the set was never the same.

The I.V. the hospital had put inside J-Ridah's right wrist put him to sleep fast. After his mother had told her story of back in the day he took another long nap. Mama Jo had already talked to Janelle and she was able to hold down the household while Mama Jo was away. She wanted to go home and take a shower later that night but she was waiting on Michael's sister Patricia. She tried to call her own sister Sharon but she wasn't picking up the phone. She finally decided to call Patricia who also lived on the East Side of Compton. She was raising two sons that were coming up in the streets banging. Her oldest son Marvin was a year younger than Jason and her youngest son Shawn was two years younger. They didn't show up until about fifteen minutes to four. Mama Jo was irritated but she had to swallow it since she didn't have a car. Mama Jo always liked Patricia from back in the day but she couldn't understand for the life of me how she could raise her sons to be Bloods.

"Girl, I'm sorry for being so late, I had to hunt these two little bad ass niggas down. They were out there running the streets and hanging up at the park. Besides this bullshit, how have you been girl?" Patricia walked in.

"I'm doing good, just a little tired. I need to take a hot shower and see what's going on with the rest of my kids. My sister is probably laid up with some man because she won't answer her damn phone. How are ya'll doing Marvin and Shawn? Ya'll can't come over here and give your Auntie Jo a hug?"

"Hi, Auntie Jo." Marvin replied while hugging Mama Jo.

"Shawn you better say hi to your Auntie before I have to beat yo ass. He's always acting like he is too shy." Patricia commented.

After Shawn hugged Mama Jo she decided to wake Joseph up so that he could speak to his cousins. She shook him a few times as he slowly opened his eyes. He looked to see four faces staring at him and he was startled.

"Joseph, I'm about to leave but I will come back tomorrow. But before I leave I wanted you to say what's up to your Auntie Pat and your cousins Marvin and Shawn." Mama Jo said.

"He's our relative." Marvin commented.

"Boy if you don't shut yo damn mouth you gone wish you never had a mouth to speak out of." Patricia warned.

Mama Jo and Patricia walked outside talking while Marvin and Shawn sat and talked to their big cousin.

"So what, ya'll suppose to be slobs now?" J-Ridah asked sarcastically.

"What, you suppose to be a crab now?" Marvin snapped right back.

"What little nigga? You better be lucky I'm laid up in this bed like this or I would whip ya'll asses." J-Ridah chuckled.

"Whatever big relative, this Piru on mine. I can't help it if ya'll chose the wrong side." Marvin replied.

"You know one of yo homeboys shot me? And they killed one of my homeboys. I was lucky enough to live." J-Ridah replied.

"Yeah but one of yo homeboys killed one of my homeboys too. I don't like that they shot you but if someone kill our homeboys we got to go back and kill one of they homeboys." Marvin said.

"You talk too much Marvin, that's on Piru." Shawn said.

"Nigga what? This is our family even if he is one of them. This is Uncle Mike's son. You know he got life and he told mama to keep us close to his kids." Marvin protested.

By this time J-Ridah was sitting up in his hospital bed watching the exchange. Even though they were Bloods, J-Ridah had to respect their heart. He smiled knowing that they believed in what they represented.

"Ya'll some down ass soldiers, too bad you ain't Crips. How old are ya'll now?"

"I'm twelve and Shawn is eleven. You seventeen now right?" Marvin eagerly asked.

"Naw, I'm sixteen but I will be seventeen later this year."

"Ya'll about ready to go? I got to take yo Auntie Jo home then we got to pick up a few things from the store." Patricia asked loudly.

"Alright then relative, you get well and don't let any of the homeboys catch you slippin'. Marvin said.

Do-Dirty had gathered four of the homeboys together a few days later. The police were hot after they got hit so they had to be cool for a few days. It was no way he was going to let it ride but patience was important. Compton police wasn't that bright and most people referred to them as the Compton dum-dums. So it was always a way to get past them. Only problem was that they started bringing the Lynwood Sheriffs to help them with investigations. Police or not it was time for them to retaliate.

It took about twenty minutes to find someone slippin' after they came across a raggedy Nissan. It was Deuce, C-Dog, Snake riding shotgun and Do-Dirty driving. He found some niggas hanging out near an alley close to Long Beach Boulevard. Do-Dirty heard them from one angle and decided to drive around the block. When he hit the corner Deuce, C-Dog and Snake were already hanging out the car with their pistols drawn. About six Pirus were hanging outside drinking forty ounces and playing oldies.

"Alondra Block Cuz,"

The shots rung out in the night as everyone hanging near the alley began to run in different directions. They must have thought that they were low key because it was a total surprise. The bullets pierced through flesh as bodies began to fall in every direction. Do-Dirty had stopped the car so that his homies could pick off anyone running away from the scene. When the last one was either hiding or lying in a puddle of blood, Do-Dirty sped off into the night.

Do-Dirty dumped the car off right on Alondra Boulevard then they walked back to the set. They all agreed to meet up at Snake's house to finish the night off with a few forty ounces of Old English Beer. Once they were secure Snake went into his garage to get the beer from out of a small freezer his mother had placed back there.

"We let those Mayo Lane niggas have it cuz." Snake chuckled.

"I know cuz, at least three or four of them niggas is meeting they maker. How they gone kill one of our homeboys and think they getting away with it." Deuce replied.

"They shot the homie J-Ridah too, don't forget that. I know that trigger happy nigga would have loved to be in on that ride." Do-Dirty added.

"I know, he would have loved handing them slob niggas they nuts. He won't be getting out the hospital for awhile though." Snake commented.

"I seen Mama Jo the other day and she told me he should be out in enough time for Shawny's funeral. I don't know if he's going or not." Do-Dirty replied.

"What we should have done was take Gangster's crazy ass with us. He's been giving them niggas the blues for some time now." C-Dog finally spoke.

"Naw cuz, he a little different with his shit. He goes off and blast on niggas on his own. I saw that nigga creep off about a week ago but I just left him alone. You know I seen him and J-Ridah get into it in they front yard one day. That nigga Gangster got the best but it has a lot to do with that nigga being a little off. He's Mama Jo's favorite though, and that's why him and J-Ridah have problems." Do-Dirty explained.

"Yeah he goes off with Mike Dog fucking with them shermsticks. Mike was telling me that Gangster hits that shit like he was doing it for years." Snake replied.

"Well whatever the fuck it is, that shit is making him crazy. It's like he got a death wish or something." Do-Dirty replied.

"What about Baby Gangster? That little nigga might grow up to be a rider just like his brothers." C-Dog said.

"Naw, he more into making money. He's probably one of them niggas that's gone be chasing after bitches and shit. He already doing little side hustles for the little homie Pookie." Do-Dirty said.

"I sure would like to fuck they thick ass sister. If she wasn't so young I would have been had her in the house trying to run up in her. What's her name again?" Deuce commented.

"Nigga you would fuck her now if you thought you'd get away with it. This nigga Deuce is a trip cuz." Do-Dirty laughed.

Everyone laughed right along with him. The beer had sunk in by then and they were starting to feel good. Even Deuce had to laugh because he knew Do-Dirty was telling the truth.

"So what is up with her anyway, Mama Jo got her on lock down?" Deuce pried.

"Yeah, but I think the little homie Pookie is fucking with her. I seen them kicking it about a week ago. He might be fucking by now." Do-Dirty replied.

"So young ass Pookie is hitting that huh?" Deuce rhetorically asked.

"Look at this nigga cuz. If Mama Jo see you anywhere near her only daughter she gone cut off ya balls and hand them to you partner." Do-Dirty laughed.

"I ain't fucking with Mama Jo; she is a rider just like her sons. They daddy is a OG nigga that hung with Raymond Washington and Tookie?" Deuce asked.

"He is OG but he's a little younger than them niggas. J-Ridah says he got life in prison without the possibility of parole. The twins are eleven I think and he's been locked up since they were born." Do-Dirty continued.

"Damn cuz, a whole family of riders." C-Dog cut in.

"CC-Ridahs!!!" Do-Dirty corrected him.

"Yeah that's them Laney Boys." Snake smiled.

That following morning everyone was up early at the Laney household. It was Saturday and everyone was excited that J-Ridah was coming home. His homeboy Shawny's funeral was Sunday and he told Mama Jo that he wanted to go. She was hurting inside from the hospital bill but glad that her son would be okay. Janelle had cleaned up the house practically by herself while Mama Jo gathered some money for an extra treat for J-Ridah. She had vowed from that day forward that she would make sure they always ate at least once a week as a family. That would give her time to talk to everyone and to see what was going on in his or her life. She knew boys were supposed to be tough so she let them be tough and there was no other place but the streets that would make them tough. But one of her sons getting killed was something she was going to avoid.

"I can't teach them how to be a man, only a man can do that." She would always say.

She didn't always just worry about her boys. She wondered about Janelle as well. She started suspecting that Janelle had a boyfriend that she wasn't telling her about. She didn't have any proof but a few signs were there. She had been coming home later than usual. She started lying to Mama Jo about little things during the day. Mama Jo chuckled because she didn't understand how Janelle would make up a lie then forget about it later on. Then say something that suggested that she wasn't where she said she was. It was the same thing Mama Jo would do when she would sneak off with Mike.

"Little girl, how are you going to try to hustle a hustler? You need to sit yo fast ass down somewhere. I know you into something and once I find out me and you are going to box." Mama Jo warned.

But she didn't stay mad at Janelle too long because her only daughter kept the household in line if Mama Jo was there or not. Janelle loved all her brothers and that was what made her the center of attention. The twins did whatever she asked of them. When she told them to stay outside until she was done cleaning that's exactly what they did. But her relationship with J-Ridah was the closest. She and J-Ridah were always close from day one. So she was really hurt when she found out her big brother had gotten shot. She made sure that the house was in order so that Mama Jo could spend all the time she needed at the hospital. Mama Jo appreciated how close Janelle and Joseph were. She even attempted to pry information out of J-Ridah while she sat in his hospital bed. If he knew anything he pretended not to know. Surprisingly only person in the family that knew was Gangster and that was only because Pookie was his road dog. Mama Jo didn't even think to ask him.

Unbeknownst to anyone Gangster was the reason J-Ridah was shot or the reason behind what provoked the shooting. He was the one that initiated the war against the Mayo Lane Pirus. He felt responsible after considering he had a fight with his brother not long before his brother was shot. He had been sneaking over to the Mayo Lane for the last three nights trying to find someone to kill. He was the only one that wasn't at home when J-Ridah was supposed to come home from the hospital. He had been looking for OG Mike Dog to maybe get a chance for that high. He wanted to smoke his problems away and that PCP always took him away. He wouldn't go on his hunt until later that night. Gangster was slowly changing into something he didn't have any control over. His appetite for murder was becoming addictive and the ghosts began to haunt him. Even though, he was her favorite Mama Jo was beginning to fear her second son. That side of Michael that she practically hated is what she was seeing more of. The despondent disposition that he carried for most of the day didn't sit right with her. Anger was more of a realistic thing to her but somber and recluse was something she couldn't quite grasp. She had too many concerns to really address his problems but she considered taking him to a psychiatrist. When J-Ridah was shot that ultimately changed her focus.

"SURPRISE!!!"

Everyone yelled when J-Ridah came walking through the door on crutches. Not only was his family there to greet him but so was most of his homeboys. His OG homeboys who he normally hung around were all present as well as most of his BG (Baby Gangster) homeboys. He tried not to smile but it was difficult. He had never had all that attention put on him at one time. Even on birthdays Mama Jo would ask him what he wanted for dinner and that was his birthday present. He didn't know anything about parties or get-togethers thrown for him.

He scanned the room trying to find where Do-Dirty was at. Do-Dirty and Snake was both sipping on some Old English over in the corner. He limped towards them but before he could make it over to them the twins rushed up to hug him. J-Ridah was more stunned than hurt initially. Then he felt the pain and he moaned which made the twins loosen their embrace. But to let them know he acknowledged what they were doing he both gave them a pound with his fists. He continued his journey over towards his homeboys when Janelle and Jason jumped in front of him.

"Damn cuz, you not gone say what's up to yo family?" Jason asked.

"Yeah, you not gone say what's up to us?" Janelle agreed.

It was surprising to Janelle that she agreed with Jason because she hardly ever did. He hugged both of them and then decided to look around. Everyone was staring at him but he couldn't find who he was looking for. Mama Jo was in the kitchen so he knew why he couldn't see her. But it was one person he didn't get to see. It bothered him a little because it reminded him that the person he was looking for had been hanging out with Mike Dog a lot lately.

"Where is Gangster?" J-Ridah asked Janelle.

"He got up this morning to leave and haven't been home since. I thought he would make it back in time for the surprise but I guess not." She replied.

"I guess not huh?" J-Ridah commented.

He embraced his two siblings one last time then continued his journey over to the corner. He quickly shook hands with Do-Dirty and Snake then started a conversation like he had seen them the day before.

"You know we served them slob niggas for what they did to you and Shawny. The police been hot but we was able to sneak out once this week." Do-Dirty said loud enough for only J-Ridah and Snake to hear.

"I figured that much. But when I get better we got to give them niggas problems for killing Shawny. We can't let that shit ride." J-Ridah replied.

"I know cuz, but we gone wait until you get better." Do-Dirty said.

"Ride or die, Alondra for life. Ay, have you seen my brother?"

6
RENT PARTY

Bitches in the living room getting it on!
Snoop Doggy Dogg

The war began two days after J-Ridah was able to walk in a normal way. He went a couple of weeks walking with a limp without his crutches. Do-Dirty had the homies putting in work against the Mayo Lane's in rotation. It continued for weeks until it leaked out that one of the Laney boys was involved. Somehow a snitch that happened to have gone to school with J-Ridah had told the police that he was the one to look for. They knew his first and last name. The police didn't have any idea that it was actually Do-Dirty calling the shots for them to put in work against Mayo Lane Pirus. So once the Lynwood Sheriffs got a hold of J-Ridah's address they were staked out across the street from his house.

Snake had everyone at his house drinking and having a good time when J-Ridah took Sheila inside the garage. He always locked the door behind them while all the homies hung in the backyard. They had just finished having sex when C-Dog came knocking on the door.

"What's up cuz?" J-Ridah yelled through the door.

"Ay J-Ridah I just need to take a piss real fast then I'll leave ya'll alone."

"Damn C-Dog you can't go in the house?" J-Ridah yelled again.

"You know his moms don't want us in her house. Fuck it though, I'll find a bush or something." C-Dog replied.

"Naw, we coming out right about now." J-Ridah said.

Sheila was still getting dressed when C-Dog first knocked but now she had put on her clothes.

68

"Before you let him in J-Ridah, I want to tell you I might be pregnant. I missed my period and everything." Sheila said.

"Aw cuz, you just now telling me this shit..." J-Ridah snapped.

"You letting me in or what nigga?" C-Dog impatiently yelled.

"Fuck it we'll talk about this shit later Sheila."

C-Dog rushed through the door once it swung open and ran to the bathroom. J-Ridah laughed as C-Dog ran past him. Sheila glanced at J-Ridah with her eyes narrowed in.

"What? We gone talk about the shit cuz, you trippin" J-Ridah sneered.

She turned around to walk away. Suddenly J-Ridah grabbed her arm so that she couldn't get too far. She had her head down then looked up at him with sad eyes. J-Ridah could see the tears well up in her eyes. He stared at her for a moment confused. He had never really known how to deal with a woman being sensitive. His mother was a soldier in her own right so this was bizarre territory for him. He barely ever saw his mother smile let alone cry.

"We got to be gangster about this shit cuz. Look here Sheila, you my bitch and everything, but all that crying and shit ain't me. There isn't a female out there outside of my family that comes before you and you know that. So if you pregnant we just gone handle that shit that's all. You know this Compton Crip on mine, Alondra Block till I die and that's what's in my heart right now. So be cool and everything gone be fine." He calmly said.

"I don't know J-Ridah; you won't even let me call you Joseph and you about to be my baby's daddy. This shit is just different for me." Sheila replied.

"Alright you can call me Joseph if you want to." J-Ridah surrendered.

"Aw cuz, this nigga letting his broad call him by his government name." C-Dog yelled while passing by the couple.

"Fuck you cuz, you need to mind yo business." J-Ridah snapped.

"Nigga don't get mad at me because I heard you Simpin." C-Dog teased.

"Aw say it isn't so? Don't tell me that Sheila got you whipped where she get to call you by yo first name?" Snake cut in.

A few of the OG homies chuckled after Snake's comment. Everybody knew he was a gangster through and through but Snake knew that it would hit a nerve.

"That's why the fuck I don't want you calling me Joseph." J-Ridah sneered.

The homies really started laughing when he said that. The liquor had gotten into everybody so something small made everyone laugh. The laughter was interrupted when Do-Dirty walked in the backyard.

"Ay J-Ridah cuz, you got that twelve gauge pump at the house right? We gone need to get that muthafucka sawed off real soon. Cut off some of that handle then put that duct tape around that bitch." Do-Dirty said while walking across the back yard towards him.

"For sure cuz, I should go to the house and snatch that muthafucka up right now."

"Naw, you ain't got to do that shit now but let's do that shit some time tonight if you see what I'm saying." Do-Dirty gestured as if he was hinting.

"You know what; I think it would be better if I got that muthafucka right now. I'll be right back." J-Ridah suddenly walked off.

As he was walking towards the backyard gate he remembered Sheila. He stopped right before he opened the gate. He turned around and walked back over to Sheila. She smiled when she realized he had thought about her. He gently touched her on the face.

"We gone be good Ms. Sheila." He half smiled.

It made her feel warm inside. She had to settle for that for the time being because he was rushing out the backyard a moment later.

70

"You got yo strap, just in case them slob niggas is riding." Do-Dirty yelled after him.

"I got the thirty-eight long barrel, I'm good."

He walked down the street looking in every direction for any enemies creeping up. He had his blue golf hat turned backwards. His all Black T-shirt was creased on both sides matching his blue Dickies pants; blue Chuck Taylor's and black shoestrings. He kept a steady pace until he got to his own street then he slowed down. He always felt a little safer on his street than any other street in his neighborhood. He drew closer to the house and he seen the twins tossing the football around. Before he could make it to his yard two white men had jumped out of their car and walked towards him. He wasn't paying any attention because he was looking at the twins throw the football.

"Aye cuz, tossed that muthafucka to me."

Jamil, who was slightly darker than his twin Jalil tossed the ball to J-Ridah and smiled. J-Ridah was the closest to a father they had ever seen. Both twins looked on with admiration as J-Ridah caught the ball.

"Tight catch Joseph, I thought you might miss the catch." Jalil commented.

"Come on now, you know I'm tight with the football." J-Ridah said while tossing the ball to Jalil.

"Excuse me, are you Joseph Laney?"

A tall white man approached J-Ridah, having brown hair with brushes of gray and a thick cowboy mustache wearing a green jacket and tight jeans. On the back of the jacket it read L.A. Sheriffs. The clean-shaven white man that walked up with him wore a brown suit but his suit jacket wasn't on. He had a pistol strapped to his shoulder over his white shirt and beige tie.

"Who's asking?" J-Ridah replied.

"I'm Detective Bush and this is Detective Miller of the Los Angeles Sheriffs Department in Lynwood." The man with the Green Jacket replied.

"We need to ask you a few questions, could you come with us?" Detective Miller said more as a command than question.

71

"Hell naw cuz, ya'll ain't taking me anywhere. I live right here." J-Ridah walked towards his house.

"Mr. Laney it would be easier if we talked to you now instead of getting a warrant and you making things much worse." Detective Bush replied.

"Well that's what you gone have to do cuz, I don't know ya'll." J-Ridah replied.

By then he had made it in the yard. The twins had already told Mama Jo so she was on the porch right after J-Ridah finished his sentence.

"Joseph come in the house. What is the problem officer?" Mama Jo asked while walking off the porch.

"We need to talk to him about some things that have been going on in this neighborhood. If we have to come back with a warrant it will be a lot worse ma'am." Detective Bush replied.

"What is he being questioned about?"

"A few homicides that have been attributed to him." Detective Bush continued.

"Attri...what? You probably got the wrong person. My son doesn't have anything to do with any murders." Mama Jo calmly explained.

By this time J-Ridah had walked inside the house. Mama Jo was outside talking to the police.

"Janelle!!!" J-Ridah yelled just loud enough inside the house.

"What nigga?" Janelle yelled back from her and Mama Jo's room.

"Bring yo ass here, that's what." He fired back.

Janelle came in the living room pouting with a magazine in her hand. Her tank top was replacing a much-needed bra while her jeans were unbuttoned and halfway zipped. Her bare feet stomped on the hardwood floor.

"What do you want Joseph damn? Where mama at?" She looked around.

"She outside talking to the police. Now here, take this thirty-eight and put it in Mama's room with you and get that twelve-gauge pump from out my room and put it with the thirty-eight."

"What if mama finds it?" She asked.

"It's better she finds it instead of the pigs."

She nodded her head in agreement and began carrying out his instructions. J-Ridah decided to go on the porch to see how everything was going. When he walked outside he saw Mama Jo in her moo-moo and house shoes still calmly talking to the police.

"You should talk to us son or it will be much worse." Detective Bush insisted.

"First and foremost, you can talk to me. You don't need to shout at my son when I'm standing in front of you right now." Mama Jo snapped.

"But you don't have any idea what your son is into. So how can you be of any good to us?" Detective Bush fired back.

J-Ridah had already walked into the yard from off the porch. He slowly began towards the street where Mama Jo was with the police.

"Watch how you talk to my moms' cuz." J-Ridah said.

"We don't even want to talk to your fucking mother; we want to talk to you. I swear to God Mr. Laney if I have to get a warrant you are going to regret you ever met me." Detective Bush warned.

"Once again you don't have anything to say to my son. I'm his mother and now you don't even get to talk to me. Joseph go inside and let these assholes go about their business." Mama Jo waived them off.

Detective Bush was fuming and before Mama Jo could walk away he grabbed her by the arm tightly.

"Watch how you talk to a Sheriff Ms. Laney. I assume you're not married, typical."

J-Ridah saw him grab Mama Jo and he snapped. He quickly was outside the yard pulling Mama Jo away from Detective Bush. When he pulled his mother closer, Detective Bush snatched her closer to him.

"I'm not done talking to this nigger bitch." Detective Bush sneered.

J-Ridah's eyes got bigger. He had heard the word nigga a million times but he had never heard the term nigger from a white person. His entire body felt cold all over. He attempted again to pull his mother away from the angered detective.

"Let go of my moms'." J-Ridah warned.

Detective Bush pulled her harder. This infuriated J-Ridah to the point where tears began to well up in his eyes. He let go of his mother and took a full swing at the face of Detective Bush. The blow landed flush on the Detective's jaw, which caused him to stumble. Detective Bush held on to his jaw and screamed in pain. Mama Jo walked over to the sidewalk somewhat disoriented. Detective Miller went into action a moment later. He pulled out his pistol and hit J-Ridah across the head with his gun. Blood streamed down J-Ridah's face while he stumbled to gain balance. Detective Miller pulled out his handcuffs and quickly put them on J-Ridah's wrists.

"You are under arrest for the assault of a police officer." Detective Miller began.

As he read the Miranda rights to J-Ridah, Janelle, Jason and the twins walked off the porch.

"What happened, Mama?" Janelle yelled.

"Go back in the house Janelle and take them with you." Mama Jo replied.

"What happened, Mama?" Janelle repeated but with more hysteria.

"Never mind, just do as I say right now. This is the wrong time to not listen to me Janelle." Mama Jo said firmly.

She was starting to get her head back as the detectives took J-Ridah to the car. She stood straight up and looked at her neighbors staring at the whole ordeal. She watched her son get pulled to the police car but before he made it inside the unmarked car Detective Bush punches him in the stomach while holding his jaw.

"You broke my jaw you fucking nigger." He struggled to say.

They stuffed him into the backseat of the car so that Detective Bush could use his police stick to beat J-Ridah bloody. Mama Jo stared helplessly as they drove off.

"Janelle!!!" Mama Jo yelled.

"Yes mama?" Janelle peaked outside.

"It is almost dark outside so I need you to run around the corner and tell Dennis that Joseph just went to jail for assaulting a police officer. Now you come right back because things are getting hectic around here. You here me?" Mama Jo said.

"Yeah, tell Dennis that Joseph got locked up for assaulting a police officer."

"Okay good. They are probably hanging out in David's backyard. Now hurry up Janelle, it shouldn't take you longer than ten minutes."

Janelle took off right after Mama Jo made her commands. Mama Jo watched her get half way down the block then turned her attention towards the house.

"Jason, come help me up this walk way and into the house. One of ya'll twins go get your mama some water." Mama Jo said sounding exhausted.

Janelle made it around to Snake's house in about three minutes flat. She walked towards the backyard breathing hard. She slowly unlatched the gate and entered into the backyard. It was loud in the backyard with the radio playing 'The Message' from the rap group 'Grand Master Flash and the Furious Five'. Janelle bypassed everyone and walked straight up to Do-Dirty. Do-Dirty was leaning on the garage wall talking to this girl that Janelle knew as Pam. She remembered hearing that she lived over in Greenleaf territory. She was a little reluctant to approach because she worried if she might give Pam the wrong impression. She stopped a few yards of where they were standing.

"Damn Janelle, what yo fine young ass doing around here with all these niggas?" Deuce said from behind her.

She knew exactly who it was, so she didn't bother to turn around. 'What this old ass nigga want with me' she pondered? She didn't have much time so she figured it would be safer to approach Do-Dirty.

"Ay Dennis, I mean Do-Dirty, I got to tell you something." Janelle blurted out.

Do-Dirty looked up from swigging his forty-ounce of Old English to see Janelle standing in front of him. He only paid attention to her a few times but he suddenly realized that she was a grown woman. She was only fourteen but she could have easily passed for eighteen to twenty. Her voluptuous body in her tomboy façade caught him off guard. For a moment he had to think about who she was.

"Who is this little bitch coming up asking for you?" Pam snarled.

"Bitch? Who you calling a bitch?" Janelle fired back.

"Chill the fuck out Pam, this is J-Ridah's little sister. What's up Big Nell what are you doing around here?"

"Mama just told me to run around here and tell you that Joseph just went to jail for assaulting a police officer." Janelle replied.

By that time people had gathered around out of curiosity. Do-Dirty had to be drunk because it didn't sink in for a few seconds. He staggered slightly as he got up from leaning against the wall.

"Aw cuz, you mean to tell me the homie got caught up by 'One Time'?" Do-Dirty slurred.

"Yeah some plain clothes police came by our house looking for my brother but my mama talked to them instead. When one of them tried to grab my mama Joseph socked him in his jaw." She explained.

"That nigga J-Ridah is a fool for firing on the police." Deuce commented.

"He was fucking with my mama?" Janelle snarled.

It suddenly dawned on Do-Dirty the severity of the situation. His senses were much slower than usual. He usually

76

didn't allow himself to get this drunk. He glanced down at Janelle with his eyes slightly open and his forehead wrinkled.

"What did they find on him?" He asked.

"That's all good, you don't have to worry about that." Janelle nodded.

Do-Dirty sighed for a moment then started moving around so that he could sober up.

"Look here cuz, the police is staking out the homies house so we got to make sure we are careful. We gone lay low tonight but somebody get word to the little homies to watch they back because 'one time' is hot." Do-Dirty announced.

Janelle turned around to leave so that she could make it back home in her ten-minute time span. She halfway made it to the gate.

"Ay Janelle that was good looking out from Mama Jo. You be sure to tell her what I said." Do-Dirty said.

Janelle nodded and headed out the gate rushing towards her house. She made it around the corner in about three minutes flat. Mama Jo was sitting at the table when she walked in. She looked more relaxed than when Janelle last seen her.

"Did you let Dennis know what I said?"

"Yeah, he told me to tell you good looking out."

"I'm worried shitless about your other brother Jordan. He hasn't been home in about three days. I didn't want Joseph to go to jail but at least I know where he's at. This shit is getting to be too much. Why don't you go in the bathroom and hand me my aspirin?" Mama Jo said to Janelle.

She walked into the bathroom then peaked into the twins' and Jason's room. She noticed that Jason was nowhere to be found. She gave the room a once over then decided to look in Joseph and Jordan's room. When she opened the door she caught Jason looking at J-Ridah's thirty-eight. She walked into the room and quickly closed the door.

"What the fuck are you doing with Joseph's gun? If mama sees that you got that gun she gone beat yo ass." Janelle whispered.

"She doesn't have to know. If you don't say shit then she won't know I got it." Jason fired back.

"Boy if you don't..."

"Janelle baby, what is taking you so long to grab some aspirins? I could have grabbed them, swallowed them and did a few other things as long as it's taking you to bring those pills." Mama Jo yelled.

"Here I come Mama." Janelle replied.

Janelle looked firmly at Jason with her lips curled up. She pointed her finger at him. He looked her right in her eye blankly.

"You better get those pills to mama."

At that very moment she understood that he wasn't giving up that gun. She came to terms with that fact then walked into the living room and handed Mama Jo her pills.

"Girl you working my nerves as long as you took."

Janelle sat across from her half smiling. She was trying to lighten up the mood. Even though Mama Jo didn't smile too much she liked when Janelle did.

"You think Joseph is going to be fine mama?" Janelle asked.

"Yeah, the pigs probably beat him up but if he makes it to Los Padrinos then he should be fine.

"Los Padrinos?"

"Yeah, that is the local juvenile hall. Jackie's daughter Monique got sent there for shoplifting last year. You remember I was going over to Jackie's house a lot last summer?" Mama Jo replied while picking at her toes.

"Yeah, but I didn't know it was because Monique was shoplifting. I thought Auntie Jackie had that good government job. Why would Monique have to steal?"

"Ya see that was why I didn't want to tell you. You looking deeper into it than you have to. That little heifer is greedy that's why. I didn't want to put any ideas in your head so I left well enough alone. My sister has always been sidity anyway. Talking about she would expect that from my kids but not from hers. I haven't talk to that little bitch since." Mama Jo snarled.

"Are you serious? She really said that to you?"

"Do it look like I'm serious?"

Mama Jo was stern and sullen then she rolled her eyes. Janelle seen that it was somewhat hurtful when dredging up the memory. Mama Jo lowered her head as if she had been wounded.

"Sister or not, she doesn't talk about my babies like they ain't shit when I'm the first bitch she calls when her babies get to acting up." Mama Jo stared at Janelle hard.

"Well Mama don't let that get to you."

"Naw I'm not. I got bigger fish to fry. I might be a little short on rent and I don't know what I'm going to do about it. You got any ideas?"

"Naw not that I can think of."

"I knew Joseph might have it but since he went to jail I don't know where I can get some money. You know what I should do? I should throw parties and charge everyone to get in. Then I can scrape up enough to pay rent this month." Mama had the facial expression as though a light bulb went off.

"You think you can get enough people to pay for a party?" Janelle asked with surprise.

"Sure could, if I get it out there word of mouth. Then we can buy a bunch of bottle six packs and sell them for two dollars a bottle."

"It just might work mama. But you gone need to tell everybody for it to really be cracking."

"It will."

7

THE CASE THEY GAVE ME

I can dance under water and not get wet!
Mack 10

Mama Jo had cleaned the entire house. She was getting ready for the biggest party she could muster. She already had a banging sound system that J-Ridah had brought to the house one day. He never explained where he got it but it would come in handy today. Somehow Jason had gotten a hold of some weed and planned on selling bags at the party. He had started running errands and curb serving for Pookie for several months now. He was saving his money that he made with Pookie plus selling a little weed on the side. He didn't have to worry about someone trying to rob him because his brothers J-Ridah and Gangster had a reputation. But just in case someone did want to make a move he kept his thirty-eight stashed away for such occasions. He helped Mama Jo with money here and there to get her started with the party. He gave her money for beer and snacks. She didn't bother to ask where he got it from because he came up with the money just when she needed it. She was ready to have her first rent party.

She had finished all the arrangements a little past seven in the evening. She told the twins that they would have to stay in the room. But since Jason gave her the money for the accessories she allowed him to be at the party. She was reluctant at first but she decided it would be best if she wanted to throw another party and he was hoarding away money. She just might need his help again. She wanted Janelle around to help her host the party. She would get refreshments for people and things like that. There was really no way she could dress down Janelle's womanly body among all these grown men so she let Janelle decide what she wanted to wear. On the day of the party she had a brand new outfit that

Mama Jo didn't recall buying. It didn't dawn on her where she could have gotten it until she seen Janelle be extremely nice to Jason. That was something that hardly happened, so it wasn't hard to put two and two together.

Jason had ran to the grocery store for Mama Jo one last time for a couple of items for just in case. He passed by the spot where Pookie and Flintstone would hustle. He seen Pookie in the alley curb serving and he stopped to chat for a moment.

"What's happening Baby Gangster cuz, are we able to go to Mama Jo's party or is it just for the OG niggas?" Pookie asked.

"As long as you paying I don't think my moms is going to trip. You will get to see my sister in that new outfit you bought her."

"Is my old road dog going to be there too? I haven't seen Gangster in awhile since he's been hanging with OG Mike Dog." Pookie commented.

"Yeah they be fucking with that Sherm. He came home for a few days the other night. I sleep in the same room with that crazy nigga now and he wakes up in the middle of the night reaching for his strap. I got love for my brother cuz, but that nigga is a little off."

"Yeah I've been hearing he hasn't been the same lately. He gone be all right cuz, he just got to get off that shit. Tell your sister I said hi and I will see her later at the party. I got to do the curb serving since you got the day off little nigga." Pookie chided.

"Alright then cuz, I'll tell her what you said."

Jason walked up to the store and quickly bought the items he intended to buy. Before he walked out the store he noticed some loud mouth Crips at the store that wasn't from Alondra Block. He didn't pay it much mind but was cognizant of what was going on around him. They walked out the store a little bit ahead of him. Once he made it outside he noticed them in the parking lot still being loud and boisterous. He decided to not even look their way. He wasn't in any mood to get into trouble and it was obvious they were looking for trouble.

"Ay young cuz, where you from with that blue golf hat?" One said to him.

Jason didn't look up and pretended not to hear.

"Cuz, I'm talking to you little nigga." The same guy barked.

"Leave that young nigga alone Nu-Nu, he got groceries and shit." The other one chuckled.

"Naw cuz, this little nigga is from somewhere, he got on a blue golf hat, he's sagging in some khakis and he got on black Chuck Taylor's with blue shoestrings." Nu-Nu barked.

"I'm from Alondra Block but I ain't tripping off all that shit cuz." Jason replied.

"Aw nigga, yo little young ass need yo ass whipped. What do you got in the bag?" Nu-Nu continued.

"Some shit for my moms." Jason stopped to reply.

"Let me see cuz."

"Nope, you ain't got a reason for going inside this bag. You might know my brothers Gangster and J-Ridah from the Block? I'm they younger brother they call Baby Gangster Laney." Jason subtly warned.

"I don't give a fuck what they call..." Nu-Nu was interrupted.

"You related to the Laney's?" The other guy asked.

"Yeah, they my brothers."

Jason could tell that Nu-Nu's homeboy knew whom he was talking about. At the very least he had a certain amount of respect for one of his brothers if not both.

"C'mon cuz, leave this little nigga alone."

"Naw Sly, this little nigga need to know who the fuck he's talking to. Like I said cuz, what's in the muthafuckin bag?" Nu-Nu barked again.

"Like I said, I don't have to show you shit." Jason sneered.

"Fuck this little nigga cuz, let's go back to the hood." Sly insisted.

"Yeah right after this young nigga give me this bag."

Nu-Nu was still a little distance from Jason but it was easy to tell that he was a little drunk. He walked straight but the way he slurred his words suggested alcohol. He took one step towards Jason but Sly grabbed hold of his arm.

"Let me go cuz, who the fuck this little nigga think he is? I'm a muthafuckin OG."

Nu-Nu snatched his arm from Sly and started walking towards Jason. Jason didn't budge from his position. He stood still as if waiting for Nu-Nu to approach. His eyes narrowed as the larger man drew closer. Just as Nu-Nu came about three yards from him he pulled out his thirty-eight.

"Aw cuz!" Sly blurted out.

"Oh shit this little young nigga is strapped." Nu-Nu realized.

He stopped in his tracks without making a move forward or backwards. He seemed to sober up immediately.

"Who you going to shoot with that strap cuz?" Nu-Nu attempted to downplay the situation.

"Come a little bit closer and find out." Jason replied.

"It ain't even got to be like that little Laney." Sly said.

"I didn't want to make it like that but yo homeboy keep trying to punk me. If this nigga wants to die then he can come running up and I'm gone give it to him." Jason replied

"Naw little Laney we about to bounce. Let's stall that shit out." Sly suggested.

"It ain't up to me." Jason firmly stated.

He still made eye-to-eye contact with Nu-Nu without flinching. Nu-Nu began to believe that he was capable of using the weapon. He slowly put his hands up as if to surrender but Jason kept his pistol drawn and pointed at him. Nu-Nu began slowly backing up trying to make it to the passenger side of Sly's car. Jason allowed him to reach the car then watched him jump in on the passenger side.

"It's cool little Laney, we about to bone out." Sly said.

"Quit fucking calling me little Laney. They call me Baby Gangster from Alondra Block Compton Crip." Jason announced.

Sly waived his hand as if to apologize then hopped in on the driver's side. Jason watched him sit down in the seat and say a few words to Nu-Nu. Nu-Nu was sitting in the passenger seat with a stone face. Jason could tell he was seething inside. He heard Sly start up the car so he started to walk away. He was only allowed to walk a few steps before he looked up to see Nu-Nu reaching out the window with black long nosed pistol. Before Nu-Nu could get out the window with the gun Jason started pulling the trigger finger back. The first two shots busted out the window of Sly's El Dorado. The third shot must have hit Nu-Nu because he heard him scream out. Jason let off the rest of the round as Sly tried to turn in the other direction. When Jason realized that he didn't have any more bullets he took off running full speed with the grocery bags in hand. He slid the gun into one of the bags because it was too hot for him to put back into his waist. He didn't stop running until he reached the alley where Pookie and Flintstone were hanging.

"Damn little nigga what the fuck happened to you?" Pookie asked after Jason ran up on him.

"Some niggas tried to rob me at the grocery store just now." Jason said while panting heavily.

"Are you serious cuz?" Flintstone flared up.

"Hell yeah but they are not behind me anymore so I think they got the hint." Jason replied.

"Got the hint?" Pookie looked puzzled.

"Yeah, I had to blast on them niggas just now. They tried to blast on me first because I drew down on them niggas. I wasn't going to shoot if they would have just backed away but one of them niggas kept trying to rob me." Jason explained.

"So you blasted on them? I knew I had heard some gunshots" Pookie chuckled.

"Where were they from?" Flintstone asked.

"I don't know. One called himself Nu-Nu and the other nigga called himself Sly."

"I know them niggas cuz. They some Greenleaf niggas. They got OG status over in they hood. Did you tell them anything?" Pookie asked.

"Yeah, I told them I was a Laney. One of them kept calling me little Laney. I told that nigga I was Baby Gangster from Alondra Block Compton Crip." Jason proudly stated.

"I know that's right." Pookie laughed.

"You a down ass little nigga, Baby Gangster." Flintstone laughed also.

"Yeah you are down cuz. But you better get back to the house before Mama Jo gets a search party to come look for you. And you know she will do it." Pookie said.

"Alright then, I'm out."

Jason looked around then looked back at Pookie and Flintstone who were still laughing at the incident. He rushed home in a fast paced walk trying to hurry without looking like he was running. He began to slow down only when he made it to his front yard. Mama Jo had her front door open and could see him walking up.

"Damn boy, did you bring back the whole store? Why did it take you so long to get them few things?" She yelled while he was walking up.

"It was crowded in the store, that's all mama." Jason replied.

"Well hurry up so I can finish up before everybody gets here."

Jason handed her every bag except the one he had slid the pistol inside.

"What's in that bag?"

"Something I bought for myself."

He hurriedly walked into the room before she could ask any more questions. Once he got inside the room he instantly realized that Gangster had been home for a moment. He slid his gun under his mattress then walked back into the living room with the remaining items that were in the bag.

"Oh mama, it was a few things in this bag for you also. Did Jordan come home for a minute?" He curiously asked.

"Yeah, that crazy nigga came in then ran back out. I tried to tell him that I was throwing a party and he acted as if he had

85

forgotten I told him. I don't know what I'm going to do with that boy." Mama Jo said.

Jason walked back in the room then went into the side of his mattress. He dug inside and realized that there was only twenty dollars gone from his stash. He was relieved but at the same time sad. He knew what Gangster was about to do with that money he had stolen. It didn't really hurt his stash because he prepared to spend a certain amount anyway. He had over three thousand saved and this was the first time he had really spent any of it with the exception of him buying weed. But he figured he wouldn't see Gangster for the rest of the night.

Right before Do-Dirty and the other OG homies were headed out to the party a carload of niggas rolled up. They knew to pull up right in front of Snake's mother's house. They were five deep in a blue 1964 Chevy Impala sitting on chrome Dayton rims with chrome knock offs. The car looked familiar to Do-Dirty so he didn't start shooting. In fact he walked up to the car thinking that they were there early to come to Mama Jo's party. The driver got out the car and walked up to Do-Dirty and they embraced.

"What's up C-Rag cuz? Are you over here to check out the party tonight?" Do-Dirty nonchalantly asked.

"Yeah we came to check it out. But I got to holla at you about some other shit too." C-Rag looked perplexed.

"What's happening?" Do-Dirty recognized the look.

"One of your little BG homies just blasted on one of my OG homies." C-Rag continued.

"You know who it was? We been beefing with those Mayo niggas so one of the homies must have thought ya'll was some off brands."

C-Rag pondered on his words for a moment. Do-Dirty and him were locked up in the County together so they had developed a rapport. C-Rag was still locked up when Do-Dirty got into a fight with Rick Rock. They had always remained cool and actually had love for each other.

"Naw cuz, the homeboy says this little nigga knew they were Crips and decided to blast on them anyway."

"Does he know his name? If he knows his name I'll check the young nigga right now. But I'm gone let him tell his side of the story first. We don't have any reason to be blasting on Crips." Do-Dirty replied.

"That's what I told the homeboy but he was sure. Glass had shattered in his face and everything. My homeboy with him said it was a little nigga by the name of Laney." C-Rag suddenly remembered.

Do-Dirty sighed out of frustration. He knew that Gangster was on that Sherm fucking with Mike Dog. He had just seen Gangster walk by about twenty minutes ago with Mike Dog about to go smoke.

"This was about thirty minutes ago. It was up at the Grocery store on Long Beach Boulevard."

"Thirty minutes ago? Naw the nigga I'm thinking about couldn't have done that shit in that amount of time. You sure his name was Laney. His brother is locked up and he couldn't have been way over there at the store because I just seen the nigga." Do-Dirty replied.

"Yeah, he called himself Baby Gangster." C-Rag explained.

"Aw snap, you got to be bullshitting me. Ay Snake tell that little nigga Ace to come here for a minute." Do-Dirty yelled.

Ace came jogging out the backyard with his golf hat tilted slightly to the side on top of his afro.

"What's up cuz?" Ace said to Do-Dirty.

"Look here, run around the corner and get Jason Laney and tell Mama Jo I want to holla at him. Let her know it's important. You got yo strap with you?"

Ace nodded then rose up his shirt to show his piece.

"Alright then make sure he is safe so that I can holler at him for a minute." Do-Dirty said.

Ace took off running to the Laney household. Do-Dirty chopped it up with C-Rag until Ace came back around with Jason walking beside him. Jason was a little scared but decided against carrying his thirty-eight since Do-Dirty wanted to talk to him. He figured what it was about and he thought he would be punished. Once he was closer to the car he seen Sly and Nu-Nu sitting inside staring at him with hateful eyes. He ignored their stares and walked right up to Do-Dirty while Ace walked toward the backyard.

"What's up Jason or Baby Gangster? Did you get into it with some niggas at the grocery store tonight?" Do-Dirty asked.

He could tell that Jason was scared but he wanted to clear this matter up without any problems. But it was highly unlikely that Jason would shoot at someone. So Do-Dirty already had it in his mind that they probably provoked him. Jason nodded his head somberly.

"Why did you get into it with them?"

Jason looked up at the unfamiliar person and didn't reply. He wanted to be alone with Do-Dirty to tell him the truth. He decided not to answer him since the stranger was present. Do-Dirty recognized why Jason was reluctant and slightly smiled.

"Aw cuz, he just wants to hear yo side of the story. He's not about to trip on you. No body is gone trip on you." Do-Dirty calmly explained.

"Well…I went to the grocery store for my mama and when I came out those two niggas in the car tried to take my mama's stuff. The nigga with the ponytail wanted to look inside my bag and I told him no. When I said no he got mad and said he was an OG so I better let him see the bag. When I said no again he started rushing at me so I pulled out my thirty-eight."

"Thirty-eight? Where did you get a…" It suddenly dawned on him that he had never gotten that gun back from Janelle. The twelve-gauge pump and the thirty-eight were still at the Laney house.

"I waited until they got into the car and everything. Then when they got into the car they tried to shoot at me. So I started shooting at them. Then I ran back to the hood. I tried to tell them about my brothers but that nigga with the ponytail, Nu-Nu didn't give a fuck who was my family."

"That's all I needed to hear cuz." C-Rag threw his hands in the air.

C-Rag walked off towards his car upset. He didn't waste any time discussing it any more because he knew how Nu-Nu was.

"Stay up C-Rag, you should come through for the party tonight though."

"I'm coming back after I drop these niggas back off in the hood. This nigga Nu-Nu always trying to rob somebody cuz." C-Rag said

Do-Dirty looked down at Jason and smiled. He didn't really say anything to him but watched him carefully. He glanced up to see C-Rag making gestures like he was pissed off talking to his homeboys. Finally he started the ignition then put the car in drive. As he was driving off he rolled the window down.

"Yo little BG homeboy got heart cuz." C-Rag said.

Do-Dirty threw up the Crip sign then turned his attention towards Jason.

"We are not going to call you Jason anymore. From now on we are calling you Baby Gangster. But don't just be down to shoot; also being down to handle it from the shoulders should be in yo heart. You understand what I'm saying?"

Baby Gangster nodded his head and fought from trying to smile. He was now down for the set officially. Do-Dirty escorted Baby Gangster to the back yard where all of the OGs were hanging. When they entered the gate people were gathered ready to go party at his house.

"Look here cuz, this is Baby Gangster. This young nigga got heart. Some Greenleaf niggas tried to rob him and he blasted on they ass."

Everyone laughed as they began to file out of the back yard. In passing everyone congratulated him by either shaking his hand or embracing him. Once everyone passed through the gate Do-Dirty and Baby Gangster followed suit. Once out front everyone was in front of Snake's house preparing to jump in his or her perspective cars.

"Roll with me Baby Gangster." Do-Dirty said.

When they made it around the corner Mama Jo had the music blasting. She was playing 'What's Going On' by Marvin Gaye on the stereo. A crowd emerged in Mama Jo's yard while Janelle collected the money at the door. Mama Jo had found a strobe light and everyone hit the dance floor. The music was loud and the party was jumping. It was Saturday night and everyone partied like they didn't have a care in the world.

Close to eleven was when people from other set's started mobbing into the party. The first ones to arrive were the Greenleaf Crips. Then the Boulevards came in next and before long the living room was crowded. By the time it hit one in the morning Mama Jo had made close to seven hundred dollars. But the party didn't stop.

Around one-thirty in the morning Mike Dog walked in with Gangster following close behind him. It was obvious that they were high off that Sherm. Mike Dog was moving through the crowd bumping into to niggas intentionally and it finally came to a head.

"Damn cuz, you better watch who the fuck you bumping into. This Boulevard on mine." Ghost snapped.

"What the fuck you talking about cuz, you in my hood. You better move the fuck out my way." Mike Dog fired back.

Ghost didn't waste any time. He swung and hit Mike Dog dead center on his chin. Mike Dog stumbled back and fell against the wall. Ghost went after following him hit the wall with a thud. Ghost's had a blue rag wrapped around his head Aunt Jemima style with a blue Pendleton, blue Khakis and Krokasaks. He hammered Mike Dog with three more punches to the face but the punches didn't seem to hurt.

"He's fucking with that Sherm cuz." Somebody blurted out.

That was what made Ghost elbow him in the chin. With that blow Mike Dog slumped to the floor. He was practically asleep but Ghost opted to stomp him even more. Before he could lift his first foot to come down on Mike Dog he heard a loud noise. It wasn't a gunshot but it was something similar. Ghost looked up from his attack to see a twelve-gauge pump pointed directly at him. His first thought was that it was someone from Alondra Block then he realized it was a woman holding the shotgun.

"Don't you know that you ain't ever supposed to pull a gun unless you gone use it." Ghost sneered.

"Well keep doing what you doing and see if I don't use it." Mama Jo calmly replied.

She stood in a stance that let him know that she was ready to fill him with buck shots. His eyes wandered for a moment because he considered seriously challenging her. But this was her house so he had to respect that.

"Tell yo homeboys not to be tripping off that Sherm." Ghost calmly said.

During the entire incident Do-Dirty was in the bathroom making out with Pam. He heard the thud but chose to ignore it. But once Janelle seen Mama Jo had come out with the twelve-gauge pump she instantly turned off the music. That's what alerted Do-Dirty that something was wrong.

"What the fuck happened?" Do-Dirty demanded.

"That nigga Mike Dog and Ghost from the Boulevard got into it because Mike was tripping on that Sherm." Deuce replied since he was the closest.

Do-Dirty looked to see Mike Dog out cold on the floor with his mouth busted open. Do-Dirty was seething with anger and went searching for Ghost who was already outside. He mobbed outside with the rest of the Alondra Block homeboys close in tow.

"Why in the fuck didn't anyone help the homeboy?" He posed the question to everyone.

"That shit was over so fast; we didn't get a chance to help him. By the time I realized who was fighting, Mike Dog was knocked out and Ghost had a twelve-gauge pump in his face." Snake replied.

Do-Dirty walked outside looking for Ghost to settle the problem. He tried to find where Ghost was among the crowd because by now everyone was leaving. Right when he spotted Ghost a distance down the street he marched toward him.

"Ay Ghost cuz, we got to settle this shit."

Suddenly he heard the sound of a police siren. He turned around to see the Compton police three cars strong pull up on the crowd of people. Do-Dirty wanted to handle the problem with Ghost but he did like everyone else and dispersed when the police said to do so.

"Damn, I'll have to handle this shit on another day." He sighed.

8
FEUDING

Remember they used to thump now they blast right!
Dr. Dre

"All I know is one of the homeboys got rushed in our own hood. That kind of shit can't happen over here cuz. So either that nigga Mike Dog gone go head up with Ghost or one of us will." Do-Dirty barked at a pack of his homeboys.

"But you know that nigga Mike was tripping off that Sherm?" Snake interjected.

"I could give a mad fuck what that nigga was on. It makes us all look bad when a nigga from another set can just come over here and rush one of ours." Do-Dirty fired back.

"We should roll over there today and handle up with that nigga. I'll do a fair one with that nigga." Deuce volunteered.

"That's what I'm talking about cuz. I could do it just the same but niggas over there know I'm a shot caller so they gone think I'm set tripping." Do-Dirty said enthusiastically.

"You are set tripping though." Snake chuckled.

"But still, it's some shit that has to be done. Damn I wish J-Ridah was out because that nigga is down for anything." Do-Dirty replied.

"Yeah, but that was sometimes his problem. He didn't know how to be cool. Now you flying off the handle over some shit that Mike Dog should have taken care of himself. Now I'm hearing that little young bitch Sheila is pregnant while this nigga doing time." C-Dog commented.

"Yeah he looking at five years behind that shit. Mama Jo told me that shit the other day. But still, we got to let niggas know when they come to our hood; a respect thing is in order." Do-Dirty replied.

93

"What we waiting for? Let's go over there and settle this shit." Deuce eagerly suggested.

"Naw Deuce, I'm waiting on Baby Gangster to roll around here and roll with us." Do-Dirty said.

"What!?!! You about to have that young nigga rolling with us? He's only thirteen or fourteen years old. Ain't that little nigga still in junior high school?" C-Dog said.

"But he's got heart. He blasted on some Greenleaf niggas for trying to jack him. I just want him to see how we roll as a set. He's over there hustling with Pookie and Flintstone but I told them to send him over here in a little bit."

"Here he comes now." Deuce said.

Baby Gangster walked up on the OGs with his black Pro Club T-Shirt, black khakis and his blue Nike tennis shoes. He was letting his hair grow out so he paid his sister to braid his hair. As he walked up Do-Dirty gave a sly smile. The Laney boys were all big for their age and Baby Gangster wasn't any different. His disposition was a little more laid back than his two older brothers. He always took the attitude suggesting that he didn't want any problems.

"Damn Baby Gangster, I didn't think you could be more gangster than yesterday. But you pulled it off little young nigga." Do-Dirty commented.

"Aw cuz I just put together what I can. But what's up, Pookie and Flintstone said you wanted to see me?"

"Yeah, that fight that broke out at Mama Jo's party never got settled. So the OG niggas is about to roll over there and settle this shit. I wanted you to roll with us."

"Alright then." Baby Gangster was flattered.

They hop into two separate cars over to Boulevard territory. Snake, Do-Dirty and Baby Gangster rolled together. While Deuce, Jay-Cee, and Cornbread who just got out Susanville, rolled in C-Dog's Cutlass Supreme. Baby Gangster sat in the back seat wondering what was about to happen. He ordinarily wouldn't feel like he had time for this but since OG Do-Dirty asked him to roll he felt obligated. He knew this was about the time when the dope fiends would be coming out in droves for that dope he was serving for Pookie. He let his thoughts wander off until he realized they were in Boulevard hood rolling up on several gangsters.

He instantly recognized the light skinned cat that beat up OG Mike Dog. He was talking loud, being the center of attention. It was obvious to Baby Gangster that this nigga was a shot caller. He wasn't that tall but he had muscles on him. He stood at maybe five foot nine inches tall. His Pendleton shirt had his arms and chest busting through it. Do-Dirty jumped out the car first to walk up on the pack of Boulevards.

"What's happening Ghost cuz?" Do-Dirty greeted him.

"Do-Dirty, damn what you doing over here in *my* hood." He sounded condescending.

"We got a problem with what happened the other night at the party. You rushed one of our homeboys when he was drunk. So it's only right that you get down with one of our homeboys head up who ain't drunk." Do-Dirty replied.

"Aw naw cuz, it wasn't even like that. That nigga we talking about was on that Sherm and he started acting crazy."

"That ain't how it was told to me. I heard you bumped into the nigga then bombed on him when he didn't get out of your way quick enough. We can settle this shit by you going head up with my homeboy Deuce."

"Fuck that cuz, don't be coming over to our hood telling us who the fuck we need to get down with." Shotgun fired back

"That's why it's head up cuz. This shit can be settled head up and then the shit is squashed. Unless yo homeboy Ghost ain't down to catch a fair one with Deuce." Do-Dirty slyly commented.

It was his subtle way of suggesting that Ghost might be scared. He knew that it would force Ghost to take up the challenge.

"Fuck that cuz, you shouldn't…" Shotgun was interrupted.

"If this nigga want a head up then let's handle the shit." Ghost replied.

Deuce was already out the car by this time. He stood a little distance behind Do-Dirty. Ghost was well known for being able to throw his fists. But there wasn't too many people around that could win a fair one with Deuce. He once was an amateur boxing champion. Anybody that went to school with him knew about his skills. Baby Gangster sat in the back seat of Do-Dirty's car staring in awe as they squared off.

Naturally the first punch was landed by Deuce right in Ghost's mouth. Ghost had been hit harder but the punch irritated him. He had a little more muscle so he decided to rush right in. He wanted to make Deuce brawl instead of box. Ghost swung his seventeen and a half inch arms in fast combinations. Deuce backed up slightly to avoid the onslaught. Do-Dirty bit his bottom lip impatiently waiting the outcome.

The second time Ghost threw his combination Deuce stood in place. With trained timing and precision he hit Ghost with a two-punch combination. The first blow was an uppercut right above his chin, and then the second punch landed flush on his nose. Ghost stumbled back in a daze. Deuce stayed on top of him and followed with a right hook to the rib cage. Ghost winced in pain. He folded under holding his stomach but no mercy was given. Deuce finished him off with a blow to the jaw and a blow to the chin. Ghost was laid out on the street unconscious. Do-Dirty smiled as Ghost's homeboys came over to aid him.

"Aw hell naw cuz. Ya'll can't just come over here and run up on one of the homeboys like that." Big Kong snapped.

"Yo homeboy accepted a fair one. He had to know he might lose. Nobody jumped in nigga, so you set tripping over some shit that was handled between those two niggas." Do-Dirty lashed back.

"Naw fuck that. Ghost got down with yo homeboy Mike Dog so that shit was supposed to be settled between them two. Everybody knows this nigga Deuce was once a golden gloves." Kong protested.

"First of all, Mike Dog couldn't be found. Second, this nigga Deuce was the one that seen the fight so he had a problem with how it went down and wanted to even up with Ghost. But if you don't think that it was fair, you and I can handle this shit for good, head up." Do-Dirty replied.

"I got to see what's up with my homeboy." Kong dismissed the challenge.

Do-Dirty turned around and smiled. He figured Kong wouldn't want a fair one. Kong was big but he didn't have any heart or skill. Do-Dirty hopped into his glasshouse then looked in the back seat at Baby Gangster.

"That's how we do niggas when you claiming Alondra Block. We ain't letting anyone come in our hood and regulate us."

Baby Gangster nodded his head but in his mind he wasn't impressed. That was the problem with his brothers he thought, they always wanted to fight someone. He could have been out on the corner with Pookie making some money. He felt somewhat honored to be hanging with the OGs but he really preferred making that money instead.

"I'm going to be the best hustler in the world. I'm going to have money, cars and bitches." Baby Gangster said to Janelle the next day.

"What makes you think you can be a Baller? Just because you are making a little money with Pookie don't mean you gone be a Baller. You still are selling for *my* man." She teased.

"Just watch and see." He replied.

She smacked her lips then waived her hand at him while walking away. He didn't care what she thought; he knew where he was going. He threw on his 501 Levis with his blue T-Shirt with matching Chuck Taylor's and went straight to the block to hustle. Pookie hadn't got out there yet because he was hanging out with Flintstone and a bunch of BGs. They would do their routine of slap boxing, 'playing body' which consisted of punching each other in the torso area until one of the two quit, or playing murder ball in the street. Murder ball was a little rough because they would throw the football up in the air and whoever picked the ball up would have to run until he was tackled. There would always be a lot of cuts and bruises after a game of murder ball. But this was the camaraderie that brought them together as a set. Baby

Gangster always bypassed the days when the young gangsters hung out like that. He would rather make that money. So while the police were jacking the BGs up around the corner Baby Gangster was making money hand over fist. Pookie would even let the young hustler keep all the dope because he would get up earlier than him to hit the block.

The same day Jason had talked to Janelle about his plans, he saw a car looking suspicious coming into the neighborhood. It was at least three gangsters in the car on the hunt. He couldn't make out who they were or if he even knew them. He hid near some bushes in the alley with his thirty-eight revolver drawn. They hadn't noticed him when they drove by but he questioned who they were looking for. They didn't look like Pirus, he could tell that much. Then he wondered if the Boulevards were rolling on the set for what happened the day before. He had a dilemma. He wanted to run around the corner and tell the homeboys to look out but he didn't know who to tell. If they were riding on the OGs he would have to cut down another street. If they were riding on the BGs he would have to go right around the corner. He decided to go to who was the closest. As he took off, Kim, a neighborhood crackhead came up to him to cop some dope.

"Damn nigga, what you hiding in the bushes for? I ain't gone bite unless you want me to." She smiled with a few missing teeth.

"What's up Kim? I got to run around the corner real fast, what you trying to cop?"

"I got twenty dollars but I'm trying to cop me a twenty-five piece. Why don't you hook me up?" She replied.

"I'll give you a twenty piece for twenty dollars. You know how the game works Kim, stop wasting my time." He sneered.

"I'll suck ya dick if you put a little extra on top. How about it baby, I'll make yo young ass cum real hard." She flashed her toothless smile.

"I don't have time for all of that right now. I'll be back in a little bit and we can work out something."

As he was walking away she grabbed his arm as if to plead. He glared at her in the most vicious way possible.

"Bitch don't you ever grab my arm like that again. Do you hear what the fuck I'm saying to you cuz?"

"I didn't mean anything by it daddy, I'm just really in need of a hit and I will do anything for it, that's all." She trembled.

"I told you that I had to…"

Blah, Blah, Blah, Blah, Blah, Blah!!!

Gunshots continued to sound off and Baby Gangster knew it was too late. He lashed out in anger and punched her in the stomach. She curled up as he ran around to where the BGs were hanging. When he made it around the corner he ran into a pack of his BG homeboys talking loudly. He quickly saw Blue laid out on the ground in a puddle of blood. Then he noticed Pookie and Ace had been shot as well. He ran up to Pookie to aid him.

"You gone be alright Pookie?"

"Yeah, they only got my hip and shit but it hurts like a muthafucka. Go run around the corner to Snake's house and tell OG Do-Dirty some niggas just blasted on us."

Before Baby Gangster could get halfway down the street a pack of OGs were coming towards him. He walked over to Do-Dirty first who was leading the pack. Some of the OGs had their pistols drawn ready to shoot. Baby Gangster seen the weapons as he drew closer.

"Ay OG Do-Dirty cuz, some niggas just blasted on the homies and I think Little Blue is dead. Pookie and Ace got shot too but they look like they gone pull through. The big homies got they pistols but the police are probably on their way." Baby Gangster quickly explained.

"Ay cuz, ya'll niggas stash ya'll straps because 'One Time' is probably on their way." Do-Dirty ordered.

Everybody moved towards hiding the guns in different areas. Before long the police were pulling up. Seeing numerous gang members gathered together made them draw their weapons immediately. It suddenly became a tense situation until Do-Dirty spoke up.

"Look here cuz, we ain't the ones that you need to worry about right now. You should be calling the ambulance because my homeboys got shot."

"I'm none of your cuz!" A fat middle-aged black cop retorted.

"The ambulance is on its way young man." A younger black cop replied.

When the ambulance came people started coming outside of their houses. The police had already called the coroner for Blue then the ambulance took Ace and Pookie to the hospital. Two homicide detectives arrived and began asking questions. Do-Dirty stood a few yards away from the crime scene without saying a word. He was seething inside but maintained a façade of cool in the presence of the police. When he seen one of the detectives looking over at him for answers he walked away. He didn't want to give the detective any impressions that he was willing to talk. The detective stared at him realizing he was the leader because the pack broke up when he walked away. The detective put it in his mind to remember the face.

"We have to serve them Boulevard niggas for what they done to our little homies. It's about to be serious rotation on them niggas, and that's on the set. Ya'll gather all the homies because we need to have a meeting about this shit." Do-Dirty firmly stated.

"That's for real." Snake co-signed.

The following night Do-Dirty, Snake and the BG Flintstone crept over to the Boulevard territory. They had stolen a Station Wagon Snake was driving this time while Do-Dirty sat shotgun. Flintstone was in the back seat tightly gripping his forty-four magnum he had just bought off the street. Do-Dirty had gotten a hold of a seventeen shot, nine-millimeter with hollow tip bullets. He was determined to murder someone from the Boulevard.

They rolled over to where Do-Dirty knew they would hang out and cut threw an alley. They came threw the other side appearing as someone wanting to cop weed. One of their homeboys sold weed out of a vacant house back yard so they were used to people coming through the alley. Everyone in the Station wagon had their faces covered with blue rags. The night air was rather warm so a pack of niggas was hanging out. As Snake reached the end of the alley Do-Dirty and Flintstone quickly climbed out of the window. It caught everyone from the Boulevard off guard.

The fire began dashing through the crowd as bodies fell in startled pain. Do-Dirty let his gun unload all seventeen shots while Flintstone had finished his round quickly. They were caught totally by surprise without any opportunity to retaliate. When the massacre was over at least six people were laid out on the asphalt.

"Roll out!" Do-Dirty barked.

Snake tried to punch out as fast as he could in the raggedy station wagon. They decided to drop the car over on Long Beach Boulevard then walk back to the Block. They had to make sure that they weren't caught slipping by any of the Mayo Lane's who they always were feuding. When they got back to the neighborhood Do-Dirty told Flintstone to gather all the BG homies so they could meet up for a hood meeting in Snake's backyard.

"Ay little Flintstone cuz, when I say everybody, I mean everybody."

Flintstone nodded then walked away to do as he was told.

Mama Jo was tired as she walked in from a long day. The bus ride to Downey was long and drawn out. Not to mention the process of sitting in juvenile court all day waiting for the hearing of her oldest son. She was somewhat relieved he was in jail because she didn't have to worry about him as much. She always considered her oldest son to be trigger happy. It was ironic to her that he would end up in jail for assaulting a police officer with his fist. They had her sitting outside waiting for him to go to court just for him to plead guilty in less than an hour for the assault charge. Mama Jo thought about having him fight the case for a brief moment then she realized she didn't have any money for a lawyer. Jason probably did, she pondered.

All she was thinking about when she made it home was getting out of her clothes and having a tall can of Old English beer. Janelle and the twins were watching television in the living room.

She didn't dare ask where Gangster was at because they probably didn't know, so she nonchalantly asked for Baby Gangster.

"Where is Jason at? Has he been home anytime today?"

"Yeah, he brought back some Taco Bell for everybody. Your Burrito Supreme is in the oven with your two tacos. But you know he probably out on the corner. Now that my...now that Pookie is in the hospital I think he is on the move even more." Janelle replied.

"Well I'm going to finish this beer, eat that Taco Bell then lay down because I've had a long day. Yo brother got five years in Youth Authority for breaking that pig's jaw."

"Damn Mama, five years?" Janelle said incredulously.

"Yeah, it might do him some good though. He didn't flinch when they handed him the time either. He's just like ya'll daddy in a lot of ways. He told me today that he got that little girl Sheila pregnant. So tomorrow I want you to get word to her that she is family."

"Yeah I already told her that the other day. She's starting to show already." Janelle replied.

"You already knew and you didn't tell me. I wonder how much other shit you keeping from me Janelle." Mama Jo retorted.

Suddenly the front door swung wide open then slammed hard with Baby Gangster being the force behind it. She stood at the front door with his head down fuming inside.

"What the hell wrong with you, slamming my door like that?" Mama Jo barked.

Baby Gangster didn't say anything as he walked into the house and right into the bedroom. Everyone's attention was on him but he ignored her question and went into the bedroom and closed the door.

"I don't know who the hell you think you are Jason Gerome Laney but you better get your ass out here and answer me when I'm talking to you." Mama Jo yelled.

Baby Gangster reluctantly got up from the bed and walked into the living room. He glanced up at Mama Jo and it was obvious to her that he was truly upset.

102

"Janelle, take the twins in the room and get them ready for bed. It's late anyhow."

Janelle glanced at Baby Gangster then done as she was told. The low murmurs from both twins were ignored as Mama Jo focused in on Baby Gangster. Janelle quickly put the twins in bed then rushed into the living room to hear what Baby Gangster had to say.

Baby Gangster had already made it to the dining room table and was sitting down. Mama Jo wanted to brace herself for some more bad news so she lit up a cigarette.

"Okay now Jason, what is your problem where you feel you got to come in this house slamming doors. Another one from the neighborhood got shot or killed."

Janelle sat directly across from Mama Jo while Baby Gangster sat between the two.

"Naw, this nigga Do-Dirty, I mean Dennis, want to start feuding with the Boulevard niggas for the next month or so. He gathered everyone from the hood, even Jordan was there and he was half sober too. He wants to do heavy rotation on what those niggas did the other night to Blue, Ace and Pookie. We already done served those niggas now he wants to keep it going. And he wants everybody involved and you know that wars are only gone bring more police. Then that's gone fuck with everybody's money." He bitterly explained.

"What!?!!" Mama Jo exclaimed.

Janelle chuckled a little bit because she knew why Mama Jo was reacting the way she was.

"Boy you ain't anything like yo daddy. I thought you came inside pouting because we lost one of our own. Instead you are upset because the war might jump off and you might lose out on money?" Mama Jo laughed.

"Yeah Mama, the police are going to start sweating everybody from the hood. Ya'll don't see where I'm coming from? I'm down for the set but I'm down to make that money first." Baby Gangster sighed.

"Speaking of money Jason, why don't you give your mama three hundred dollars to take care of some things?" Mama Jo slyly asked.

"How you want it, in twenties or hundred dollar bills?" Jason replied.

Mama Jo shrugged her shoulders as she watched Baby Gangster pull out a wad of money from his pocket. He licked his tongue then peeled off three crisp C-notes and handed it to her. She quickly stuffed it into her bra and dragged on her cigarette. She leaned back in her chair studying the face of her third oldest son. He had grown to become a handsome young boy. She hadn't really looked him in his face since he was a toddler. She identified her babies by their personalities and not their looks. She looked over at Janelle who was studying her every movement. Mama Jo didn't mind because Janelle had been doing it for several years now. She still had that tomboy mannerism at times but she was trying to learn how to be a woman.

"Let me tell you a story about when we were coming up on the east side of South Central."

Janelle and Baby Gangster leaned in closer to eagerly hear what Mama Jo had to say. Mama Jo dragged on her cigarette then leaned forward on the dining room table.

9
SUNDAYS

A Sunday, a gun day, rolling down a one way!
Mack 10

Yo daddy and I were renting out the back house of a duplex on the east side. He had started working at the tire factory plus slanging weed on the side. This was right before I had gotten pregnant with Janelle. Michael was supposed to be the weed man around the neighborhood because he had this connect. His connect was this cat that owned a liquor store around the corner from where we lived. For some reason or another he took a liking to Michael. So everyday after work Michael would run around to the liquor store to chop it up with Frankie. They grew to like each other. The only problem with Frankie giving Michael weed to sell was the fact that Michael wasn't a hustler. Michael had always been a gangster and always had fighting on his mind. Joseph and Jordan are just like him when it comes to fighting. But no matter what, Frankie would still front him weed whenever Michael would blow his cop money. After weeks of seeing this happen, I decided to do something about it. Michael always talked about this man at the liquor store who was real cool. So I decided to pay this Frankie man a visit. I got my stuck up sister to watch Joseph and Jordan while Michael was at work. She would only do it for a couple of hours so I had to make the most of it.

When I made it to the liquor store on Avalon I studied the outside of the store before I entered. It was somewhat of a grocery mart but it mostly sold liquor. I started drinking with Michael every now and then so I liked the idea of him being cool with someone owning a liquor store. Though Michael started smoking a lot of weed my preference was alcohol and cigarettes to get me high. So I slowly walked into the store with my eyes trying to study every detail. Suspicion would probably best describe my emotions once I had gotten inside. He had the basic food that one would have on a miniature grocery store shelf, but everything looked old. His shelves were dusty and his walls needed cleaning. His food wasn't molded but it was too old for someone to want to buy anything. If you bought any type of food you more than likely would buy condiments like ketchup, mustard or mayonnaise. Only items that appeared to be fresh were the candy and potato chip section. After looking around for a minute and studying everything that I could possibly study I finally walked near the front counter.

A middle-aged man that looked somewhat familiar to me gave a halfhearted smile, which I returned. I figured I had seen him around the neighborhood.

"Can I help you find something you want?" He continued to smile.

"Yes, I wanted to know where I could find Frankie." I replied.

"Who wants to know?"

"Could you tell him that I am Josephine Laney, the wife of Michael Laney?"

"So you are the mother of Mike's two sons. It is a pleasure to meet you. Mike comes through here and talks about his family all the time."

"So you must be Frankie?" I asked.

"Yeah I'm Frankie, how can I help you Jo? I hope you don't have a problem with me calling you Jo."

"Naw, that's cool. I just wanted to discuss some business with you, if that's cool." I said.

"Well what kind of business are you talking about?"

"The kind that involves smoking." I slyly replied.

He nodded his head fully understanding where I was coming from. He looked around appearing to be a little reluctant to talk about it. Then he gave a sigh as if to surrender.

"What is it you want to talk about? Now when asking you this question I want you to keep in mind that when a customer comes in we quickly change the subject."

"Of course."

"Okay, well what's on ya mind?"

"To get straight to the point, instead of giving Michael the weed that you give him why don't you just give it to me? I believe that you would get a better return that way. Besides, I'm at home most of the time while he is either at work or running the streets." I explained.

"What makes you think I give Mike weed?" He looked puzzled.

"Come on now Frankie, I thought you and I could be straight with each other." I replied.

He studied my face vividly before making a response. He rubbed his chin as he contemplated. I began to look around because I didn't want to appear too eager. He stepped from behind the cash register and walked toward the end of his counter. He leaned down and came back in a couple of minutes with a bag full of weed. My eyes got big as he walked from behind the counter then motioned for me to come closer.

"I think this bag will fit into your purse. My next question, what happens when your husband comes into my store looking to re cop?" He asked while slipping the bag into my purse.

"Don't worry about that. Let me handle all the details when it comes to Michael. As long as there is some for him to smoke and enough for us to make a profit I can keep him from asking you for anymore."

"You are a good woman Jo. You take care of Michael, you here?"

I smiled from the compliment then walked out the door.

When I made it home my sister was eager to leave until I told her that I had some weed to smoke. We sat on the porch and talked while Joseph and Jordan played in the yard. Michael was doing a little overtime at the Tire Company on that Saturday. His routine was pretty basic. After work he would take a shower throw on some clothes then hang out with the homies until two or three in the morning. Most times Saturday nights was cool because he might get too drunk to want to have sex which was most of the time. He didn't bother me on Saturday nights because that was his time to hang out until he passed out. By Sunday he would usually be out of weed to sell but I had the back up without him knowing about it this time. When his homeboys came around trying to get some weed he would tell them that he was sold out but I would tell them I had a little left over. They usually could get Michael to smoke with them but since I had the weed it was strictly for sell.

Two weeks after that Sunday everybody knew to buy the weed from me instead of Michael. I had told Michael not to ask that man Frankie for any more weed because we don't want to ever have to owe him, so he stopped asking. I never told him that I was buying it on a regular from Frankie; he just assumed I had a connect while he was at work. He would see the money flowing in so he never complained. Michael wasn't the kind of man that you could tell him something and he would just do it. He was a rebel by nature. So you had to suggest thing through action. He had to see you do something better than he did and accept it. And that is exactly what happened for the next couple of months.

Money was flowing so good I decided to buy a new furniture set. I had found out that I was pregnant with Janelle by then so we bought a brand new baby bed. I had about three thousand dollars saved up after buying the couch and love seat. I would always find time during the course of the week to pass by Frankie's liquor store and cop more weed. We had developed a friendship and he had to respect my hustle.

One afternoon I had sold out quicker than I expected. So I carried Joseph and Jordan with me in tow. Once I hit the block of the liquor store I realized that something was seriously wrong. It was a Thursday afternoon and the sky was sort of gloomy. The lukewarm weather seemed a little depressing but there was also something different about the corner. Fear rose up in me but my legs refused to stop walking toward the store. When I made it to the front of the store all the windows were busted out. The store had been cleaned out of any good inventory and everything else was laid out on the floor. I was seriously hurt because for the life of me I couldn't think of anyone that would want to do this to Frankie. It was painfully obvious that it wasn't the police doing a raid. It was more like some knuckleheads that just picked a random store to vandalize. My stomach dropped as I pondered on what could have happened to Frankie.

For the rest of the week I was depressed. I hadn't felt good about what happened in days and the pregnancy gave me highs and lows. I couldn't smoke or drink so I decided to put the boys to sleep and step on the porch for some fresh air. I was on the porch for about twenty minutes when a familiar white Cadillac pulled up to the curb. Out comes Frankie from the driver's side smiling from ear to ear. I hadn't been that happy to see a man in my life. I walked off the porch and gave him the tightest hug I could give considering my pregnancy. We both stared at each other for a moment and smiled. Words were hard to come for the both of us. Finally seeing that he was safe and sound I spoke up.

"Damn Frankie, I thought something had happened to you when I seen your store vandalized like that."

"Yeah some little punks put me out of business but it wasn't a big deal. I did what white folks done and put out some insurance for the place and it worked out fine." He grinned.

"But you still are going to miss your store ain't you?"

"I'm going to miss talking to you Mrs. Josephine Laney."

"That's right honey; you know I was named after Josephine Baker. She didn't take any mess and neither do I." We both laughed.

"I just came by to say my farewell to you. I plan on leaving this here state and move to Las Vegas. You can buy you a house for real cheap right about now because it's out in the desert."

"Since your store is burned down you plan on just leaving us? Aw Frankie you can set up another store somewhere around here." I replied.

"I'm about ready to call it quits in this here state. I've never been any good in the state of California. I was down in Memphis doing big things before I came back out here."

"That's right you did say you lived out there for a few years. You know Michael got some peoples from out that way." I commented.

He didn't really reply to my statement. He had probably heard it before as much as I repeated myself. He lowered his head and after a few moments he looked up at me.

"I wanted to give you a few extra dollars to get you by for a spell. I won't be around for you to get any weed so I want to give you a stash just in case you come across another connect."

"Naw Frankie you don't have to do that. I'm thankful for everything you've done for my family."

"Look Jo, I've done really well with this insurance, so I insist that you take this little bit of change. I won't feel right not helping you out just a little bit. If you want an old man to feel guiltier than he's already felt then you will refuse this money."

I thought about what he said and he didn't have to twist my arm for free money. He pulled out a wad of cash already rolled up and ready and handed it to me. He made me promise not to count it until he left. We talked for a few more minutes then he drove off in his white Cadillac. When I went inside to count the money it was five thousand dollars. At that moment I realized that if I would have known how much was in that wad I would have refused it. I promised myself that I would save it and only use it for something important. It was Saturday right before dark.

As usual Michael came in that morning drunk as hell. He didn't make it in the house until two or three in the morning. But he was different this time. He was still stinking drunk but he had felt bad about something he had done. He tossed and turned letting his inebriated words fly out of his mouth.

"You gone be just like yo daddy, a Memphis hustler and pimp. You keep it up you gone be no good just like he was no good." He cried out.

I wanted to hold him but I didn't because he would shake violently when he was drunk. I stared at him because I was not able to go to sleep.

"I shot down my daddy's store. Why did I do that to my daddy?" He screamed.

That same morning I allowed Michael to sleep in as usual. He didn't wake up until noon. Once he was up and functional I talked him into taking the kids and I to his mother's house. It was only a few blocks away but I wanted us to go as a family. Once he had gotten inside the house he kissed his mother then stepped outside with his homeboys. I decided to talk to Ms. Peterson for awhile.

"Why you only had two children Irma?"

"Shit you got enough grandchildren for me. That's all I ever wanted was a girl and a boy. After I had Patricia I was through." She replied.

"What happened to their father? Where is he at right now?" I slyly asked as if it was out of curiosity.

"Please, that nigga was nothing but a pimp and a hustler. That's all he wanted to do. He wanted to get married but I told him if he didn't get a job I was going to leave him and go to California. Patricia had to be about two while Michael was about four or five. That nigga followed me to California and lasted six months out here. He couldn't keep a job. So I eventually kicked him out of my house and he went back to Memphis. It was good for me any way because he couldn't have been a good man for Michael. I figured I could be a better man than he could." Irma explained.

"What was his name?"

"Franklin Laney."

My mouth dropped. I couldn't believe my ears. It couldn't be the same Frankie that I had been dealing with for some time now. It couldn't be the one who just moved to Las Vegas. What a coincidence. I never asked Frankie his last name. I never saw a need.

"What!?!" Irma replied.

111

"Did Michael remember his father and how he looked?"

"I doubt it. Michael was too young to remember his father. He would get curious every now and then and I would just tell him his father is in Memphis."

"You never tried to keep in touch?"

"What for? He was good for nothing in my book." Irma waived her hand.

"Good for nothing?" I replied in disbelief.

"For nothing but hustling. The one thing I would say he was good at was being a hustler."

Mama Jo woke up that Sunday morning playing her favorite album. She always woke up every Sunday to 'Harold Melvin and the Blue Notes' the 'Wake Up Everybody' album with Teddy Pendergrass singing lead. Janelle woke up shortly after, once the music started playing. It was as if it was on cue, because one after another everyone would wake up in the Laney household. No matter how many days Gangster was out on the streets he would always find his way home on Saturday nights. It was one of his ways of letting Mama Jo know that he was still alive. The household was always more pleasant because Mama Jo was more pleasant. She never was religious but she stuck to her rituals. She halfway wanted Gangster to go to jail so she wouldn't have to worry about him as much. She wanted him to get clean. She had thought about kicking him out the house but every time he returned she was glad he was home. But he actually participated in the household cleaning. For most of the morning she would play Marvin Gaye, Diana Ross, The Stylistics, The Temptations, The O-Jays and The Dramatics.

"The twins were conceived off 'Be My Girl' from the Dramatics!" Mama Jo would say from time to time.

Janelle cleaned up the house for the most part during the week but Mama Jo would do what she called a 'thorough cleaning' on Sundays. Even Baby Gangster who was always ready to hustle would stick around a little longer before hitting the block. Everyone would sing along to the music while they attended to the chore they were assigned. J-Ridah was the only one that wasn't present in recent times. He had been sent up to Youth Authority up in Stockton California.

Mama Jo's routine would play out until about one in the afternoon. By that time everyone would carry on with their day. Baby Gangster was the first to leave the house. He had stacked up a nice little bit of change since Pookie had gotten out the hospital. He was able to cop on his own so him and Pookie became more like partners. It had become painfully obvious that Baby Gangster was a much better hustler than Pookie. He just wanted more than anyone else on the block.

"Baby Gangster, you are a hustler through and through cuz. You are out here serving when everyone else is asleep." Pookie chided.

"Shit, my grandpa was a hustler. That nigga was hustler all the way out in Tennessee. He came to California and opened up a liquor store from the money he made from hustling. I'm gone try to open me a grocery store for all the homies in the hood." Baby Gangster laughed.

"Shit I can't see you selling food...but then again the way you slang this dope I figure you could sell bananas out yo ass too."

"That's what I'm saying. When you selling legal shit the police can't fuck with you then. So when did the doctor say you don't have to wear crutches anymore?"

"In a couple of more weeks. I've wanted to ride on those Boulevard niggas with the homies but OG Do-Dirty say I should wait until I'm off the crutches."

Suddenly C-Bone comes running up on Pookie and Baby Gangster. He was bent over with his hands touching his knees panting hard. When he finally catches his breath he rises up to look at Baby Gangster.

"Ay cuz, OG Do-Dirty told me to tell you to come around to Snake's house so that he could holler at you. Them Boulevard niggas want to stop warring with us, so one of them niggas is begging Do-Dirty to stall they set out." C-Bone bragged.

Pookie and Baby Gangster fell out in laughter. C-Bone gave them time to recover because he thought that it was funny too. After getting their laughs for a few more moments C-Bone got serious.

"Naw though, on the real, Do-Dirty wants you to clear something up with him."

"Do he want me too?" Pookie asked.

"Naw cuz, he only said Baby Gangster."

"Alright then, I'll hold it down while you handle that shit." Pookie replied.

When C-Bone and Baby Gangster got around to Snake's house a crowd of the Alondra Block's were posted in the front yard. There were two men standing outside that wasn't from the set Baby Gangster didn't know. The third one standing with them was the light skin one that beat up OG Mike Dog but lost in a fight to OG Deuce. Baby Gangster glanced at his brother Gangster and seen the black nine-millimeter he was brandishing. He knew his brother wouldn't hesitate to start blasting and he wasn't trying to get anyone killed. He shook his head at his big brother indicating that there was no problem. Gangster nodded but still looked at the three Boulevard Crips like he was ready to put them down. Baby Gangster looked up at Do-Dirty who looked at his young comrade with admiration. There was a mutual respect.

"What's up cuz, C-Bone said you wanted to see me?"

"Yeah cuz, does any of these niggas look familiar when you seen that car pull up on the set. They saying that they wasn't the ones that blasted on the little homies."

"Naw, they don't look like the niggas I saw, but it was too dark. Whatever car they were in was stolen so I know I couldn't remember the car. But that don't like them."

"You sure Baby Gangster? I'm a fair nigga cuz, and if these are not the niggas that done that shit then we can squash that shit right now." Do-Dirty passionately explained.

"Naw that ain't them, I'm sure." Baby Gangster shook his head.

Do-Dirty walked over to Ghost so that he could finish resolving the matter. Baby Gangster seen he was no longer needed and walked back to the dope spot.

Later that night around ten o' clock Pookie called it a night and left Baby Gangster outside alone. Baby Gangster didn't mind he was used to being done like that. Besides, the crack heads had to be served at least until four in the morning.

Around the corner the OG homies ran out of beer. They had ran through four or five 40 ounces and was ready to go to the store for some more.

"Ya'll niggas chip in cuz, and I will go around the corner to get some more." Do-Dirty announced.

He held out his black baseball cap that matched his black Chuck Taylor's with thick blue shoelaces. His black khaki suit hung loosely over his tall but stocky frame. Once everybody put into the pot he scooped the money from out of his cap then quickly exited the backyard. He had a little buzz already so his mind was in a haze. He took his time getting outside the gate because he didn't have the clearest mind. After struggling with the gate he went to the side of the house and pissed on the side of Snake's neighbor's house. He slowly walked across the front yard grass to get to his car, which was across the street.

His buzz had him feeling good and relaxed. His eyes were blood shot red while he attempted to sing 'Computer Love' from Roger Troutman. When he made it to his car he thought he heard something in the bushes. He looked around but couldn't see anything. Then it suddenly dawned on him he didn't have to pull his forty-five out of his glove because they just made a truce with the Boulevard's. He smiled when he thought of that.

"You a cold ass hood when you make niggas beg to get a pass. This is Alondra Block until I die."

That was when he heard footsteps. He didn't have time to react because the footsteps were coming from both sides of his car. He looked and seen that the faces were familiar. They tried to cover them with blue rags but he had gone to school with all three predators. Their guns were lowered to the side until they were close enough to shoot. Do-Dirty's buzz suddenly evaporated as the gunmen raised their weapons. He was able to count every millisecond until the first gunshot was fired. Everything from his vantage point was in slow motion. Then the first shot pierced his chest. The next three shots riddled his chest and his abdomen. He stood as countless bullets crashed into the upper part of his body. He didn't make a scream or a sound. He allowed one tear to fall from his face as his body was finally forced to the pavement. His smooth dark brown complexion was smeared with his own blood. His six-two-frame was filled with multiple holes. His neatly cropped small Afro had a hole on the side from a fatal shot to the head. Without glimpsing at the corpse his killers quickly ran away.

By the time his homeboys could react, the assailants were long gone. Snake actually allowed tears to fall when he seen his road dog laid out. The homies from Alondra Block gathered around Do-Dirty's lifeless body as if to protect it. No one touched it until the police arrived. They were then forced to stand back while the police proceeded to put out yellow tape to seal off the area.

About thirty minutes after the murder two detectives roll up in a black unmarked Crown Victoria. Detective Miller began to study the crime scene while Detective Bush looked for shell casings. It took about ten minutes at the crime scene before Detective Miller reacted.

"Fuck!!!" He blurted out.

"What happened?" Detective Bush asked, not bothering to look up from what he was doing.

"This is one of the shot callers from Alondra Block. This is a major fucking problem."

"Aww shit, this is Dennis Jones AKA Do-Dirty. We have a lot of work cut out for us in the weeks to come."

"Or it could be the other way around. If the head is cut off the body will fall." Detective Miller sounded hopeful.

"We'll know in a few days." Detective Bush attempted to support his partner's optimism.

10
CRACK COCAINE

So he can go and score him some coca-ine!
Juvenile

Four years later

Baby Gangster hopped out of his all blue El Camino with the gold Dayton's rims and gold knock offs. He leaned on the driver's side door and pulled out a joint of skunk weed. It was the strongest form of marijuana at the time. He only puffed on it while he sat patiently waiting in an empty parking lot. He shouldn't have to wait too long he pondered. Just as the thought ran through his head a burgundy 1964 Chevy Impala with hydraulics came bouncing into the vacant lot. The driver hops out the Impala smiling. He walks over to Baby Gangster and they embrace. Baby Gangster gives him a once over as he notices the thick red shoelaces in his Reebok tennis shoes that matched his red belt. His brown corduroy Levis creased with heavy starch and an all white T-Shirt.

"What's happening relative?" Marvin said in a jovial spirit.

"You know we cousins, so why don't you just go ahead and say cousins?" Baby Gangster chided.

"Naw, you my Blood relative. We got the same Laney Blood pumping through our veins." Marvin chuckled.

"So how is everything? Are you able to buy a whole bird (kilogram of cocaine) now?"

"I told you I was gone get that shit off fast. That's exactly what I did once I hit the block; they were coming after that shit. It's some niggas that got some dope over in the hood but it ain't fucking with yo shit." Marvin replied.

117

"Cool, well I got a whole bird in the car waiting for you. You lucky we related nigga or I wouldn't be giving yo slob ass the same price that I'm getting it for."

"Awww, just because we family you got to talk shit? I ain't calling you all kinds of crabs and erickits nigga. So anyway, when is Joseph getting out? Mama was telling me that he was getting out any day now."

"Oh tell Auntie Tricia I said hi. J-Ridah supposed to get out Thursday. We were thinking about throwing a party for his crazy ass but you know you can't come." Baby Gangster replied.

"I know, I know, but it would be good to holler at my big relative. Last time I seen that nigga he was in the hospital because he had got shot by some Mayo Lane niggas."

"Yeah, he went to jail right after he was able to walk again. I made sure there were money on his books as well as money on my Pop's books. But he's not seeing daylight though."

"Yeah, moms be getting on me and Shawny-Ru because we chose to be Pirus instead of Cra...Crips. She says our family has always been on that side since Uncle Mike started up in the seventies." Marvin commented.

"Yeah, but ya'll can't help where ya'll grew up at. So they calling my baby cousin Shawny-Ru huh? And they call you Bamm. Ya'll grown up to be Ridahs for ya'll hood. But you need to worry about getting that paper and say fuck that gangbanging shit. Claim your set but don't let that shit make you stupid where you can't make that money, you understand where I coming from?"

"Yeah, I know where you coming from. When it's time to ride I ride but other than that I'm about my paper. I try to tell Shawny-Ru that shit and he doesn't listen."

"Well look, I ain't trying to keep you too long. So grab that bird from the passenger side under the seat and I will holla at you later on. So Cee up cuz and ya better keep it Crippin Bamm." Baby Gangster smiled.

"Naw relative, it's Big Bamm because I be knocking Crabs out with a big boom Bamm." Big Bamm nodded in arrogance.

118

They embraced right before Big Bamm walked over to the passenger side and tossed a bag on the passenger side while grabbing another bag from under the seat. Baby Gangster nodded to confirm that was the dope then they jumped in their cars and sped off.

Baby Gangster decided to go straight home from meeting with his cousin. He was tired and didn't really feel like dealing with anyone. He was hoping the twins were out in the streets as well as Mama Jo and Janelle. He would have no such luck. When he walked inside he realized that he was dreaming to think the Laney household would be peaceful. Right when he walked in the door his nephew Joe Jr. came running past him into Mama Jo's room. He ran right back into the living room shooting his gun making gun noises.

"Damn boy, you trigger happy like yo daddy was before he got locked up." Baby Gangster commented.

"Don't be telling that boy any shit like that." Mama Jo yelled from the kitchen.

Baby Gangster ignored his mother and headed towards the room. Last thing he needed was drama from her.

"Jason that little heifer Kisha keeps calling here and it's getting on my damn nerves. You need to call her back so she won't be so damn paranoid. She called at least four times, huh, Janelle."

"Yeah Jason, you better see what she wants." Janelle yelled from the kitchen.

"What ya'll in there cooking?" He asked.

"Frying some chicken, with some mashed potatoes and some spinach. I'll make you a plate in a little bit." Mama Jo replied.

"Cool! Kisha didn't say what she wanted?"

"Hell naw, you know she don't trust mama and I." Janelle laughed.

"Uncle Jason, where did Uncle Jamil and Uncle Jalil go? They were supposed to hang out with me." Joe Jr. cut in.

119

"Boy sit down at the table and get ready to eat. I told you they was out in the streets, if it ain't too late you can play with them when they get in." Mama Jo replied.

Baby Gangster looked at Mama Jo as she sat down a plate in front of him. They made brief eye contact because they both knew that they weren't coming until long after he was asleep.

"Oh by the way mama, Bamm... I mean Marvin told me to tell you hi. You know he wanted to see Joseph when he got out." He commented.

"Oh yeah, next time I see him tell him that I love him. He loves his auntie, he called me on my birthday and we talked for an hour. Too bad Patricia moved him over to the wrong side because I would have had him come to the party for sure."

She sat down next to Baby Gangster after fixing herself a plate. He could tell the way she was looking that she wanted something from him. He always was amused at how she would set it up to ask. Mama Jo was the type of woman that didn't like asking for anything. Even though she was on welfare since her husband Michael went to prison she still didn't like to ask anyone for anything. He glanced at his mother for a brief moment noticing the creases beginning to show in her face. Her beauty was still there but she was beginning to show signs of aging. He worried about her because from time to time she would develop a cough.

"You know it would be good to look at a big screen TV every now and then. I'll bet you the twins will want to stay home more if there was one in the house. And yo nephew with his bad ass could watch cartoons in the morning before he goes to school." Mama began.

"I would have been bought a TV for the living room if that is what ya'll want." Baby Gangster replied.

Suddenly the doorbell rung and there was a loud pounding on the front door. It startled everyone because the Laney household door is usually unlocked. It was silence with the exception of the TV for a moment.

"Who's knocking on my door like that?" Mama Jo yelled.

"It's Kisha; I came to see if Jason is home. I seen his El Camino parked outside when I was passing by."

"Here I come Kisha!" Baby Gangster yelled.

Mama Jo sighed because of the distraction. She never got to drive her point home. He glanced at her before he rose from the table. Her forehead was wrinkled and she slightly frowned.

"Mama don't worry about it, tomorrow me and Janelle will go down to the convenience store and pick up a new television. You let her know what you want and we will get it." He assured her.

As he walked towards the door he smiled back at his family. He was one of the only Laney's that was known for smiling. He opened up the front door to see a scowl on Kisha's face. Her body language suggested that she wanted to devour him. But her facial expression was more of contempt. She could tell that he observed her resentment so she quickly tried to mask it. His eyes scanned her from head to toe. She reached for both his hands while he studied every curve.

Her eyes were hazel and her complexion was golden brown. She had full lips and a beauty scar right under her left eye from a junior high school fight. Her voluptuous frame accentuated her white blouse and her tight mini skirt. She had her hair freshly done in a hairstyle known as dookie braids. Every strand of hair was in place as the baby hair gently laid across her forehead in perfect position. He was infatuated. This is why I put up with this crazy bitch, he pondered.

"What's up Kisha, why in the fuck you knocking on my door like you were the police or some shit?" He firmly asked.

"Because I've been calling you all day and I know yo mama or your sister didn't tell you." She replied.

"Yeah they told me you called like three or four times."

"They lying, you ain't all that for me to be calling like that. I've called yo ass twice."

Baby Gangster chuckled for a minute and lowered his head. She smiled in response playfully grabbing his arm. She slowly drew closer so that her lips could touch his. She pressed her lips to his mouth and stuck her tongue inside. He had his arms around her waist slowly sliding his hands down to her ass. They stood up grinding on each other until they heard the phone ring from inside the house.

"So what's up Kisha, I want some pussy?" He whispered in her ear.

"Go get a room and we can do what we do." She replied.

Baby Gangster opened the front door to announce he was leaving. Kisha grabbed his arm trying to suggest that he didn't tell anyone. Her eyes tried to meet his but he was obligated to his family.

"Mama I'll talked to you tomorrow, Janelle will let me know what kind of TV you want." Baby Gangster yelled.

"Jason I wasn't done talking to you yet. You think that little fast tale girl can wait a few minutes before ya'll run off." Mama Jo replied.

The door was wide open so Kisha and Mama Jo made brief eye contact. Kisha quickly rolled her eyes at Mama Jo. It was somewhat appalling to her because her own children had never disrespected her like that. Everybody knew and respected Mama Jo.

"Go ahead and go Jason. But tell yo little heifer that if she wants to roll her eyes at me she needs to know how to bring grown woman whip ass. I'm not a child that you can roll your eyes at; I'm a grown ass woman." Mama Jo said so Kisha could hear while frowning.

Baby Gangster glanced at Kisha with both disdain and shock. Then his look turned to anger.

"Who the fuck you rolling yo eyes at? You ever roll yo eyes at my moms, I will…"

By now he had grabbed her by the neck. She was genuinely scared as his grip got tighter and tighter.

"Naw Jason, just tell her to watch what she does around me. Take your hands from around her neck." Mama Jo consoled.

"Naw mama she done lost her damn mind."

He extended his arm with his hand still around her neck. She began to cough slightly so he loosened his grip. Her eyes watered up as tears fell down her face. His eyes full of anger he waited for her to catch her breath. Then he lifted his hand with his fingers spread out and slapped her across her mouth. She whimpered as he focused his eyes on her. Mama Jo had made her way to the door by then. She grabbed Baby Gangster by the arm he used to slap Kisha with and held it tightly.

"You acting just like yo daddy used to act with me." Mama Jo stated while dragging him into the house.

By now Kisha is crying her heart out. Tears profusely fell from her face as she seen him walking away.

"No! Jason don't go inside. I'm sorry, I'm sorry Mama Jo." She pleaded.

Baby Gangster ignored her and began to close the door in her face. She walked closer to the door trying to stop him from closing it.

"Don't you want to spend time with me baby?" She pleaded.

"Hell Naw bitch, you disrespected my mama so I'm going to call one of my other bitches." He barked.

She screamed at this point. He slammed the door in her face and walked into his bedroom that he had to himself. His head was hurting by then so he decided to go to sleep earlier than usual. Mama Jo knew he was pissed and decided to leave well enough alone.

An hour into his sleep the door swung open in his bedroom. He was asleep when a voice came barking into his bedroom.

"Ay Jason, Ay Jason, wake yo ass up." Jalil who was known as Laney Twin deuce loudly whispered.

"What nigga? You see the light is off which means I'm sleep." Baby Gangster said in a drowsy tone.

"Ay cuz, what did you do with that three-fifty-seven you had the other day?" Laney Twin deuce replied.

Baby Gangster took a moment to reply. He was irritated for being waked but more frustrated that his younger brother ignored him. He considered doing the same but he knew he wouldn't get a moments rest. He slowly rose from the bed then placed his feet on the floor.

"What the fuck you want with my strap? Ya'll niggas want to be stupid with it."

"Aw come on cuz, quit tripping. Some of the homies is talking about blasting on some slobs. I ain't even asking you for that Uzi I seen yo ass with the other day. Just let me hold the tray-five-seven and we good. You act like you only got one gun." Laney Twin 2 persisted.

"Where is Jamil? That nigga supposed to do some shit for me." Baby Gangster finally stood up.

"Aw that nigga went to go fuck with that bitch Neicy, you know Cornbread's sister. Speaking of females, why was that broad Kisha walking down the street crying about an hour ago? I thought she was coming to see you then the next thing I know she was walking back down the street with tears in her eyes." Laney Twin 2 chuckled.

"That bitch went off the wall and disrespected mama. I had to slap the shit out of her punk ass. Now that I'm up, I'll probably call up Tina that stays over there in Greenleaf hood."

Baby Gangster handed him the three fifty seven while cutting on the light. He had to rub his eyes from the sudden light.

"Aye cuz, where is that box of bullets you got?"

"Look under the bed. After I pick up Tina, I'm cutting off my pager so if you need anything yo punk ass better ask me now."

"You about to go over to Greenleaf territory? Fuck them niggas; I don't trust any of those shady ass niggas. Cee Careful when you go over there because some of they homeboys is scandalous." Laney Twin 2 passionately replied.

"Yeah I don't trust them niggas either. I always thought those were the niggas that smoked Do-Dirty and Blue, rest in peace." Baby Gangster yawned.

"Well give me a C-Note before you go and watch you back. After we serve these Mayonnaise Lanes they might try to come right back." Laney Twin 2 laughed.

"You still out here gangbanging but you asking me for a hundred dollars. You need to be making that money for yourself."

"Miss me with the lectures cuz. I'm trying to handle my business against these slobs. Then after that we gone gather with the homeboys, get some drink and smoke some skunk weed." Laney Twin 2 waived his hand.

Baby Gangster peeled his brother off the money then went into the living room to find Janelle on the phone. He waived to her to let him use it. She grudgingly got off the phone and handed it to him. Baby Gangster took the phone and glanced at Joseph Jr. laid out asleep on the couch. He untangled the long phone cord and took it into his bedroom. He called up Tina and was headed out the door to pick her up.

The next morning after he dropped Tina off from the motel he came home to a house in chaos. He had almost forgot the day but the activity around the house had quickly reminded him.

"I think just you and Sheila should go pick him up since only three people can get inside yo El Camino." Mama Jo suggested in passing.

"Where is Sheila?" Baby Gangster looked around the house.

"She's in my bedroom getting make up put on her face by Janelle. She's going to be ready in…Jamil if you don't finish cleaning off that damn table. Ya'll act like you not happy to see yo oldest brother get out of jail." She yelled.

Baby Gangster glanced at Jamil half cleaning the table then noticed that Jalil was doing a half hearted vacuum. He smiled as Mama Jo tried to give directions as if it was Sunday. He knew she had thrown them off key by cleaning up on a Thursday. She had total power on Sunday when her music could calm the savage beast. Now she was making everyone resent that J-Ridah was coming home. Baby Gangster felt the tension in the air. He had seen enough.

"Ay Sheila, you ready to go? We got about a two hour drive."

"Here I come." She yelled from the bedroom.

She walked out looking done up like a pretty china doll. Her light brown complexion matched evenly with her light brown highlights blending into her perm. The lip-gloss accentuated her thick juicy lips. Her one-piece jean button down top and mini skirt complimented her petite but voluptuous frame.

"Go tell yo mama how beautiful she looks." Mama Jo whispered in Joseph Jr.'s

He ran up to his mother and wrapped his arms around her legs. She giggled when she seen him trying to hug her so tightly.

"You look beautiful mama!" He yelled enthusiastically.

"Thank You baby, I'm going up to see yo daddy and I'm going to bring him home with me." She smiled.

Baby Gangster smiled proudly as if Joseph Jr. was his son. He knew he had a drive ahead so he got to the point.

"We need to hit that road right now Sheila."

"Okay I'm ready."

"Ya'll hurry back because I'm cooking a big dinner and even Jordan and his girlfriend what's her name is coming through to see Joseph." Mama Jo commented.

"Felicia!" Janelle cut in.

"Who?"

"Felicia mama, who is the girl, Jordan is staying with."

"Yeah Felicia." Mama Jo cynically replied.

Mama Jo didn't talk too much about Gangster after kicking him out the house several years' back. He was a name that she didn't want to say or hear that much. She always felt he was weak because of his addiction to Sherm.

Everybody waived as Sheila and Baby Gangster walked out the door. He didn't know what to expect from his brother's baby mama so he figured he would keep the radio playing until they arrived at his prison.

When they made it to the prison J-Ridah was already waiting outside sitting on a bench. Baby Gangster pulled up in his El Camino glancing at the familiar man turned the other way. He kept glancing through his peripheral because the man sitting on the bench had massive arms. Even his forearms were big. But

126

something drew him to keep staring at the large man with the humongous muscles.

"Wait a minute, are you Joseph Laney?" Baby Gangster poked out the window.

"Aw cuz, I didn't think that was you but that is you Jason. I'm tripping cuz." J-Ridah stood up.

He stood about 6'1 and had the penitentiary stroll down to a science. Sheila instantly jumped out of the passenger side door and threw her hands in the air.

"You don't remember me baby?" She practically yelled.

"Aw shit Sheila, I didn't know that was you. When I spoke to mama last night she made it seem like she was coming up by herself." J-Ridah said with a deep resonating voice.

After Sheila hugged and passionately kissed him Baby Gangster had seen enough. He was ready to hit the road.

"C'mon we can talk on the ride back home cuz." Baby Gangster replied.

Everyone hopped inside the El Camino. For a few moments down the road it was just as quiet as it was when Sheila and Baby Gangster were alone. J-Ridah would glance at Sheila then at Baby Gangster then look at the road. He was never good with words but he had much love for both of them. At that very moment he was at peace. War wasn't on his mind which was a luxury he couldn't afford behind the walls. He always had to consider who might try to shank him in the yard. He could relax for a change.

"What's Up Jason cuz, you done grown like a muthafucka? I've been hearing a lot of good things about you. C-Bone from Boulevard was telling me you doing big things nowadays cuz." J-Ridah proudly said.

"I'm just trying to make a little money that's all big brother. I've been hustling for a little while now. Matter of fact look under your side of the seat and it should be a brown paper bag."

J-Ridah struggled to reach under the seat because of his large arms. In a matter of seconds Sheila reached under the seat and grabbed the paper bag and handed it to him.

"What's this?"

"Open it up cuz." Baby Gangster laughed.

J-Ridah reluctantly opened the brown paper bag to find a wad of cash inside. It was more money than he had seen in his lifetime. With a bewildered look on his face he glanced over at Baby Gangster.

"What you want me to do with this cuz?"

"Keep it nigga. You, Sheila and Joseph Jr. can you get you a spot now that ya'll a family. That's to get ya'll started but it's a lot more to come with that."

"That love cuz, that's some real shit Jason. How were you able to get that much money?"

"Crack Cocaine!!! That's the new hustle right now and it pays good."

11
KNOCKED UP

Mommy's knocked up because she wasn't watched over!
Jay-Z

The California night air felt good to Janelle as she waited for Pookie to come pick her up. It would normally be colder but it was unusually warm as Janelle stood outside with her cousin Monique. They were both supposed to be attending a sleep over at her best friend Rachelle's house. Janelle had every intention on sneaking off with Pookie so they could do their thing. She resented having to baby sit her shoplifting cousin who was only a year younger than her. Monique had gotten caught stealing at a department store so her mother thought that Janelle might be a better influence. Janelle smirked because she knew that Mama Jo couldn't stand her sister Jackie most of the time. But since they were family Mama Jo felt obligated which meant that Janelle was obligated as well.

"So when yo boyfriend coming through? Shouldn't he be here by now? Does he have any fine ass homeboys?"

"Damn Moe, one question at a time. Pookie should be coming up any minute. As far as homeboys he got a bunch of homeboys but you gone have to decide who is fine. Now listen to me Monique, I'm stepping out with Pookie so you on yo own. Don't talk any shit to my homegirls because I don't want to beat anyone's ass because of you. Cee cool and everything will be fine." Janelle firmly explained.

At that moment Pookie pulled up in his Cutlass Supreme. Janelle smiled as he rolled up close enough to the curb for Janelle to get in. Janelle opened the door and pulled the front seat forward so that Monique could get in the back seat. Janelle climbed in and stared at her man with the eyes of a tiger.

"How are you doing Pookie baby?"

"Crippin'! How are you baby and who is this in my backseat?" He grinned.

"Aw that's my cousin Monique, but we call her Moe." Janelle waived her hand.

"So Pookie are you going to introduce me to some of your homeboys?" Moe said over the music.

Janelle glared at the backseat venomously. She then turned to see if Pookie would respond. Moe sat in the backseat smiling and basically ignored her cousin's glare.

"I got a few homeboys that would fuck with you. Let me see what's up once I drop you off over Rachelle's house."

Pookie turned the music back up until they got to Rachelle's house. He had 'Cinderfella' Dana Dane blasting as he hit the corner to Rachelle's house. They actually could have walked since it was right around the corner. But not only did Pookie and Janelle want to hook up; J-Ridah had gathered some of the homies to ride on the Mayo Lane's. The Block was hot so they opted for the safest route. Pookie had already gotten a motel and was ready for Janelle to spend the night. When they pulled up in front of Rachelle's house, Janelle smiled.

"I'm running in to let Rachelle know that my cousin is spending the night and then we on our way. You ready Moe?"

"Yeah, I'm ready, but why can't I hang with you and one of Pookie's homeboys?" Moe protested.

"Bitch I told you what we was going to do; now you pull this shit? Get out the car so I can take you inside to meet everybody."

"But I don't know any of your friends except for Rachelle. That's fucked up when I could roll with you and one of Pookie's homeboys." She frowned.

"Girl if you don't…"

"Wait a minute baby, I can pull Turtle from off the block and he can kick it with her." Pookie suggested.

"Yeah, but I don't want them fucking up what we trying to do. She can stay her ass over here for one night damn." Janelle replied. The irritation was evident in her tone.

"Naw, I was thinking more like they got they own room and kick it together. We get some drink and some bud and while they doing they thing we will be in the other room doing our thing." Pookie shrugged his shoulders.

"Come on Janelle, you can do your thing while I do my thing and we won't even fuck with ya'll. But yo homeboy Turtle better be cute or I'm going to be pissed." Moe cut in.

"Beggars can't be choosers. You better be glad I'm even thinking about bringing yo ass along." Janelle snapped.

They jumped back inside Pookie's car and he drove around the block where Turtle was curb serving. Turtle stood outside with his blue Khakis and blue Fila tennis shoes. He had on a blue sweatshirt with creases, one on the front and two on the back. There was a blue New York Giants Starter jacket lying on the small brick wall. His light brown complexion matched with his dark sandy brown cornrows that were freshly done. He had just gotten out of Camp Kilpatrick, which was a lockdown camp in the hills of Malibu so his muscles bulged through his sweatshirt.

"Oooh Janelle, that nigga fine." Moe whispered.

"What's Up Turtle cuz?" Pookie said from the driver's side.

"Alondra Block till I die." Turtle announced nonchalantly.

"Well check this out here cuz, I got a homegirl in the back seat that wants to meet you. So we were thinking about going to a motel and hang out for a while. We can get some drink and I already got some weed, so are you with it cuz?"

"Hell yeah I'm with it cuz. Where's the broad that wants to meet me?" He eagerly asked.

"She's in the backseat." Pookie pointed with his thumb.

Turtle glanced into the car but the tinted windows made it difficult for him to see. He kept trying to look over Janelle until she finally got irritated.

"Look cuz, you rolling or what?" She snapped.

131

"Damn Big Nell, you ain't got to come at a nigga like that. I was about to get in." Turtle mumbled while climbing in the backseat.

Once Turtle made it to the backseat him and Moe hit it off instantly. They chatted in the backseat together as if they knew each other for years. They whispered in each other's ear until Pookie drove inside the motel parking lot.

"Look here Turtle cuz, I already got the room for us so just get a room for ya'll."

"Alright then cuz just let me out."

Everyone followed suit and climbed out the car. Pookie and Janelle went towards their room while Turtle and Moe went up to the caged window. Turtle felt Moe walking up on him while he was paying the man behind the window.

"Ay Moe cuz, tell Pookie to let you get some of that weed he was talking about." Turtle said without turning around.

Moe ran towards the room to catch them before they got inside. Panting she took a few breaths then finally spoke.

"Turtle wanted to know if you got any of that weed you were talking about?"

"Yeah but tell that nigga we going to the store to get some zig zags. Then I can pick up some drink also. Let me get Janelle inside of here then we gone make that move."

Janelle rolled her eyes at Moe but she was too preoccupied with Turtle to notice. After Pookie sat some things down in the room he came back outside to roll with Pookie. Janelle cut on the television and sat on the bed. Moe stood at the door with puppy dog eyes looking at her.

"Janelle is it alright if I stay in here with you until they get back?"

Janelle frowned then looked up at Moe.

"I don't care."

Moe came bouncing in as if she had been granted a million dollars and sat next to Janelle.

"Damn Moe, scoot down, you act like we fucking or something." Janelle sneered.

"Damn Janelle why you always got to be so mean? You act like we aren't family sometimes. I can't help that mama and Auntie Jo don't get along a lot of times but I love ya'll and my auntie." Moe protested.

"It ain't like that Moe, it's just I was expecting to be alone with my man and if it ain't one thing it's another. I guess I'm taking it out on you." Janelle reached over to hug her cousin.

Janelle grabbed the remote from off the bed to cut on the television. When she cut on the television there was a porno already playing. They both looked at each other and started laughing.

"I'm glad I get to hang with you Janelle. Since mama and Auntie Jo got their problems we don't get to see each other. It's boring out in north Long Beach. Mama insists that we stay out of Compton." Moe rambled.

"I know, mama was telling me that she thinks she's too good to come out here to Compton and only reason she let you come out here is because you had gotten into some trouble. What happened with that shit anyway?"

"A few of my homegirls went up to the Long Beach mall and they wanted to steal some shit. It was a few things I liked and I knew mama wasn't going to give me the money for it so I said fuck it. But they had cameras all over the place, and before we could make out the store a bunch of security guards rushed all three of us. I was scared, girl I ain't even gone lie. So to make a long story short they put me on probation and that's when mama said that I need to get away from my friends for a while." Moe lowered her head.

Janelle put her arm back around her cousin and smiled. Moe leaned inward and put her head on Janelle's shoulder.

"You don't have to be ashamed around family. It wasn't what you did; it's that you got caught." Janelle chided.

At that moment Pookie and Turtle came through the door. Janelle smiled as she stood up to greet Pookie. He sat down a couple of 40 oz bottles of Old English then sat the sack of weed next to the zigzags.

"I'm gone roll up a couple of joints for Turtle then we gone do what we do baby. Is that cool?"

"Yeah, I'm not tripping. Matter of fact we got all night so let's smoke some together before you go in the other room." Janelle suggested.

After all four of them smoked two skunk weed joints together Turtle and Moe went into the other room. Right after Turtle shut their door Pookie reached over the bed and grabbed Janelle. Being just as eager she drew her body close to his as they slowly undressed. She hadn't been intimate with Pookie for some time and she missed him being inside of her. Pookie cut off the television so that they could do what they do.

Turtle took off his blue NY Giants Starter Jacket and sat next to Moe on the bed. She wiggled a little bit trying to relax. He looked at her with a devilish grin.

"So what's up Moe?"

"So what's up Terrance or should I call you Turtle?"

"Turtle is cool. But are we gone do this or what?"

"What do you want to do?"

"You ever sucked a nigga's dick?" He said as smooth as it could possibly be said.

"Naw, I ain't ever done that?"

He unzipped his pants and pulled out his dick. Her eyes got big as he slowly stroked it.

"All you got to do is put your lips around it without biting it with your teeth." He explained.

He grabbed the back of her head and pulled her mouth down toward his pants. She grabbed hold of his dick and slowly began doing as she was instructed. Before long she had got into a rhythm. He kept his hand on the back of her head as she went up and down.

"Now take off your clothes so I can hit that ass." Turtle lustfully demanded.

She was undressed in a heartbeat. Turtle threw her on the bed and spread her legs from east to west. He plunged inside of her ravaging her at his will.

"I got this bitch now!" He thought.

Days later J-Ridah paced back and forth while Snake puffed on a Camel cigarette. J-Ridah's eyes were blood shot red from taking a bottle of Thunderbird to the head.

"Fuck that cuz, we gone ride on them Mayo Lane niggas for what they did to the homeboy Do-Dirty. That's why the war is cracking. We can get the little homies to put in work and earn them muthafuckin stripes. That's on the set cuz." J-Ridah vented.

"I'm just telling you cuz, 'One Time' been hot lately because we've been riding on those slob niggas. They bumped up Little Sham and Drama the other day asking what sparked the war. They tried to tell them that there isn't a war but they knew cuz, they knew."

Snake nonchalantly puffed on his cigarette. He had just got out of the County on a warrant. He was trying to avoid going back to the pen but he knew J-Ridah well.

"We got to find a way to get at them niggas without having to worry about the pigs."

"We can chill for a while then ride on them niggas later." Snake suggested.

"Aw cuz, you sound like my brother Baby Gangster. He is talking that shit about it fucking up business for niggas in the hood. As if the hood doesn't come first. I had to check that nigga about that punk shit." J-Ridah vented.

"You do have a son now cuz. Look here J-Ridah, this is Alondra Block until I die but we don't even know if those niggas even killed Do-Dirty. It could have been those Boulevard niggas or those shady ass Greenleaf niggas."

"Fuck it then, we should ride on all those niggas until we find out who did it." J-Ridah replied.

C-Dog, Jay-Cee and Gangster walked up during the discussion. They seen J-Ridah in one of his moods so they were reluctant in their approach. They weren't scared of him but they knew his temper had a short fuse.

"Damn Gangster, come holla at your brother for a minute." J-Ridah's mood suddenly changed.

They walked over to corner so that they could have some privacy. They stared at each other for a moment. They had an undying love for one another that couldn't be spoken in words. Every fight or disagreement was quickly looked at as the past.

"Are you staying off that Sherm cuz?" J-Ridah asked.

"Yeah since Mike Dog got eight years I've been trying to stay clean. I'll smoke a little weed but that's about it. Between you and me though, I have nightmares a lot. Ever since I've been off that shit, I think about all the dirt I've done and that shit comes out in dreams." Gangster sighed.

"Yeah you always were down to put in work, even if you had to do it by yourself." J-Ridah commented.

"What you doing over here acting all heated about?" Gangster asked.

"Naw, Snake was telling me that Drama and Little Sham came up to him saying the police was wondering why we started all of a sudden warring with those Mayo Lane niggas."

"Yeah they've been getting hot lately. We haven't had a war with anybody since Do-Dirty got smoked. I'm telling you though cuz, I think it was those Greenleaf niggas." Gangster said.

It was like a new revelation to J-Ridah. He leaned against a nearby tree and thought about it. Gangster gave him a little time to collect his thoughts.

"That's the second time I've heard that shit today. But I'm not quick to blast on other Crips like them L.A. nigga do. Besides, why would them niggas ride on Do-Dirty when he had homeboys from they hood that he was locked down with?" J-Ridah reasoned.

"That doesn't mean shit. They will set trip on they own homeboys. Plus I don't think them niggas ever really forgot about the time Baby Gangster blasted on two of their homeboys. That's a trip to hear about Jason blasting on some niggas huh?" Gangster chuckled.

"Yeah, but he got that Laney family in him like the rest of us. Did he tell you that story he said mama told him and Janelle about Grandpa Frankie? He told me that he thinks he takes from that side of the family. That nigga is a trip but I love that muthafucka though."

"Yeah I love that nigga too. Do you remember when Janelle couldn't stand his ass? Now she's got the utmost respect for him. Oh yeah, before I forget, what time did mama want us to meet up Saturday for that family picture?"

"She told me two o' clock." J-Ridah replied.

He still leaned on the tree lost in his thoughts. He patted Gangster on his back as they walked back over to the rest of the homeboys. It was getting dark and he had contemplated sending some of the young homies to blast on the Mayo Lane set but now he had doubts. The OGs had gathered around him by now because he was a well-respected shot caller. It was obvious that he replaced the void that was created when Do-Dirty was killed. It was a new era of Alondra Block Compton Crips. J-Ridah had every intention on letting the world know that they were one of the coldest sets in the world. He had already set it up with his brother Baby Gangster to get hold of an Uzi and other high caliber weaponry. Since his brother was a shot caller he grudgingly obliged.

"Where in the fuck is the little homies cuz?" J-Ridah asked.

"I over heard those niggas talking about pulling a train on this toss up bitch. Some little bitch Turtle is fucking with." C-Dog replied.

In a small motel room on Long Beach Boulevard a party was taking place. Not a regular party but a sex party involving four Crips and one female. The pretty young girl with the dark caramel complexion and sexy thick lips told Turtle she would do anything he asked after a week of knowing him. She couldn't get enough of him. When she told him she would do anything he told her that he didn't believe her. Time and time again she swore to him that she would do anything he likes. So one day he asked her to prove it. Her eyes stared directly in his eyes not budging from his position.

"I want you to fuck my homeboys and me. If you down to do that then I will believe you." He calmly suggested.

She never considered doing that before. But she had never loved a man like she loved Turtle. She went back and forth about it.

"Just once then you will believe me?" She sounded hopeful.

"Just once, and I will believe you from now on." He winked at her.

Now she is at the third homeboy because Turtle made sure he got his first. The third homeboy plunged inside of her and she felt a tear in her vaginal tissue. She winced in pain as he sweated on top of her steadily pushing his dick into her almost dry vaginal cavity. She finally couldn't take it anymore and let the tears fall from her face. The pain was unbearable but the weight of number three was too heavy to push off. She cried in silent agony wanting to be set free but there was no one there to aid her. She tried to scream but found that she was too weak and her voice would only give out a low wine.

"This is a nasty bitch! You hear her moaning and shit cuz?" One voice said in the dark.

She didn't reply. All she could hope for was that number three hurried and number four was quicker. Suddenly she felt a hard dick pushing her mouth open.

"By the time this nigga through she gone be all dried up. I just get some head from the bitch." Another voice said in the dark.

She swallowed him in her mouth until finally she felt semen leak into her throat. She began choking and coughing as number three released similar fluids inside of her. He moaned with relief then finally climbed off of her. They didn't even take the time to clean up. They quickly zipped their pants and ran out the motel room. She laid on the bed left all alone in the dark. The muscles on her body ached so much that she couldn't move. With all the will she could muster she rose from the bed. She stumbled into the bathroom and quickly vomited inside the toilet. She held tightly to the commode for fifteen to twenty minutes allowing all the impurities to leave her body. Tears still fell profusely from her face as semen leaked from her vagina down both legs. She crawled over to the stand-up-only shower passionately turning on the faucet. She lifted herself up and climbed in the dingy shower and bathed long and hard with cheap motel soap. Her tears never stopped pouring. When she finally crawled out of the shower her legs shook as she slowly and carefully tried to reach the bed. Her legs buckled once. Her legs buckled twice. She finally was able to reach the bed that had the remnants of cigarette smoke ingrained in the odor of the bed cover. She rolled over on her back and fell into a deep coma like sleep. She didn't awake until the cleaning lady banged on her door for clean up at eleven in the morning.

12

GRANDMA JO

I grew up around some niggas that's not my homies!
50 Cent

Moe came strolling into the Laney household around eleven thirty in the morning. She could hear the commotion before she even walked inside. She was praying that Auntie Jo would either be gone or too preoccupied to notice her coming home in the morning. After hearing her voice she could only hope for the latter. She slid inside the house and went straight towards Mama Jo's bedroom. It was the first bedroom to the right once you walked into the house. She didn't want to be noticed and it sounded as if Auntie Jo and Janelle were having their own issues.

"So what the fuck happened to you going to Cosmetology school Janelle?"

"I can still go to school Mama, damn. You act like it's the end of the world for me because I'm pregnant." Janelle fired back.

"Things change when you become a mother Janelle. You can't just up and go when you feel like it anymore. You have to make sure that someone else is taken care of. This mama shit ain't easy and now you are about to fuck up your life over this Pookie nigga."

"See Mama there you go putting down Pookie. He is going to be there for me. That nigga loves me and I love him. Plus I'm a grown ass woman now Mama."

"How the fuck you know he's going to be there for you? You say some of the stupidest shit I've ever heard. That nigga sells dope Janelle he doesn't have a job. Ain't no telling when he's going to see the penitentiary then you is going to be carrying the weight by yourself. Then he's going to expect you to send him packages and all kinds of shit. This shit ain't easy...fuck I wish you would have waited until you were married or something." Mama Jo showed her frustration.

"You were pregnant at sixteen mama with Joseph and I'm nineteen years old now." Janelle sassily replied.

"That's what the fuck I'm talking about Janelle. I don't want you going through the shit I went through. I wanted it better for you but you don't want to listen. You hard headed just like yo damn daddy."

"Look mama I plan to finish cosmetology school like I promised. I've always wanted to do hair and that's what I'm going to do."

"No one in our family has ever gone to college and I was just hoping that you would be the first to do that." Mama Jo's voice strained.

Janelle felt bad after those words. She silently vowed to finish school no matter what.

"Monique don't think because Janelle and I are talking that I didn't notice you walking in this early in the morning." Mama Jo interrupted her thoughts.

Mama Jo peaked out of the kitchen door giving a quick glance at Moe after she heard the door open. Janelle didn't pay attention at how Moe was walking until Mama walked into the living room.

"Come sit down and have something to eat so we can talk about you staying out…what happened to you?"

Moe painfully walked towards both of them. Her face winced at every step. She felt like her entire body had pinched nerves. She had cried enough so the tears no longer fell.

"What happened to you baby? Tell us and we will make sure it's taken care of." Mama Jo softly spoke.

"Come on Monique we will love you no matter what. Tell us what happened to you." Janelle said while gently touching Monique's hand.

The tears began to fall all over again. Not only from the pain but the embarrassment. She looked at both Mama Jo and Janelle with deeply saddened eyes.

"It was my fault. I should have proved myself a long time ago. I promise Auntie Jo I told him I would do it. It was all my fault." Moe said while tears covered her face.

"What was your fault? Tell me what happened so I can help you." Mama Jo grew impatient.

"You have to promise that you will not hurt him."

"All I can promise is that I won't kill him. Now tell me Monique what happened to you?" Mama Jo firmly asked.

"Okay, I told Turtle…I mean Terrance that I loved him and would do anything for him. He didn't believe me Auntie Jo. I kept telling him that I would do anything he asked. So finally he asked me to prove myself by doing something with his homeboys too. I didn't want to do it but I had to prove to him that I really did love him. Now that it is all over he will know the truth. I just wish it didn't hurt so bad." Moe desperately explained.

Mama Jo sat at the dinner table seething inside. Janelle leaned back in her chair and slowly let out a sigh. She was more stunned than anything. No one said a word for a minute. Everyone was lost in their thoughts.

"Janelle take Moe into the room then run her a hot bath so she can soak in it. If she starts bleeding or anything then we will have to ask Jason to take her to the hospital."

Janelle did as she was told slowly walking Moe into the bedroom with both arms wrapped around her. Moe got close to the bedroom door then turned around.

"Auntie Jo please don't tell my mama about this."

"Don't worry baby we gone handle this together. Your mother doesn't have to know." Mama Jo nodded.

She leaned back in her chair and pulled out one of her cigarettes. She wanted to cry for her niece. She wanted to kill for her niece. Her thoughts raced back and forth as she seen Janelle walk in the bathroom to turn on the bath water. She sat there stiff only moving her arm to put the cigarette to her mouth. How was she going to handle this?

"What's Up Mama, I was tired as hell. I know it's late as hell right now. What time is it, around noon?" Baby Gangster walked into the living room.

"Look here Jason, it's a plate of food on the stove but I need to talk to you about something important while you are eating." Mama Jo replied.

"What's up Mama, you need some money?"

"Naw nothing like that. Just grab a seat so that we can talk for a minute.

Turtle was down to his last of the package he had copped from Pookie. It had just gotten dark and he was hoping to sell out before the night was over. It was the fifteenth so the fiends were spending either paychecks or County checks. He glanced at the Cadillac Seville pulling up on him. The car was familiar to him so he smiled when it pulled up to the curb right next to him. Damn I wish I were Ballin like this nigga do, Turtle pondered. He wasn't driving the El Camino today; he was driving the all white with the blue pearl painted Cadillac.

Baby Gangster hopped out of the driver's seat with his 501 Levis creased to the Tee. His one-inch cuff had a split on the side that made his jeans easily lay over his blue Fila shoes. His crisp new white Pro Club shirt hung over his frame. Barely peaking out of his shirt on his belt was his beeper. He walked up to Turtle with his pistol drawn but lowered to the side. As soon as he was in arms reach his pistol slammed into Turtle's head. Turtle stumbled back, half dazed from the blow to encounter a second blow following behind the first. He dropped to one knee as Baby Gangster bent over to speak to him in low tone.

"I should kill you cuz. I promised my mama that I wouldn't shoot yo punk ass. If Moe hadn't agreed to do that dumb shit you would be dead. Don't you ever think about violating my cousin again nigga." Baby Gangster said in a low but sinister tone.

"Naw Baby Gangster cuz I didn't know that she was related to you. I thought she was Janelle's homegirl…"

Baby Gangster's pistol crashed into his forehead interrupting his words. He didn't want any explanation. There was nothing that he could say to explain this. He gave Turtle time to regain his sense.

"Look here cuz, if I was to tell my brothers J-Ridah or Gangster they would have smoked you on the spot. So you getting a mercy pass because of a few things. First off she didn't get raped and she agreed to do it. So my moms thinks you should live because of that. She came to me because any other brother would have killed yo ass cuz. So listen and listen good. You come around Monique or anything I won't tell my brothers shit. I will smoke yo punk pretty ass myself and that's on Alondra Block."

Baby Gangster stood up totally erect waiting to get a reply. After a few seconds he walked to the driver's side of his car still looking at Turtle. Turtle slowly lifted himself from the ground holding his forehead. Baby Gangster looked at Turtle one last time before getting into his Cadillac.

"Don't fuck with my family!!!"

He hopped into the driver's seat and sped off. Turtle decided it was time for him to pack it up for the night. He needed to tend to his wounds. Baby Gangster looked in his rearview to see what Turtle would do but he had driven too far. He drove over to Snake's house to meet up with his brothers. All of his brothers were hanging out over there with the OGs and he needed to drop something off.

When he arrived everyone was in the backyard drinking, playing dominoes or leaning against the garage wall.

"What's happening Baby Gangster?" C-Dog shouted.

"Hella Bella Skella." J-Ridah announced.

J-Ridah just scored fifteen points on the domino table then glanced up at Baby Gangster. Baby Gangster nodded then walked over toward the garage wall where the Twins and a few of the young homeboys were hanging.

"You want some of this Night Train?" Laney Twin ace asked.

"Bolts and Screws cuz." Snake announced.

144

Baby Gangster grabbed hold of the bottle then turned around to see Snake score twenty points.

"How in the fuck you get twenty points like that cuz." J-Ridah said with playful frustration.

"Because nigga, I knew you was trying to get rid of that big three you just so happen to get some points. All money ain't good money J-Ridah cuz. I knew you had it because I was reading the board."

"I try to tell some niggas all money ain't good money." J-Ridah jokingly glanced at Baby Gangster.

Baby Gangster gave him the finger as he swigged the Night Train. He mingled with the homies until he heard Snake holler domino. Everybody gradually got up from the table cursing and whatnot. J-Ridah glanced at Baby Gangster then waived at him to come to the front of the house. Once they reached the front they walked toward the Cadillac. Baby Gangster popped the trunk and J-Ridah smiled.

"Good work! We gone have to put that Uzi to use. This is a small little artillery. We can fuck around and fight the police with some shit like this." J-Ridah commented

"Aw nigga you talking about fighting the police?" Baby Gangster asked.

"Naw, I'm just bullshitting. But we gone give those Mayo Lane niggas the blues." J-Ridah replied.

"So you think they the ones that killed Do-Dirty?" Baby Gangster asked but not really caring about the answer.

"I don't know but I figure like this, we should blast on them niggas just in case they did. More than likely it was those slob niggas anyway." J-Ridah commented.

He turned around to see Laney Twin ace walking up on them. He was with one of the little homies named Pokey. Him and Laney Twin 1 were road dogs unless Laney Twin 1 was out chasing some ass. It was always odd to J-Ridah because he always thought that Laney Twin 2 would be more like a road Dog to Pokey. Pokey was a young shooter that didn't mind shooting at anyone. J-Ridah liked the young comrade the moment he met him.

"What's up cuz…aw shit you got some heat up in this trunk. Let me see that machine gun." Laney Twin 1 reached for the gun.

J-Ridah smacked his hand away instantly. He quickly put his finger to his mouth and sternly stared at his younger brother.

"You ain't about to do shit with it so what you reaching for?" J-Ridah retorted.

"Fuck you Joseph cuz, I'm down to put in work for the set." Laney Twin ace fired back.

"Well we will see if you selling wolf tickets or not. We about to handle it with these Mayo Lane niggas so we gone find out if you down or not. What about you Pokey? You down to ride on these Mayonnaise niggas?"

"I'm down for whatever OG homie. You tell us to ride on them slob niggas then we gone ride." Pokey calmly replied.

"See that's what I'm talking about cuz. This nigga right here is a ridah for real." J-Ridah passionately pointed at Pokey.

"Well put this shit in yo car or stash it somewhere because I'm about to roll out. While ya'll niggas is riding I'm gone have Kisha riding on top of me." Baby Gangster lightheartedly replied.

"Whatever nigga. Ay Jamil, tell Snake to bring me a brown paper bag from out of his house so we can put this shit somewhere. Good looking out little brother, you came through with the heat." J- Ridah grinned.

Baby Gangster walked up to his older brother and they embraced. They had different philosophies about the street but there was still a mutual respect. J-Ridah's eighteen inch arms wrapped around Baby Gangster firmly.

"How many of those pictures you took of the family? Mama was telling me she only had four or five of them left." J-Ridah asked.

"As many as I like cuz, I paid for them." Baby Gangster remarked.

"Money ain't everything Jason; sometimes it's about your comrades. It's about your loved ones and that's on Compton Crip."

"And that's why I paid for them. But to tell the truth I only took two. I think mama was passing them out to everybody she knew. She will probably have to order some more." Baby Gangster said while climbing in his Cadillac.

J-Ridah was leaning on the Cadillac so he quickly rose once the engine was fired up. The trunk was still open as J-Ridah and Pokey quickly loaded the weaponry in a large brown paper bag. J-Ridah pointed to the backyard so that Pokey could stash them there then he closed the trunk. He hit the back of the car twice so that Baby Gangster would know to drive off.

Baby Gangster went looking for the closest phone booth so that he could call up Kisha. He figured he would get a motel room so that they could chill for a little while. Before he could hit Compton Boulevard he noticed Pookie at another spot they just opened up. It looked like everything was buzzing when he got out the car. Pookie nodded towards him when he seen him walk up. They embraced for a moment.

"So what's up with you pistol whipping the little homie cuz?" Pookie asked.

"Damn news travels fast. That pretty ass nigga should have gotten his ass hit up side the head. He got some of the homies to pull a train on my little cousin Monique." Baby Gangster said with disgust.

"You bullshitting? They raped her?"

"Naw, she agreed to do the dumb shit but then she couldn't handle it once it started happening. That nigga Turtle wanted her to prove that she would do anything for him and that's what he got her to do." Baby Gangster explained.

"That ain't the little homie's fault, that's yo cousin's fault. She decided to be a toss up for the homies. It ain't like he forced her to do it." Pookie defended Turtle.

"That's the reason why I didn't smoke him. I would have peeled his cap back if it was a rape. That stupid ass girl is still my cousin. That shit is off the chain with my family. On my mother's side of the family I got two naïve cousins that don't know shit. On

147

my father's side of the family my cousins is slobs. I love them two niggas know matter what they are though." Baby Gangster smiled.

"But I got to say this though; he didn't know that was yo cousin. If Turtle would have known that was yo cousin do you think he would have done that dumb shit? I think you overreacted on the little homie cuz." Pookie replied.

"Not really. He should have checked out who she was related to before he even thought about doing that crazy shit. My moms was even hot about that shit." Baby Gangster replied.

"Mama Jo knew about that shit?"

"Yeah she knew; that was how I knew. She knew not to tell J-Ridah or Gangster because they would have peeled his cap with no hesitation. I showed his pretty ass some love. That nigga needs to stop trying to be a pimp and start being a man."

"What the fuck is a man anyway? Most niggas sixteen and older claim they are men. What makes Turtle less than a man?"

"A nigga that takes care of his peoples. I can take care of my whole family. I can hustle what I need to make sure my family has what they want and need. That's a man to me." Baby Gangster said with pride.

"So a nigga with money is what makes you a man?"

"Naw not just that but also willing to take care of your own." Baby Gangster replied.

"But Turtle been copping from us since he's been out and he got money to take care of yo cousin. Because he got other bitches on the roster he less than a man?" Pookie persisted.

"But he also got to be willing to do it cuz. What's with all the interrogation? That nigga violated my family so he had to pay for that shit. It's that muthafuckin simple." Baby Gangster voice revealed irritation.

"Naw cuz, you say the nigga needs to be a man but you didn't give him a chance to be a man. Just because she's yo cousin he ain't a man. You've been down to pull a train on a toss up bitch before. But the little homie got to get chastised because he didn't know it was yo family but yo cousin chose to be a toss up." Pookie fired back.

148

"What's yo point?"

"My point is that everybody got their meaning of what a man is. Getting bitches and money is what Turtle is about. You are about the same thing but just because yo cousin was involved he has to get pistol whipped." Pookie explained.

"You muthafuckin right. Maybe he is a man but he's a man that's gone think twice before he pulls a train on a bitch." Baby Gangster replied.

"Damn it looks like yo mind is made up. Do you think I'm going to be a man to Big Nell?" Pookie asked out of curiosity.

"Yeah, you've always been an up and up nigga. It's just we have to instill the code in these young muthafuckas. You a nigga that done proved yourself time and time again. But when I think about it, I don't know what a man is supposed to be. My father been locked up since I could barely walk. The closest I've had to knowing what a man is like is from my brothers Joseph and Jordan. And I'm about as close to being like them as the earth is from the moon. So I try to live by my own idea of what a man is supposed to be." Baby Gangster replied.

He looked down from gazing in the air because his pager went off. He noticed the familiar number.

"I'm out! I'm copping three of those birds tomorrow so we can have that raw for the rest of the month." Baby Gangster said while climbing into his car.

"That's cool cuz. I got enough dough to get a place for me and Janelle when the baby comes. So the rest of the money is going to be for extra shit." Pookie replied.

"That's good. It's already too many people living in the house as is. I was thinking about getting a place with Kisha but I don't know if I can live with that crazy bitch."

They both started laughing while Baby Gangster started up his engine. He quickly tapped the roof of his car then threw up the Alondra Block gang sign. Pookie did the same as Baby Gangster sped off towards Compton Boulevard.

Nu-Nu and Sly was sitting at a gas station off of Compton Boulevard. They were sharing a bottle of Thunderbird when a white Cadillac Seville pulled into the gas station.

"Man that nigga got some nice ass rims on that Lac. He even got gold knock offs." Nu-Nu commented.

Sly didn't say anything as he observed the man getting out of the car. The Thunderbird was starting to get to him but he thought the man looked familiar. He blinked his eyes several times then leaned closer to the windshield to get a better look.

"Ain't that the young nigga from Alondra Block?" Sly asked.

"That sure in the fuck is. Aw that nigga is slippin big time cuz. We got to get this nigga." Nu-Nu keenly replied.

"I'm down!"

They both pulled out straps. Nu-Nu had a nine-millimeter with sixteen in the clip and one in the chamber. Sly was carrying a black long nose forty-five six-shooter. They crept out of the car closing both doors as quietly as possible. By that time their intended victim was using the pay phone and wasn't paying them any attention. They squatted down low so that he couldn't see them. They patiently waited for him to walk back to his Cadillac Seville. Once he had gotten the keys from out of his pocket he walked quickly to the driver's seat door.

"Break yo self Blood. Break yo self Blood." Nu-Nu yelled.

He had the nine-millimeter pointed directly at his victims head. Sly slid from the other side of the Cadillac with his pistol drawn as well. The victim raised his hands in the air and let his keys drop to the ground.

"Look homies who ever you are I probably got family that know ya'll. You can have the Lac I just don't want any problems." Baby Gangster said.

"It ain't gone be any problem if you don't make any problems Blood." Sly followed what Nu-Nu had said.

Baby Gangster knew they were familiar but the black handkerchiefs over their faces threw him off. His hood normally wore black rags but now he knew they weren't from his set. Why would some Pirus carry black rags he pondered?

"Fuck that cuz, we gone let this nigga know who the fuck we are." Nu-Nu sneered as he pulled off his black rag.

Baby Gangster made a gesture of surprise but it all made sense to him. He thought about running because at this point he figured they had to kill him.

"Fuck cuz, everything was cool without him knowing who we were." Sly whispered.

Nu-Nu slowly picked up the keys from off the ground with his gun pointed at Baby Gangster's head. He opened the Cadillac then pointed his head towards his parked car.

"Drive my car cuz so we can roll out." Nu-Nu instructed.

Baby Gangster kept his hands up as Nu-Nu climbed into his car. He didn't move because he could easily replace the car. He would chalk it up as a loss and move on to bigger and better things. Before the door closed to his Cadillac his mind went blank. He didn't hear the loud gunfire. Each bullet pierced his skull before he had time to think. Six shots pounded into his brain as his body collapsed to ground. His body still shook as the nerves all over his anatomy reacted to the sudden shock to his brain. Then his heart slowly murmured away until his body was totally stiff. The Cadillac had sped off before the body had finished moving.

13

ONE LESS MOUTH

It wasn't yo brother to brutally die!
Ice T

The living room was thick with tension and concern. Kisha had called the Laney household several times saying that she had just spoken to Baby Gangster. No one knew why he wasn't answering his pages. So finally Janelle paged Pookie who promptly drove around to the Laney household.

"What's up Nell you having problems with the baby?" Pookie came inside.

"Naw, I wanted to know have you seen Jason because Kisha called here saying that he was supposed to meet up with her but he never showed up." Janelle stood up when he walked in.

"How many times did you page him because he might have decided to fuck with another one of his females? I just seen him a couple of hours ago and we had a long talk." Pookie sternly glanced at Moe.

She lowered her head in shame.

"We called him three times with 911 on the pages and he still hadn't called back."

"Let me see what's up. Where did Kisha say he was at when he called her?" Pookie sighed.

"She said he was at the phone booth on Compton and Long Beach Boulevard at the gas station." Mama Jo replied.

"I'll roll up around that area and see what I can find." Pookie walked out the door.

He hit the corner on Compton Boulevard making that left towards Long Beach Boulevard. Once he hit the corner of Long Beach Boulevard he noticed a number of police and a coroner truck. As he got closer he also seen the yellow tape but kept going to avoid the police. He was hoping he would find Baby Gangster maybe talking to someone or observing the police. After circling the block he decided to park and get closer to the murder scene to see who was killed. He parked behind the gas station so he could walk up like any observer. For a moment he had forgotten that he was supposed to be looking for Baby Gangster. He figured that he was messing with another one of his broads and didn't tell Kisha. He must have cut off his pager, Pookie reasoned.

As he got closer to the crime scene he noticed the body the coroners were lifting from the scene. The top of the victim's head was blown off but the build and clothing looked familiar. He peaked a little closer to get a better look.

"Fuck no, that's the muthafuckin homeboy." Pookie blurted out.

He ran towards the coroner so that he could observe the body but was stopped by two police.

"Refrain him fellas." A plain clothes cop said.

The detective walked over to him with his pen and pad pulled out. Pookie tried to break free but in vain.

"Calm down young man or you'll be charged with obstruction. Now tell me your name and address. Do you happen to know the victim?"

"That's my muthafuckin road dog."

"Wait a minute, I don't know your name but I know your face. You are from the Alondra Block set. What is your name?" The Detective persisted.

"Patrick Carter, now can I see if that is my homeboy?"

"Do you know your homeboy's legal name?"

"Yeah, his name is Jason Laney."

"That was the name on the victim's driver's license. We wouldn't have been able to recognize him without his ID."

Pookie yelled as though he had been stabbed in the heart. The two police officers held him tighter to restrain him. He tried in vain to escape as the coroner began to close the van. Tears fell down his face as they drove off with his homeboy.

"Now Mr. Carter, I'm Detective Miller and have to ask you a few questions before I release you. Is the victim also an Alondra Block Compton Crip as well? Is he...oh shit, is he related to Joseph Laney?" Detective Miller suddenly realized who the victim might be.

Pookie nodded his head suggesting he should have known by now. That instantly knocked the wind out of Detective Miller. He wasn't in the mood to ask any more questions. The thoughts began to race through his head of all the murders that were implicated with the Laney name involved. Pookie remained quiet because he knew the cop finally understood.

"Detective Miller I need to go and tell his family. They are going to want to know what happened to him." Pookie calmly said.

Detective Miller waived his hand to indicate to the cops holding him that he could be released. Pookie walked back to his car and sat in it without cutting on the motor. He did not want to be the bearer of bad news. He couldn't think of how to break it to them. He didn't want Mama Jo to have to go through that. Even though he knew she didn't like him that was his girl's mama and his dead homeboy's mama. He let the tears flow down his face.

"My last word with him was over Turtle's bitch ass." He said aloud.

He started the engine and the music from the radio surrounded the inside of his car. 'In the Rain' from Keith Sweat was the song that appropriately played on the radio. He let the song play as he turned the corner to his neighborhood. When he pulled up in front of the Laney house he slowly cut off the engine. He hated having to be the one to give them the news. He got out the car and dragged his feet. His mind was racing so much that he didn't realize how he made it to the front door. He reluctantly knocked on the front door.

"It's open." A female said.

He slid the door open without looking anyone in the face. He wasn't able to focus on anyone so he used his peripheral. Finally he raised his head and staring right at him was Mama Jo.

154

"I could feel it, I could feel it." Mama Jo screamed.

Her voice shook him out of his sad slumber. Mama Jo threw her hands in the air and almost fell to the ground. Janelle caught her half way down while Pookie also came to her aid. Mama Jo was hysterical as Pookie had to use all his strength just to hold her up. Tears flowed from her face and it shocked everyone present. No one had ever seen Mama Jo cry until now. Her face was soaking wet as she released all her pain, espoused all her anger, she had totally surrendered her mental faculties to pure emotion. Pookie suddenly realized he was around nothing but women. Mama Jo was in his arms barely able to stand. Janelle held on to her mother while crying herself. Moe was sitting at the table balled up crying. Pookie didn't know what to do. He quickly escorted Mama Jo to the couch and softly sat her down. She was beginning to regain her composure. She panted hard trying to say something.

"Moe get my aspirin out the medicine cabinet and Janelle get me some water."

As they scurried off to follow Mama Jo's instructions she glanced up at Pookie who was still standing above her.

"I felt it Patrick, I felt that my baby was dead. Look I need you to do something for me."

"Anything Mama Jo."

"I need you to go around to Snake's house and tell my son to come around here to see me. Tell him to bring the twins and Jordan as well. Now listen, I don't want you to tell him about Jason. I want to tell him you hear?"

She then swallowed the aspirin and water that she had just gotten. She waived for Pookie to hurry up and carry out her words. He scurried off without saying a word.

When he pulled up at Snake's house he noticed that J-Ridah was outside talking to Pam who was Do-Dirty's baby's mama. She glanced up before J-Ridah did to see Pookie coming towards them.

"What's up Cuz, did you know that this is Do-Dirty's baby mama Pam? Do-Dirty had to get off in a Greenleaf nigga's ass over her." J-Ridah lightheartedly reminisced.

"Yeah I remember that. I was there when that shit went down." Pookie replied.

"That's right you were there. All the homies is in the back getting twisted." J-Ridah subtly suggested that he let Pam and he finish talking.

"Naw cuz, I came to see you."

"About what?" J-Ridah sounded irritated.

"Mama Jo told me that she wants to see you Gangster and the Twins ASAP." Pookie replied.

"I'm a grown ass man, what did she say she wanted." J-Ridah stubbornly replied.

"She told me to tell you it was real important. She needs you to come around there right now and bring your brothers." Pookie insisted.

"Alright then cuz, damn. Pam, I'll holla at you later. Is that cool sweetheart?"

"Call me when you get everything straightened out and you got time to talk."

They exchanged numbers then Pookie followed J-Ridah to the backyard.

"Gangster and Baby Gangster are gone somewhere but both the twins are back here." J-Ridah commented to Pookie.

Pookie didn't bother to go inside the backyard. He just patiently waited for J-Ridah to get his twin brothers and head back to the Laney household. His mind was wandering anyway so he wasn't in the mood to speak to everyone. The twins grudgingly followed J-Ridah out the backyard and into his Regal. He had put some gold spoke rims on his all black Regal Supreme. Once the twins got inside the car they dipped around the corner with Pookie following behind them in his car.

J-Ridah pulled up in front of the Laney household and hopped out his vehicle with the penitentiary walk down to a science. He was a Crip to the heart. He walked, talked and breathed everything he represented and his confidence showed as he strolled up the porch steps. He opens up the door as though he was a king entering his court.

"What's up mama, Pookie come running around the corner saying you need to see us right away." J-Ridah said with power resonating in his voice.

"Come in my room for a minute so we can talk." Mama Jo replied.

They walked into the front bedroom. Mama Jo was careful to leave the light off. She wasn't sure if J-Ridah could tell if she had been crying but with the light on she felt it was too obvious. The light from the living room was enough to suit her needs.

"I'm just going to say this straight out so brace yourself. Jason just got killed earlier tonight." Mama Jo stated.

"What the fuck did you just say?" J-Ridah replied in disbelief.

"You heard what the fuck I said."

"You got to be making that shit up mama. That can't be the truth, I just seen the nigga earlier today. Naw, fuck naw cuz!"

J-Ridah paced back in forth trying to understand what he heard. He grabbed his forehead as though he instantly suffered a migraine. His eyes quickly watered up as he began to imagine life without Baby Gangster. Mama Jo tried to stop his hyperactive pacing but he was blank for a moment. Mama Jo forcefully grabbed his broad shoulder with both her hands and looked him in the eye.

"Look Joseph, I know you one of the shot callers around here nowadays. We haven't always seen eye to eye about a lot of things. But this is family and we lost one of ours from our own family, ya hear? Find out who did this shit to Jason and you serve they muthafuckin ass. This ain't any blind gangbanging shit. This is for our family so we need to find out who's the ones responsible and make them pay." Mama Jo firmly said.

"Where did it happen? Where is his body?"

"Pookie told me that the coroner took his body away from the gas station on Compton Boulevard and Long Beach Boulevard." Mama Jo explained.

"That could be anybody that did that shit. That's neutral territory. It could have been those niggas from the Park; the Mayo Lane's and even some Crip niggas trying to jack him." J-Ridah pondered.

"Well you find out. You talk to Marvin and Shawn and see if any Pirus came up on a Cadillac because Pookie said his car wasn't there. If any nigga all of a sudden starts wanting to sell Cadillac parts you investigate that shit. Listen to me Joseph; I want the niggas that did this shit. Only the niggas that did this shit." Mama Jo insisted.

"Okay Mama, give me Auntie Pat's number so that I can holler at Marvin and Shawn."

"Yeah okay, make sure you talk to Marvin because he loved Jason like he was a brother instead of a cousin. They were thick as thieves. He's going to want to get to the bottom of this just as bad as you are."

"Oh yeah, I didn't know that. I haven't seen those little niggas since I was in the hospital. They were some down ass slobs even when they were little." J-Ridah commented.

"Yeah they got that Laney blood in them too."

When J-Ridah and Mama Jo walked back into the living room everyone was crying including the twins. Mama Jo felt somewhat relieved because she didn't have to break it to them. The household was thick with sorrow as J-Ridah went to a corner and pondered on the loss of his brother. He leaned on the corner wall with his hand on his forehead lamenting. J-Ridah didn't go home to Sheila and his son that night but slept in the room Baby Gangster had slept in.

The following morning the entire household was awakened by the phone ringing loudly. Maybe it was a bad dream that Baby Gangster had gotten killed last night. J-Ridah was the first to awake and pick up the phone in the kitchen.

"Hello?" He said with a distinct morning voice.

158

"Jason?" A hopeful voice said through the phone.

"Who is this?" J-Ridah said in frustration.

"This is Kisha!"

"Kisha who?"

"Kisha, Jason's girlfriend."

"This is Joseph, Jason's older brother. You hadn't heard what happened to Jason?" J-Ridah replied.

"What happened to Jason?"

"I forgot to call Kisha back to let her know what was going on. I was dealing with my own shit so I forgot all about her." Mama Jo interjected.

"What happened?" Kisha said. Her voice showed signs of hysteria."

"Somebody killed my little brother last night."

"Fuck no!!!" Kisha screamed through the phone.

J-Ridah took the phone from away from his ear suddenly as if his eardrum had been damaged. He looked at the phone and shook his head somberly. Mama Jo snatched the phone from him.

"Hello Kisha?"

No one answered. She could hear Kisha screaming in the background. Her voice carried as Mama Jo patiently waited for her to pick the phone back up. After three or four moments Kisha finally got back on the phone. She was panting hard and her words were hard to understand.

"Calm down Kisha, I understand that you are hurt baby we all are." Mama Jo calmly spoke.

"My man is dead. My man is dead." Kisha cried.

"I know, baby I did all my crying last night. It's hard on all of us so come over here so that we can deal with this together."

Kisha finally hung up the phone. Mama Jo gave J-Ridah a look to start moving on what she talked about last night.

"I'm going down to the coroner's office to claim the body. Then tomorrow I'm driving to San Quentin to visit your father so that I can tell him the bad news." Mama Jo explained.

"Mama would it be okay if I rolled up there with you?" Janelle came into the living room.

"If you want to. As a matter of fact start getting dressed so that you can come down to the coroner's office with me."

"Auntie Jo is there anything you need me to do?" Moe asked.

"Stay here and clean up what best you can. Do me a favor and fix everybody some breakfast, Janelle and I will pick something up on the way to the coroner's."

J-Ridah was already on the phone with Big Bamm while she was giving out instructions. He had arranged to meet up with him in a couple of hours at the Compton Indoor Swap meet parking lot. They talked for a few moments after the arrangements were made.

"That nigga Marvin was on one when I told him about Jason getting killed. He vowed to help us find the niggas that done that shit." J-Ridah commented to one of the twins.

"Yeah them niggas is riders both him and Shawn. Only thing bad about them is that they slobs." Laney Twin deuce replied.

"Well right now they not Crips or Pirus, they are family. And together we gone find out who did this shit to our family." J-Ridah replied.

They met up in front of a pager shop right outside the Compton Swap meet around four in the afternoon. The wind blew softly as if to reaffirm the gloomy skies. The weather set the mood for a sad time in the Laney family. J-Ridah pulled up in his Regal about five minutes before four. He got out the car and leaned on the side of his car. Even though the wind blew he was still wearing a tank top with Levi jeans and black Chuck Taylor with thick blue shoestrings. His tattoos were evident of the set he was from. Alondra Block written in bold letters was on his left arm. On the opposite arm his name J-Ridah with Compton Crips boldly showing under it. He leaned on his car with his arms folded puffing on a Camel cigarette.

Moments later Big Bamm showed up in his burgundy 1964 Chevy Impala leaning to one side. On the passenger side was his brother Shawny-Ru. They looked just alike except Marvin was a little darker and a little taller. They both hopped out the car after pulling up next to J-Ridah's Regal. Out of respect for there big relative they both wore brown but Shawny-Ru had on white Chuck Taylor's with thick red shoestrings. His brown khakis laid over them nicely with a thick white T-Shirt. Big Bamm had on brown Pendleton with brown khakis with brown leather K-Swiss. They walked up to J-Ridah and he gave both of them a once over. Then he embraced both of them.

"Ya'll some grown ass niggas now. It's been a long time since I've seen ya'll. It's fucked up we got to meet on these terms." J-Ridah said.

"Yeah but I swear to you big relative, whoever did this Crip or Ru I'm riding on them niggas. This is family we talking about." Big Bamm replied.

"I know! We all loved that nigga. But what I need you to do is find out if any niggas is selling parts to a Cadillac or if any sl…Piru nigga is bragging about killing a Crip at the gas station on Compton Boulevard and Long Beach Boulevard."

"I'll be able to let you know that in a few days. I'll even check with some of my homies in the pen to see if they heard anything." Big Bamm replied.

"We even know of fools that be jacking cars on the East Side big relative." Shawny-Ru added.

"Alright then get at me as soon as you find out what's up with that." J-Ridah opened his car door.

"For sure Joseph and tell Auntie Jo we love her and we gone find out who did this to our family." Big Bamm replied.

"Will do! Ya'll niggas stay safe and we'll talk later. And tell Auntie Tricia I said I love her. The twins wanted to holla at ya'll but I told them not to come this time." J-Ridah started up his engine.

"Well tell them niggas it's much love on this end." Big Bamm replied.

They escorted Mama Jo and Janelle towards the back where the bodies were being held. They walked towards the back feeling the cold from the air-conditioned building. It sent chills down Mama Jo's spine because this is where the dead were housed. She kept it pushing reluctantly going to find her son's dead body. When the escort walked them towards the body he pointed towards Baby Gangster's corpse. There was a white sheet placed upon the body while sitting on a roller bed. Mama Jo nodded her head for the female escort to take off the sheet. When the body was exposed Mama Jo's knees buckled. Tears began to fall from her face. Janelle had already started crying herself with her hand over her mouth.

"Maybe this isn't the image you should have of your brother you being pregnant and everything." Mama Jo cried.

"Naw Mama I'm strong enough to be here with you. That was my little brother." Janelle insisted.

The top of his face was blown off and all you could see was some of his nose and his mouth. It was like his head had been hit on top with a thick axe. Mama Jo continued to cry on Baby Gangster's chest. She rubbed her face on his chest while weeping.

"If I would have told you I loved you more. If I would have let you know that I was proud to have you as a son. I miss you already Jason. Why did you have to leave me baby?" Mama Jo cried.

The escort left giving them room and space to mourn their loss. Janelle rubbed Mama Jo on her back as they both cried. There was now one less mouth to feed in the Laney household but that was the mouth that fed everyone else.

14
A MINUTE TO PRAY

And a second to die!
Scarface

"Hello?"

"What's happening relative this is Big Bamm?"

"What's happening with you?"

"I told you I might come across something in a few days."

"You already done found out some shit?"

"It's a lead, but I think it's something to look at. My homeboy got an uncle that owns an auto body shop in Crab...I mean in Crip territory. He said his uncle told him some niggas came up into his shop trying to get rid of Cadillac parts for real cheap. They even said that they had gold Dana Dane's (Dayton rims) to sell." Big Bamm explained.

"So you saying it might be some Crip niggas that smoked my little brother?" J-Ridah said in disbelief.

"I don't know but they supposed to bring the rims back through on Monday so my homeboys' uncle can see if he wants to buy them. When I talked to my homeboys in the pen no one spoke up on killing an Alondra Block. And no one has been gossiping in the street from my side about a killing at a gas station. And trust me Joseph I would have heard about it because too many niggas want that name and that street fame."

"So it probably was some Crip niggas trying to rob Jason. He must have known who they were so they had to kill him. They still some dumb muthafuckas trying to sell some shit to a mechanic in Compton. They would have been better going to L.A. or Watts." J-Ridah said with disgust.

"But they probably don't know a mechanic that will buy they shit outside of Compton. So how you want to handle this shit?" Big Bamm got to the point.

163

"Find out what time they supposed to meet up with yo homeboy's uncle and we will post up near the shop so we can see who the niggas are."

"Alright I will hit you later on today. I'm telling you big relative you need to get you a pager." Big Bamm jokingly suggested.

"I ain't into that shit. That's you and Jason's thing. Oh yeah, mama told me to tell ya'll the funeral is on Thursday. She figured I would be talking to ya'll before she will. She probably told Auntie Tricia but she wanted me to make sure ya'll know to come."

"That nigga was my favorite relative. There isn't any way I'm not coming to his funeral. Shawny-Ru and I will be there just tell us the time."

"One o'clock"

Two days later J-Ridah and Big Bamm met up at the Compton swap meet again. This time Big Bamm got in the car with J-Ridah so that they could park across the street from the auto body shop. They showed up about twenty minutes before the time they were told the two salesmen would show. J-Ridah had a tape of the Delfonics playing in the tape deck. The volume was turned down low as they sat quietly in his Regal. Their angle was in a way where they could see everyone that walked into the shop.

"Look, there is two niggas walking up right now. Those look like some Crip niggas too." Big Bamm pointed.

"Aw shit, that looks like Nu-Nu and Sly from Greenleaf. If they are the niggas that killed my brother they are about to have problems cuz that's on everything I love." J-Ridah's temper flared.

"Let's wait a few minutes and see if they come back with some gold rims in hand. Then we can at least know they got something to do with it." Big Bamm spoke sensibly. He recognized the fire in his cousin's heart.

"I already know them niggas love to jack fools. I wouldn't put that shit past them." J-Ridah replied.

A few minutes passed while they waited for them to return to their car. Sure enough they came back from the car with four gold rims. Sly was carrying two and Nu-Nu was carrying two.

"We should smoke them niggas right now cuz. That's on everything Bamm. We should smoke those niggas right now." J-Ridah flared up again.

"In broad daylight? You want to smoke some niggas in broad daylight when there is a thousand witnesses?" Big Bamm replied.

"Yeah nigga in broad daylight. What you scared?" J-Ridah glared at his cousin.

"I ain't ever been scared and that's on Piru. But I ain't trying to get caught for killing those niggas either. You know how many potential snitches you got lurking around this muthafucka? If we got to smoke them now let's at least follow them back to they hood so it won't be on a Boulevard."

"Alright fuck it we can follow those bitch ass niggas back to their hood and then let them have it." J-Ridah grudgingly replied.

"You grab the tech nine while I grab this Uzi and right when they turn on any residential street we light they asses up."

Nu-Nu and Sly walked outside the auto body shop splitting money between the two. They were laughing and talking totally oblivious to what was taking place across the street. J-Ridah started up the car as Big Bamm started loading all the weaponry. They dipped down a few lanes on Long Beach Boulevard as they pushed towards Greenleaf. A block before Greenleaf, Nu-Nu turned right onto a residential street. That was when J-Ridah made his move and dipped on the same street with the quickness of power steering his Regal provided. Once he hit the block he sped up and cut Nu-Nu off at the stop sign. Nu-Nu and Sly were startled for a brief moment thinking someone was just driving crazy. They took a deep breath when the car wasn't damaged. Their disposition changed when they seen J-Ridah and Big Bamm jump out the Regal. They both realized what was taking place and why.

"That muthafuckin mechanic set us up cuz." Nu-Nu yelled.

J-Ridah and Big Bamm instantly began firing into the Nu-Nu's Buick. Numerous shots went into the windshield and driver's side door. Nu-Nu tried to crawl on top of Sly who was obviously dead by now. He managed to get the passenger side door open as he fell out. He quickly crawled away from the car sustaining several wounds. Big Bamm admitted to himself that the Crip was strong. At least he's fighting to live like a soldier. J-Ridah and Big Bamm ran up on him seeing that he was still alive.

"Why the fuck you smoke my brother over some rims cuz?" J-Ridah asked. He said it only loud enough for Nu-Nu to hear.

"Fuck you cuz. This is Greenleaf Crip Gang till I die." Nu-Nu defiantly replied.

J-Ridah was ready to let him have the rest of the shells but Big Bamm waived him down.

"Hold on big relative."

Big Bamm slammed the butt of the Uzi on top of the head of Nu-Nu. Nu-Nu grunted from the pain and began to laugh.

"Who the fuck else was involved with smoking my relative?" Big Bamm asked after kicking him in the face.

"So you Alondra niggas are fucking with slobs now huh. It figures but you killing me anyway so I don't have to tell you shit…But I will tell you this. Three of my homeboys smoked yo punk ass homeboy Do-Dirty. Fuck you and yo hood cuz."

J-Ridah couldn't be held back at that point. His bullets pierced through Nu-Nu's body. Big Bamm grabbed his arm so that they could quickly leave the murder scene. They hopped into the car and J-Ridah put the car in reverse and sped off until he hit Long Beach Boulevard. They turned down the Boulevard then made a quick right on Greenleaf. As they cruised down Greenleaf the sirens began to scream in their direction. The Compton Police two patrol cars deep rolled past them screeching tires and hitting hard left turns on Long Beach Boulevard.

The car was quiet as J-Ridah cruised down Greenleaf until he hit Wilmington Boulevard. They drove down Wilmington

166

headed towards Rosecrans so they could go back up to the Compton swap meet.

"Ay big relative, you know you gone have to get rid of this car. If someone seen us the first thing the police gone do is look for a blue Regal. You might want to dump it somewhere or break it down so that you can sell the parts." Big Bamm suggested.

"Yeah, it's not in my name anyway. I'll get rid of it. I can get another ride but when I get back to the hood we riding on all Greenleaf niggas. These niggas done started a full scale war with us but they are not going to see it coming. We gone give these niggas the blues forever. They killed my nigga Do-Dirty too." J-Ridah viciously replied.

Big Bamm didn't say anything but he understood. He allowed his big cousin time to ponder on recent events. When they pulled up in front of Big Bamm's car another word hadn't been spoken. It was obvious that J-Ridah was hurt and upset. Nevertheless he got out of his car and embraced his family.

"I'll see you at the funeral."

"For sure." Big Bamm nodded.

J-Ridah grabbed a plastic bag from the back seat and loaded the still warm weaponry. Then he popped his trunk and stashed it under his spare tire the best he could. By then Big Bamm had already taken off so J-Ridah thought it would be best to do the same.

J-Ridah decided to park his car in the back garage where Sheila and he lived until he figured out what he would do with it. He figured he would take Big Bamm up on his offer. Once he parked inside the garage he slowly got out of his car. He was tired. He was emotionally, mentally and spiritually drained. He wanted to go inside the house and sleep. The gloomy sky had reappeared like the day after Baby Gangster was killed. It definitely reflected his mood. When he walked inside the house Sheila was in the kitchen cooking. J-Ridah was pleased from the aroma that filled his home. Sheila came out of the kitchen when she heard him come in. He gave her a half hearted smile then went towards the bedroom.

"Joseph, Joe Jr. is sleeping in our bed...what's wrong with you?" She suddenly seen the discontent on his face.

"I got some shit on my mind that's all." He replied.

"You still tripping off of someone killing Jason huh? Joe Jr. loved his uncle and I had to explain to him why he wasn't going to see him again. It seems like life ain't the same." Sheila sighed.

"Yeah something like that. Out of any of us he was the last one I would think would get killed. He wasn't really that type of nigga. I didn't know if he would even grow up to be a real man. But now I'm not sure if I know what a real man is. He was probably the best of us and he is the one that gets smoked. Shit don't make sense anymore." J-Ridah lamented.

"Yeah, and when Do-Dirty got killed I thought things were bad then. And we never found out who did that punk shit."

J-Ridah stayed quiet. He didn't want to tell her about his new revelation. He was more of a doer than a talker. He waived his hand indicating he was going into the room for a nap. Sheila went back into the kitchen to finish cooking.

J-Ridah woke up around three hours later. He noticed that his son had gotten up earlier. He must have slept hard he pondered. He put both feet on the floor and sat on the side of his bed. His face was in the palm of his hands as he rubbed sleep from his eyes. He stretched his massive arms before standing up. He had fallen asleep in his 501 Levi jeans and a tank top. He slid on his gangster corduroy house shoes and strolled into the living room to see his son at the dinner table picking at his food.

"What's up daddy? Jamil taught me how to throw up Alondra Block so I wanted to show you." Joe Jr. eagerly declared.

"Show me later but stop picking at your food and finish the plate." He replied.

Sheila had already started fixing his plate once she heard Joe Jr. say what's up to his daddy. Moments later while J-Ridah was sitting at the table she sat down his plate in front of him.

"Snake called you while you were sleep but I could tell you didn't want to be waked up." Sheila said.

"What did he say?"

"He said some Greenleaf niggas got smoked in broad daylight. He said he didn't know everything but he just wanted to holla at you."

"That nigga was speaking up on murders over the phone?" J-Ridah asked.

"Naw he just was saying he heard about it through the grapevine. He wasn't talking about who did it. He just mentioned it like in passing." Sheila replied.

"I'm gone holla at that nigga about speaking on shit over the phone even if he heard it through the grapevine." J-Ridah said in a disgruntled tone.

He stared at her then glanced at his son. For a brief moment he felt contentment. For a brief minute he felt peace. But all he had ever known was war. All he ever experienced was combat and conflict. It was somewhat refreshing to see his family sit before him. Things weren't entirely bad he pondered. He gobbled down his food then jumped from the table and called Snake.

"Ay cuz, come around here to pick me up."

"What's wrong with yo Regal nigga?" Snake asked out of curiosity.

"Look cuz can you come and get a nigga?"

J-Ridah walked into the bedroom to grab his blue Pendleton from out the closet. He was buttoning it when he was met in the hallway by Sheila.

"Something's wrong with the Regal?"

"Naw, but we gone have to get another car real soon. Don't drive it anymore. I have it parked in the garage."

"How am I going to take Jr. to school?"

"Ask moms if you can use Jason's El Camino for that. Don't worry I'll have a new car in a little bit. I got to break though; Snake's coming around to pick me up."

"What time you coming home tonight? Are we going to spend a little time together?" Sheila desperately asked.

"Come on Sheila not now. I got some shit to take care of then I will come home right after that."

Sheila had taken her arms from around his waist. She had seen that look before and knew not to push the issue. When J-Ridah stepped outside to the street Snake was already waiting outside for him.

He hopped in on the passenger side and drove off around the corner. For a few minutes the music was up loud so neither one of them said a word. Finally J-Ridah turned down the music. He glanced over at him and nodded his head.

"We took care of those Greenleaf niggas cuz."

"What?"

J-Ridah waited until the car was parked and they had both gotten out the car. Snake passed him a Camel cigarette then pulled out a bottle of Night Train. J-Ridah took a couple of swigs from the bottle then puffed on his cigarette as they walked to the front of the drive way.

"Yeah cuz, we smoked those Greenleaf niggas in broad daylight. Those niggas Nu-Nu and Sly was the ones that killed my brother. So we made sure those niggas paid for that shit." J-Ridah explained.

"How did you know they were the ones that did it?" Snake said in disbelief.

"Because they tried to sell Jason's gold rims plus some Cadillac parts to this mechanic my cousin knew about. Word got back and we went and handled that shit."

"Aw shit I just thought about it. Back in the day when you first got locked up Baby Gangster had to blast on those same two niggas when they tried to jack him at a grocery store. Do-Dirty had to talk to C-Rag to straighten that shit out because they was once locked up together. We thought we was going to have beef back then." Snake explained.

"Yeah well we about to go to war with those Greenleaf faggots for smoking Do-Dirty. That nigga Nu-Nu admitted that shit right before I finished his ass off. He laughed about it like it wasn't shit. We got to serve those scandalous ass niggas." J-Ridah sneered.

"You bullshitting me cuz? That nigga admitted killing Do-Dirty? Yeah we got to put in work against them niggas. I guess we fighting against other Crips now like those L.A. niggas do." Snake sighed in disgust.

"Yeah that shit kind of fucks with me too cuz. But they started some shit we gone have to finish. So we about to gather the troops and start giving it to these niggas."

"Some of the little homies are hanging out in the backyard right now. We can tell them to get the rest of the homies so we can start riding on those punk ass Greenleaf girls."

They walked towards the backyard and once inside they saw Laney Twin Deuce slap boxing with the little homeboy Meechie. They threw numerous slaps to each other's face in a lock up exchange. Then they broke apart when they seen J-Ridah and Snake walk in.

Laney Twin turned around and walked over to his big brother. He embraced him.

"You let Meechie serve yo ass in slap boxing cuz." J-Ridah teased.

"Yeah right. Let me show you how Meechie got served."

Before Laney Twin Deuce could turn around to face off with Meechie, J-Ridah grabbed his arm. He looked back at his big brother and J-Ridah shook his head.

"Naw cuz, I need you to gather the homeboys because we about to blast on Greenleaf niggas."

Laney Twin Deuce smiled even though he didn't totally understand why they were blasting on some fellow Crips. J-Ridah recognized the look.

"Those are the niggas that smoked Jason." He whispered in his ear.

"So that's why we ain't been riding on anybody yet. We didn't know who to ride on. How you find out it was those niggas?" Laney Twin Deuce asked.

"Bamm found out about the nigga trying to sell parts of Jason's car. But I'll give you the rundown later; go get the homies so we can handle this shit cuz."

Laney Twin Deuce ran off to gather the troops. The few homeboys that were present continued to hang out without a clue to what was going on. A few of the OGs gathered gradually to Snake's backyard before all the little homeboys arrived.

When all the homeboys that Laney Twin Deuce could gather arrived in Snake's backyard J-Ridah took over. He prepared himself for the speech of his life. He waited until Snake and C-Dog quieted everyone down then he walked into the center.

"Look here cuz, what set is this?" He passionately asked.

"This is Alondra Block Compton Crip!" Everybody shouted.

"That's right! We ride on niggas to let them know what set we from. Well I just found out that those Greenleaf niggas killed two of our comrades. Now is you niggas down to serve these niggas or what?" He said.

After the shock settled in they began to nod and scream yeah. J-Ridah gave them time to settle down then he continued.

"When Raymond Washington, Tookie and all the other founders of the Crips started they probably didn't think we would start blasting on other Crips. My pops came up with them niggas and they meant business but times have changed. We gone make each of those Greenleaf niggas pay for what they done to Do-Dirty and Baby Gangster, you hear me cuz?" J-Ridah ardently espoused.

He turned to Snake and C-Dog when his brother Gangster walked into the backyard. J-Ridah smiled and they embraced each other immediately. He looked at him with love.

"We found out who did that shit to our family cuz!"

Gangster nodded because he had been waiting for a report. Him and Mama Jo had made amends since the death of Baby Gangster but he was ready to ride a long time ago. J-Ridah knew it too.

"We about to do rotation on these niggas."

That night J-Ridah chose four little homies to ride on them the first night. They were on beach cruisers and they all carried pistols. Some of the little homies knew where they hung out. Laney Twin Deuce, Dino, Meechie and Face rolled the first night.

172

They quickly drove over to the Greenleaf territory then split up into twos. Before long they came across where they were hanging out and decided to roll from both sides.

Laney Twin Deuce and Dino were the first to roll up on the Greenleaf hang out. Without any hesitation they started blasting into the crowd of Greenleaf Crips. Whatever wasn't finished by twin and Dino was finished by Meechie and Face.

An array of bullets was flying at a vacant house where they hung. When the massacre was over at least four were dead while other were bleeding. It was strategically set up to confuse the Greenleaf Crips. The sets of two went into opposite directions.

For the rest of the month J-Ridah would decide to blast on the Greenleaf Crips by choosing different little homies from the set. It had gotten so bad that the streets were empty in Greenleaf territory at night. J-Ridah decided to start blasting on them in broad daylight. If he knew of someone from Greenleaf that went to Dominguez High School he would send someone to catch them coming home from school. He was completely relentless. They had killed two people that were extremely close to him so he wanted to make their hood extinct.

The new generation of Alondra Block was really down for shooting. They were quick to shoot before fighting so J-Ridah used that to his advantage. His eyes were sullen and his face was twisted, as he became a fierce general against the Greenleaf Crips.

Gangster had decided to go on a solo mission on a day J-Ridah told everyone to chill out. The police were getting hot and he didn't want anyone to catch any time and get to snitching. He didn't have any intention on letting up but he did want to avoid law enforcement. But Gangster wanted to make sure another Greenleaf nigga felt the pain he felt for losing his brother. He had been off of PCP for years now so he walked over into enemy territory with a sober mind.

When he walked into Greenleaf territory for about twenty minutes he couldn't find anyone. It was extremely dark and the police had rolled down Greenleaf while he walked on a side street. He hid behind a car by leaning against it until they passed. Then he noticed a man's shadow walking down the street. He went across the street so that he could walk up on the shadow. He had on a black sweater he loved to wear that had two front pockets and a hoodie. He walked up on his victim with his nine-millimeter tucked into one of his pockets and casually walked up to the victim as if he was just going to walk by. The young Crip tried to recognize him assuming he was one of his homeboys. But since his homeboys had been getting smoked he decided to take precautions and keep his hand on his thirty-eight revolver.

"What's up cuz?" The man said with his hand on his pistol.

"Nothing cuz, what's up with you?"

"What set you from cuz? I haven't seen you around here?"

"Alondra Block on mine."

They both drew their pistols like a scene in the Wild, Wild West. With a quickness of Billy the Kid one of them got their shot off first. The second took a bullet wound to the stomach. He dropped his pistol and grabbed hold to his stomach. He collapsed to the ground then began to cough. The winner of the draw down looked downward at his foe.

"Maybe if you were a little quicker you would have gotten me."

The fear was definitely apparent on the face of the loser. He was struggling to breath and still coughing. The winner pointed his gun at his intended foe and squeezed the trigger. The bullet went through his forehead and blew out the back of his head. He picked up the gun lying next to the loser and ran off into the night.

"This is Alondra Block on mine!"

15
VISITATION

Watch for 'One Time' as I speak because they do dirt like fools in the street!
PaPa Sak

Mama Jo stepped outside of her dead son's El Camino after a long and tiresome drive. She stretched her legs and pulled out a cigarette. She wanted to smoke one more before she went inside. All of those gates and searches she had to go through were annoying. She wasn't eager to be practically molested just to see her husband. It had been many years and Mama Jo had streaks of gray hair now. She had lost a little weight so her face hung a little bit. She reminisced when her beauty was of high standard. As she was finishing the last of her cigarette she walked up to the gate so that she could be let in. Her bones ached nowadays so she took her time. Her heart also ached because she was carrying a heavy burden. She decided to request a conjugal visit so hopefully Michael would be happy about that. She took one last sigh then flicked the cigarette butt into the yard.

She had finally gotten past all the gates and suffered through all of the body searches. She always wondered if those female correctional officers were lesbians. They escorted her down the hall and into a private room where she would wait for Michael. She relaxed and tried to make the best out of the situation. It had been many years since she had laid eyes on him and she wondered how much he would look the same.

After thirty minutes of waiting the door finally opened. A correctional officer peaked inside.

"Mrs. Laney, Mrs. Josephine Laney?" He asked.

She nodded then he let Michael walk inside the room. His hair was totally gray and cut short. She always saw him with braids or an Afro. Even though he had a head full of gray hair he had aged gracefully. He still had that stern and sullen look that she would often times see in Joseph. She half-heartedly smiled even though she was really glad to see him. His broad chest bulged out of his state issued T-Shirt. His arms were as large as tree trunks with veins popping out of them. Mama Jo didn't think it was possible again but she suddenly became moist between her legs. He walked over to her with his eyes locked on hers. He didn't say a word at first. He was trying to read into her and feel what she was feeling.

"You still are beautiful Jo."

"Thank You Mike."

She was genuinely flattered as he laid his hands on her shoulders. He was so gentle that she shuttered at his touch. He smiled as though he had seen paradise.

"It has been a long time since I have laid eyes on your face Mrs. Josephine Laney. I am in love with you all over again."

"And I with you."

They softly kissed each other and intimately embraced. They had a lot of catching up to do. Each sensual kiss and passionate touch was heartfelt. As they undressed one another soft kisses were exchanged. Finally Michael laid Mama Jo on the bed. Their bodies connected in rhythmic motion. Taking each step carefully and meticulously Michael held his woman. They both took their time until they both were completely satisfied.

"I really needed that Michael." Mama Jo admitted.

"We both needed that Jo. This is a hard place to grow old."

"I know. But then again maybe I can't imagine what kind of hell you've gone through in this hell hole."

"I made my bed so I have to lay in it. I don't hold any ill will towards anyone. When you told me you couldn't come up here to visit me anymore I understood. I'm the one who did the crime so you shouldn't have to suffer for what I did."

"But I have been suffering also Mike. Things are different for me right now. I am not as strong as I once was."

176

"You've always been strong and that is something no one can take away from you." Michael replied.

"I have some bad news for you. And I don't know any way to tell you but straight out." Mama Jo's eyes watered.

"Give it to me straight."

"Jason got killed about a week and a half ago. Some guys robbed him at a gas station." Mama Jo blurted out.

Michael lay back on the pillow as a tear fell from his face. For a moment he was in total shock. He remembered getting the picture of everyone in the mail a few weeks ago. Now one of his sons is dead. He shook his head back and forth in disbelief. The tears began to fall from his face more than before.

"The sins of the father will visit the son." He mumbled.

"What did you say?" Mama Jo struggled to hear.

"The sins of the father will visit the son. My sins have brought down death on my son." He repeated.

He was halfway in a daze lamenting the loss of his son. He looked upward as though he was staring into space. Mama Jo gave him enough time to recover. When he finally came out of his astonishment Mama Jo crawled on the small bed to lay her head on his chest. He stroked her hair like he used to do back in the day.

"I thought I knew how to raise boys into becoming men but I don't have a clue Michael. I tried the best I could of what I thought a man should be. A Black man growing up in the ghettos of America has to be strong. They have to be soldiers so I made sure they were that but I haven't accomplished much else." Mama Jo said.

"Don't say that. We are in a world that is against us becoming men so we become everything else. I should have been there with you but instead I done something that will have me in prison for the rest of my life. That was unfair for me to lay that heavy burden on you to carry alone." Michael replied.

"The last time I seen you I was so confidant that I would do so much better by myself but I was plain stupid."

"Quit beating yourself up. I've grown old in this place and I can't necessarily say I know exactly what a man is. They say that society is protected from us but I wonder if we are protected from society. I don't know Jo…if I would have been free would it have been just one boy raising five boys and a daughter? A bunch of Laney boys that never matured to become men." Michael sighed.

"You are the only man I have ever loved." Mama Jo firmly replied.

"And I still misused and mishandled the love you gave me. Josephine I want to apologize for all the wrong I've done to you. There is no woman in my eyes that is greater."

"We have both wronged each other." Mama Jo said while lifting her head from his chest.

"I want you to know that if I could do it all over again I wouldn't have had babies by any other man." She smiled.

She gently touched his face and it soothed his entire being. He didn't want her to stop.

"How are Joseph, Jordan, Janelle and the twins?" He asked while his eyes were closed.

"Joseph is a shot caller in the neighborhood now. He acts like he is some kind of general or something. He, Sheila and Joseph Jr. stay in an apartment duplex around the corner from where I live. Jordan is the one that acts most like me in personality but he is the one I least understand. He goes off on these fits where no one can find him for days. He lives with this older woman named Felicia. She is only seven or eight years younger than me but he has been off dope for some years now. We weren't on talking terms for a few years because he was fucking with that Sherm. Now that he is off he is still to himself but he acts much better."

"What's going on with my little girl?"

"Well you know she is about to have a baby in three months. She should be finishing up cosmetology school soon as well. She had to quit for a little while because she couldn't be standing like that while she was pregnant. As for the twins, they look just alike but act totally different. Jamil is more like Jason was; he wants to chase after women and whatnot. But Jalil will follow Joseph into a pit of fire. He tries to be just like Joseph in every way. It gets on my nerves because of all the shit I went through with Joseph and Jordan. But those are our boys Michael."

Michael had his eyes closed trying to visualize everything Mama Jo had explained. He pulled out the picture of his family and studied their faces for the millionth time. He could define them a little better after Mama Jo talked about their personalities.

"Laney you have five minutes." A correctional officer announced.

At the Linwood Sheriff's office two determined detectives were pouncing on a gangster. He had been caught for a drug charge and was looking at some time. But he wasn't the one they really wanted so they tried to get him to talk.

"Look here Mr. Turner we don't really want you. If you give us what we want we can let you go with a slap on the hand. We want to solve all these murders that have been taking place." Detective Bush pried.

"I don't know what you are talking about."

"Come on Mr. Turner you look too pretty to go to the penitentiary. Except for that beauty scar across your head some knuckle head might take you for a woman in prison." Detective Miller teased.

"I ain't a snitch cuz."

"We ain't asking you to testify, we just want to find out about these murders. You give us something that we can use and you won't have any problems from us. I'll get the charges thrown out. But you will still owe me if I do. You just won't have to do any time. We know you did Youth Authority time but it ain't the same as going to the pen."

"Alright look, it's a bunch of niggas that's putting in work against those Greenleaf niggas. You might as well lock up all the young gangsters in my hood if you want to know who is blasting on those fools. What you might want to ask me is who is making them do it."

Both detectives leaned in closer to hear what the potential informant had to say. After he looked around as if watching his

179

back Detective Miller grew impatient. He gestured with his hands for him to spit it out.

"J-Ridah is the nigga calling shots right now. He got the homies putting in overtime against those punk ass Greenleaf niggas."

"J-Ridah?" Detective Bush vaguely remembered the name.

"Ya'll know him as Joseph Laney. His brother just got killed a couple of weeks ago."

"That's right he is the piece of shit that broke my jaw many years ago." Detective Bush bitterly replied.

"Yeah all those Laney muthafuckas are a trip. The one that got smoked gave me this scar. And it was over his cousin and that bitch wanted me and the homeboys to fuck."

"What are you talking about?" Detective Miller asked.

"Never mind. If you want to stop the shooting then you got to stop J-Ridah because that nigga is a problem."

"Does he always carry a gun? Because if he does we can violate his ass right now." Detective Bush replied.

"He don't have to carry a strap because niggas is doing the dirt for him. Ya'll don't get it, he's a shot caller now so there is all kinds of little niggas trying to prove that they down. He ain't had to carry a gun since he been out."

"You know anything about two Greenleaf Crips getting killed in broad daylight about a block away from Greenleaf?"

"Naw I don't know anything about that. I told ya'll what ya'll need to do so is it cool for me to raise up out of here?"

"Yeah, but remember Mr. Terrance Turner you still owe me one."

Turtle got up from the chair and nodded his head. Fuck them Laney niggas anyway he thought. If J-Ridah gets locked up the police won't be as hot as they been. Besides I don't have to testify so no one can call me a snitch.

Once Turtle was gone the detectives pondered on their new information. How were they going to get to Joseph Laney? If they rolled up on him there would be about twenty people that would let him know that they were coming.

"I say we jack him up to see what we can find." Detective Miller offered.

"Naturally we need to do that but he is going to know that we are on to him. If he is the problem we need to get him off the streets. The murder rate is going to be in the red this year and that little nigger got something to do with that." Detective Bush venomously replied.

"What do you suggest?"

J-Ridah hopped out of his brand new black Monte Carlo. He had just taken it to the car wash. He kept money in his household by having a few of the little homeboys cop dope from him. He also had a part time job so that he could keep his parole officer happy. But there was no doubt that he was still banging hard on the Greenleaf Crips. Even though he had lost his brother for the most part life was good. His wife Sheila was pregnant again. He had decided to make it official so they went down to the courthouse to make it legal.

He leaned on his car smiling to himself. The Greenleaf niggas tried to go to war but overall they were having problems. Since the Alondra Block neighborhood had introduced Tech-Nines and Uzis into the war that became a problem. He felt good knowing that his enemies were suffering. He had the Regal broken down and sold so there was nothing that could trace him to shit. His thoughts were sublime for a moment. He stared up into the sky wondering what the day might bring.

"Ay OG J-Ridah cuz, yo brother Gangster was looking for you." Meechie came up to him.

"What did he say?"

"He needed to holla at you for a moment. He told me if I see you to let you know."

J-Ridah thought about going over to Felicia's house until his pager went off. It was his cousin Big Bamm. He suddenly remembered that he needed to holla at him about some business. He opted to see his brother when he got back from that. He made it up to the liquor store to use the pay phone. He had been using Baby Gangster's pager and he learned quickly that it was useful.

"What's up Bamm?"

"Meet me over there in the cemetery. We can pay respect to Jason while we talk."

"Alright I will be over there in fifteen minutes." J-Ridah replied.

He jumped into his Monte Carlo quick when he seen some Mayo Lane's rolling down Rosecrans Boulevard. He seen them but they didn't notice him. It was a nigga named Turk that he knew personally. If Turk would have seen him he might have tried to blast. And for once J-Ridah wasn't strapped. He had left his pistol at Snake's house and never got around to picking it up.

"Damn I'm slipping cuz." He said aloud.

When he pulled up into the cemetery Big Bamm was already there. He pulled up right behind him. Big Bamm was already walking towards Baby Gangster's grave site. J-Ridah decided to meet him there.

"What's up J-Ridah? Is everything good?"

"Yeah to tell the truth all is good right now. I still miss Jason but other than that I can't complain."

"We all miss Jason. But what can you do? Only God can tell you when you gone leave the earth." Big Bamm sighed.

"Do you sometimes wonder what this shit is all about? Why we got to live fucked up like this. This whole Crips and Bloods thing that we do. I got much love for you and you are a Blood. Then there are Crips that I hate. I remember when I was locked up I met some cool ass Bloods."

"Yeah Damu, Blood or Piru is all the same but now niggas is beefing with each other in the County Jail, Module 4300. I don't know big relative what we do it for. I guess we do it for what Bartender, Low, Tamm and Puddin started. They were the first to stand up against the Crips when ya'll was like a wave. You know during that time when Uncle Mike was putting in work. They started what I represent today and that is probably why I bang." Big Bamm replied.

"What is a Damu?" J-Ridah asked.

182

"It is the word Blood in Swahili. Nowadays I hear niggas saying that shit representing the United Blood Nation."

"So those niggas you just named started the Pirus or the Bloods like Raymond Washington and Tookie started the Crips?"

"Yep!"

"That shit was on the West Side?"

"Yeah but all the East Side Pirus started from the Park."

"So I guess I'm representing for my pops and for Raymond Washington and Tookie. I don't know Bamm; I think I'm getting tired. This shit is in my heart but I'm about ready to slow down. We gave those Greenleaf niggas the blues and I'm cool with that. I think I'm going to tell the little homies to chill out." J-Ridah said.

He was contemplating his own words while Big Bamm wiped away some weeds that had grown nearby Baby Gangster's grave.

"It ain't always up to you big relative. These young niggas are going another way. I'm seeing niggas coming up today without a code. It's really our fault if they don't get taught the code. We are the men they look up to. Just like we looked up to the ones before us. But now they are smoking they big homies and all kinds of crazy shit. You might tell them to stop but that don't mean they will."

"I've been fighting all my life and now I'm getting tired."

"Yeah it's starting to fuck with me nowadays too. I'm trying to be all about that paper like Jason used to always stress. But it ain't easy sometimes."

"Speaking of money, did you take care of that?"

"Yeah, we can get a bird for fifteen-five like before. I went with Jason a few times so he remembered me but I had never gone by myself. He was sad to hear that Jason had gotten killed. It wasn't a problem for him to do business with me." Big Bamm glanced up at J-Ridah.

"Well I will holla at you later. Jordan wanted to talk to me about something but I wanted to get back to you first."

"Aw it was good to see that nigga at the funeral. It had been a long time since I seen him. He's been off that dope for a while now huh?"

"Yeah but I got to keep him strong. He's got a lot of demons and that Sherm helps him deal with that shit. So I try to keep his mind moving closer to some sane shit." J-Ridah replied while walking back to his car.

"Alright then Joseph holla at me in a few days so we can straighten out how we gone do it."

J-Ridah nodded then hopped into his Monte Carlo. He took his time rolling down Compton Boulevard. He liked seeing his brother but sometimes it could be depressing. He was in a good mood and didn't want it to be ruined by depression. But J-Ridah was a soldier so he faced all his duties head on. As he hit the residential block of his neighborhood he noticed one of the spots were empty. That was weird for someone not to be hustling on a corner that was hot like that. He ignored his paranoia and continued to roll down the street. When he got about a block away from his brother's place he noticed a car driving slow. He cursed because he didn't have his strap on him. He didn't know if the people that were creeping would notice his face. So he leaned a little lower than usual hoping to be overlooked if they were seeking to blast.

As the car drove near he began to notice that they weren't hanging out the window or anything that signified a drive-by. He relaxed a little when he realized it was an unmarked Crown Victoria driving that slow. Then he considered if he had anything in the car that might catch him a case. He gave it a once over in his mind then realized he was clean. They passed by him and looked right inside of his car. They kept going so he released a deep breath.

"I don't want them fucking with me."

Before he could make a left turn towards Felicia's house he noticed blue lights flashing in his rearview mirror. He quickly turned around to see the same car behind him.

184

"Mr. Laney we need you to put your hands on the steering wheel after you cut off the engine and throw your keys outside. J-Ridah followed the instructions and waited in the car. He knew that if he tried to get out he would catch a number of bullets.

"Reach outside of the window and open your car door from the outside."

He did as he was told as neighbors began to walk out on their porches. Once the door was open J-Ridah quickly put his hands back up in the air.

"Now I need you to step outside of the car with your hands still in the air."

Once again he followed their instructions to the letter. When he was totally outside the car one of the detectives walked up behind him and handcuffed him. The detective put his knee in J-Ridah's back but all he did was give a brief grunt. The detective then through him on the ground.

"Let's see if we can find anything in here that would be considered contraband Mr. Laney. Or should I call you OG J-Ridah?"

J-Ridah decided to keep his mouth shut. Since he knew that he was clean he didn't want worry about talking any shit. Even though the detective was picking at him he didn't pay it any mind. They searched high and low inside the Monte Carlo but couldn't find anything illegal. They did at least three thorough searches of his car and came up blank. He still was laying face down on the ground when they walked back to the Crown Victoria. They walked back to his car then looked one last time.

"Look what we have here? This looks like a Forty-Five long nose to me." Detective Miller announced.

He showed it out in the open as if the neighbors were his witnesses. J-Ridah for the first time looked up at them in anger.

"That's not mine." J-Ridah yelled.

"We found it in your car."

"You didn't find that shit in my car. I just washed my car today from top to bottom and I didn't have a gun."

Detective Bush walked over to where J-Ridah was lying on the ground. He squatted so only J-Ridah could hear.

"Who do you think the judge will believe a nigger or an officer of the law?"

J-Ridah was fuming as they took him into the police car. He wanted to swing on Detective Bush like he had done before.

"You are about to visit your second home Mr. Laney." Detective Miller teased.

"Yeah you are looking at fifteen years or better Mr. violent offender twice." Detective Bush smirked.

"How is your jaw detective?" J-Ridah sneered.

16
WHAT TOMORROW BRINGS

I wish pops would have let me off on the mattress!
Ice Cube

"Push Janelle Push!" Mama Jo yelled.

"Mama I am pushing but this shit hurts like hell. You are not the one laying on this bed."

"I did it six times now keep pushing. It stops hurting after the third." Mama Jo replied.

"This is my first and only one." Janelle screamed.

"I said the same thing when I was in labor with Joseph." Mama Jo chuckled.

Janelle continued to push while Mama Jo held her hand. After a while Mama Jo stopped feeling blood circulate through her right hand. Janelle was gripping onto it so hard that she had lost the feeling. Janelle screamed and pushed. She was trying to endure the pain as much as possible but this was impossible to bear.

"When is this baby going to come?" Janelle screamed.

"I see the head." The doctor announced.

Janelle's face was filled with sweat as the baby began to make progress. She shook her head and bit her lip trying to deter herself from the agonizing pain. Though Mama Jo couldn't feel her hand she still held tightly to her only daughter.

"We gone get through this together baby."

"Looks like I'm getting through this by myself. I don't know how you had six of us."

Mama Jo chuckled trying not to openly do it. She knew Janelle wouldn't think anything was funny. She smiled at her realizing probably for the first time that Janelle was now a woman.

As the baby pushed out Janelle continued to scream. The doctor made gestures to prepare his staff for the birth.

Finally after hours the entire body of the baby came flowing out of Janelle. She heard the baby cry but was too exhausted to look up. She laid her head on the pillow and felt like going to sleep. Mama Jo released her hand and walked over to where the staff was cleaning the baby.

"It's a girl Janelle." Mama Jo announced.

Janelle did not reply. She wanted to sleep for a couple of days. Mama Jo glanced at her and she was sound asleep with her mouth wide open. She turned her attention to her second grandchild. The baby had stopped crying but was still making noises. The infant was very observant, looking around at everyone in the room. Mama Jo could tell she had Pookie's complexion and eyes but everything else was Janelle. She had a light brown complexion and a head full of hair. She had chubby cheeks with deep dimples like Janelle. Mama Jo grabbed the newborn baby and walked over to the head of Janelle's bed. Janelle had yet to open her eyes and she had started a light snore.

"Janelle, wake up baby so you can see your daughter."

Janelle slowly began to open her eyes. She blinked a few times then yawned. When she seen Mama Jo holding the bundle she sat up slightly and smiled.

"This is your baby Janelle."

"What is it a girl or a boy?"

"It's a girl silly. You didn't hear me when I said you had a girl?"

"To tell the truth mama all I heard was sleep."

"Here, hold your daughter."

She reached up to grab her daughter and smiled. It finally dawned on her that the little bundle had come from out of her. She looked around at the doctor and staff elated.

"Her name will be Janette Rochelle Carter." She proclaimed.

"Carter? Oh yeah that's Patrick's name. Where is that nigga at by the way?" Mama asked.

"I didn't want to tell you because I didn't want to hear I told you so. But Pookie caught a dope charge a couple of nights ago. Jamil told me the other day and I made him promise not to say anything to you. He said somebody must be snitching." Janelle explained.

Mama Jo wanted to say that it figured but she bit her tongue. Something she hardly ever did. Since this was a joyous occasion she decided against speaking her mind.

"Well whatever the outcome you still have family that will support Janette and you."

"Thank You Mama!" Janelle grinned.

Laney Twin Deuce had heard that Gangster was back on that Sherm so he decided to pay him a visit. He always respected his brother as a killer but he didn't always enjoy their interactions. He always thought Gangster had a few screws missing. He had highs and lows that were hard to predict. Twin knocked on Felicia's door then rung the door bell. Because of his big brother Laney Twin Deuce always stayed away from Sherm. He would only smoke weed even though he had some homeboys that would mess with crack. No one answered the door so he thought about leaving. He decided against his better judgment to knock one more time. As he was about to walk off the porch the front door swung open.

"Damn cuz, why you knocking on the door like you the police?" Gangster snapped.

"I knocked and rung the doorbell so I thought either you couldn't hear me or you weren't here." Laney Twin Deuce replied.

"Naw I was just thinking about some shit. Come in so that we can talk little brother. Where is Jamil?" Gangster looked around for his other brother.

"He's probably with that broad he's fucking with. You know Karen got that nigga all sprung and shit. Where's Felicia?"

"She had to go to work. She said she was going to bring some shit back you want to stay around to hit some of that shit?" Gangster offered while cleaning his thirty-eight six-shooter.

189

"You know I don't fuck with that shit. I only fuck with weed. Damn Jordan you take care of that bitch like it's a pet."

"I got this piece from this Greenleaf nigga I smoked. It was like we were cowboys or some shit cuz. I beat him to the draw though. This is my little souvenir."

"You ain't told anyone else about your souvenir, have you?" Twin Deuce asked.

"Hell naw, you the first person I told about this. That nigga be coming to visit me. We both got respect for each other but I was quicker." Gangster replied.

"Who comes to visit you, Jamil?" Twin Deuce looked confused.

"Naw I haven't seen that nigga in a while. I'm talking about the nigga I got this thirty-eight from. We talk about all kinds of shit. He told me I was the most down enemy he had to face. He wasn't even scared to die."

"Nigga you are tripping cuz. If that nigga is dead how it is that he visits you? You dream about him or something?" Twin Deuce asked in a somewhat perturbed manner.

"Nope! Not any dreams. A few niggas that I've smoked come to visit me from time to time. Some of those niggas like me and some hate my guts. Those Mayo Lane niggas really hate me so I don't hear too much from them except when they calling me a crab or something. But fuck them slob niggas. A few of the Greenleaf niggas are cool they just was caught slipping so they understand the game. But then again it's that one Mayo Lane nigga that comes to visit me and he was saying that I put him out of his misery. He was a shot caller and everything." Gangster explained.

"Why are you making this shit up cuz?" Twin Deuce sneered.

"What the fuck I got to lie to you for? You are my family."

There was a moment of silence. Twin Deuce agreed with that statement but didn't really know how to respond. He looked around the living room to observe how his brother was living. Everything was cluttered with a small color television with a bunch of papers piled on top of a VCR player. The walls were white so you could see hand prints in different places on all four walls. The dark blue couch and loveseat was worn and old. It was a little uncomfortable because some of the springs were broken. Twin sat on the edge of the couch because he had noticed a few roaches since he had been there. As twin observed he noticed Gangster was still cleaning his thirty-eight. He had pieces of the gun lying on Felicia's nappy blue carpet.

"You need to stop fucking with that Sherm Jordan." Twin Deuce said it more as giving an order.

"I started hitting that shit when I smoked that nigga from Greenleaf. I don't know but I needed to escape."

"Well stop trying to escape and deal with reality. Mama finds out you on that shit again she's going to be through with you forever." Twin Deuce replied.

"I'm a grown ass man. I do what the fuck I want to do cuz." Gangster snapped.

"You still act like a kid if you don't know how to kick that dope."

"Who the fuck you talking to cuz? I remember when you couldn't even piss straight. I remember when ya breath was smelling like similac. Now that you done put in a little work you want to tell a muthafuckin OG how to act. Miss me with that shit Jalil." Gangster replied, dismissing his younger brother's comments.

"I love you cuz, so I don't want to see you like this. Joseph is locked up facing some serious time and Jason is dead so it is just you, me and Jamil." Twin said emotionally.

Gangster was touched by his brother's words. He sat the gun down for a moment and looked up at the ceiling. His thoughts wandered off into guilt.

"How is Janelle?" Gangster changed the subject.

"She is supposed to be coming home today from the hospital. Mama told me over the phone she had a little girl named Janette. Since Pookie got locked up on a dope charge Janelle is going to stay in ya'll old room with the baby while she finishes cosmetology."

"Sometimes I wish I was dead. This is a fucked up world we live in and I've done so much dirt I think I'm made to stay alive to suffer." Gangster said out the blue.

"You want to die?"

"It's easier than living."

"Yeah but your family will be hurting behind that kind of shit. You are a Laney and we are soldiers. We don't die we multiply. We grew up as soldiers and even our daddy was a soldier." Twin Deuce passionately replied.

"That's what I've told myself time and time again but the shit I've done still fucks with me. I still think about the niggas I killed. Then I think about Jason who didn't want any trouble. All he wanted was to make money to take care of his family and he is dead then a muthafucka. If anybody should have gotten smoked in our family it should have been me. Like mama would say about if there was a God. If there is a God what the fuck is he doing? Why do I have to grow up a soldier? Why in the fuck did he take Jason and not me?" Gangster cried.

Laney Twin Deuce considered what his older brother said. He didn't understand for the life of him why Jason was killed of all people. For Gangster to be a dope head he sure made sense. He couldn't imagine God being real and let shit happen the way it did. That was why Mama Jo always ran off those 'Jehovah's Witnesses' even though they were so nice.

"You still deserve to live. You did what you had to do at the time. Since this is the life that was given to us we have to swallow what comes with it." Twin Deuce tried to reason.

"I wish my guilt would understand that."

Mama Jo proudly pulled up into the drive-way with her daughter and granddaughter. Janette sat in the middle of her mother and grandmother in her baby seat. She was sleeping most of the short trip from Martin Luther King Jr. hospital off of Wilmington.

192

Laney Twin Ace was in the room butt naked with Karen. No one was in the house so this was a cool opportunity for sex. He hadn't heard his family walk in the house. He had Karen bent over the bed hitting it doggy style. She was moaning loudly and saying his name. Karen had a pretty light brown complexion and was affectionately known as Ms. Redbone. She always wore dresses but her ass protruded so she couldn't hide her shape. Laney Twin Ace was totally in love with her. But so was she with him. They were high school sweethearts that stayed with each other after school. Karen was what kept Twin from getting into trouble like his brother Laney Twin Deuce.

He continued to hit it from the back grabbing hold of that plump round light skin booty. She had her face in the pillow. Even though her moaning was muffled she was still loud enough to wake up the neighbors. Mama Jo walked into the house excited and feeling good about the new addition to the family. The room right next to the Twins was already set up. She knew that Janelle would make a good mother. If there was one thing about her children she understood it was the fact that Janelle would be alright. She doubted it at times but she realized that Janelle was strong as her. In some cases she was stronger.

"You hear that mama?"

"Yeah it sounds like it's coming from the Twins' room."

Mama Jo walked toward the bedroom and opened the door. Her mouth dropped as Twin began to cum. He collapsed on top of Karen asshole naked.

"Are you out yo goddamn mind? If anybody is going to be fucking in this house it's going to be me." Mama Jo snapped.

Twin jumped from off of Karen and grabbed for his boxers. He tried to hide himself. Karen began to get dress making sure not to be make eye contact with Mama Jo.

"I'm sorry Mrs. Laney." Karen said.

"You don't have to apologize because Jamil knows better." Mama Jo kindly replied.

"Sorry about that mama I thought you were going to be at the hospital for a while." Twin replied.

"Oh that should make me feel better? Don't let me catch you doing that shit again." Mama Jo demanded.

Laney Twin Ace and Karen quickly rushed out the door while Janelle smirked at them. Twin gave her the finger while laughing under his breath. Mama Jo looked back at Janelle laughing and started laughing herself.

"Can you believe him? Fucking in my house." She chuckled.

Laney Twin Deuce was hanging out with Meechie and Face when Laney Twin Ace walked up. They were swigging on a couple of 40oz bottles of Old English beer. Laney Twin Ace had on his blue Chuck Taylor's, Blue Khakis and a tank top. They quickly passed him one of the bottles of beer. He took a couple of hits and laughed.

"Ay cuz, did you know that Janelle was coming home with the baby today?" Laney Twin Ace asked.

"Yeah, mama called from the hospital when you were in the shower. I was gone by the time you got out." Laney Twin Deuce replied.

"If I would have known that shit I wouldn't have been fucking Karen when mama got home. She walked in on us and everything. Good thing I busted my nut right before she stopped us." Twin Deuce admitted.

"Aw shit cuz, mama caught you and Karen in the room fucking? Aw nigga I'm clowning yo muthafuckin ass about that shit nigga. What she say?" Twin Deuce laughed aloud.

"The only person that's going to be fucking in my house is me." Twin Ace imitated her."

Face, Meechie and Twin Deuce instantly began laughing out loud. They were in stitches as Twin Ace stood smirking. They were laughing and falling out all over the place over the incident.

"That's what yo ass get for being all sprung and shit." Twin Deuce laughed.

"You act like you don't like pussy or something." Twin Ace replied.

"Yeah nigga but you stuck on one bitch. You've been in love with Karen since high school nigga and you ain't trying to fuck with no one else. That's why she got you by the balls cuz." Twin Deuce continued to laugh.

"What that got to do with mama catching me at the house?"

"If yo ass had some other bitches you could have fucked them at they house. Instead of getting caught at our house." Twin Deuce kept laughing.

"Whatever!"

After a few more moments of laughter everyone finally settled down. They finished the two 40oz of beer and was deciding who should go get some more. After everyone chipped in Meechie and Face decided to roll.

"You know I went to see Jordan today?" Twin Deuce commented.

"Oh yeah…how is Felicia and he doing?"

"Bad! I wanted to snatch that nigga out of that house and make him take a hot shower at mama's house. He's back on that dope again." Twin Deuce sadly admitted.

"I figured. I seen him a few days ago over Snake's house zoned out. He didn't recognize me at all. I left him alone." Twin Ace replied.

"Yeah that nigga is talking some suicidal shit. He's dwelling on all the dirt he's done. I told him that we were soldiers and he shouldn't worry about that punk shit."

"What did he say when you told him that?"

"He got to talking about him getting killed instead of Jason. He believes that it should have been him instead."

"It shouldn't have been anyone in our family. That damn Sherm got his head twisted." Twin Ace said.

"I know but what can you do? Ay, we were thinking about riding on those Greenleaf niggas later on tonight. Are you down?"

"What for, didn't Joseph do enough of that before he got locked up?" Twin Ace said with indifference.

"And now that he's locked up we got to continue where he left off." Twin Deuce passionately replied.

195

"I'm straight!"

Around the corner from where the Twins were hanging Felicia stepped out for a while. She wanted to take care of some things before all the stores closed. Gangster sat down after puffing on a ten hit of PCP. The Sherm had his mind hallucinating.

"Fuck you cuz, I had to blast on you because you were slipping. You would have done the same to me if I would have been slipping."

He would wait for the response.

"Yo hood killed my brother cuz. I had to serve yo ass. What am I supposed to do if my family gets smoked? My brother Jason never did anything to anyone. If two of your homeboys wouldn't have jacked him for his Cadillac I would even be talking to you about this shit."

His eyes wandered to the other side of the room. He couldn't answer everyone but some he wanted to address.

"Bloods and Crips are supposed to kill each other. I know you were only sixteen but you shouldn't have been from the other side. Plus you Mayo Lane niggas shot my brother and killed my homeboy Shawny." Gangster fired back.

He lowered his head and began to sob uncontrollably. He felt surrounded by all of his victims. The tears kept falling from his face. He wouldn't wipe his face making his tears cloud his vision. He was tired of staring at his victims.

"You fucking act like I'm scared to die. The death doesn't scare me cuz. I'm an OG nigga from Alondra Block Compton Crip. We don't die we multiply. Maybe that was why ya'll got smoked because ya'll was scared of getting smoked. What man deserves to live when he is scared? Watch I will show you I ain't scared of dying. I didn't fucking ask to be born in the first place."

He grabbed his favorite thirty-eight revolver and put one bullet inside. He spun the chamber a few times then put the gun to his head. He squeezed the trigger and he heard the hammer slam.

"What the fuck are ya'll talking about cuz? I told you I'm a muthafuckin OG. Do or die on mine." He yelled.

Then he spun the chamber once again. He put the gun to his head and squeezed the trigger another time. He got the same result. He laughed to himself amazed off of the irony.

"I don't care about dying and I can't die. I found all you niggas because you were afraid to die. I feed off of fear cuz...I know you drew your gun too but I was faster because I wasn't scared and you were. You don't know me like that to be disrespecting me like that. Fuck Mayo Lane, this is Alondra Block till I die. Ole scary ass slob niggas. Watch this." He yelled.

He squeezed the trigger again and nothing happened. He squeezed the trigger one more time and still nothing happened.

"I would gladly join you muthafuckas but I can't die. You see what happens when I..."

His brains were plastered all over the wall. His body was leaning against the side wall while his brain stuck to the back wall. His lifeless body lay in the corner with blood all over his black Pro Club T-Shirt. Sprinkles of blood reached his black khakis but missed his black Chuck Taylor's. Now he would join his victims and settle their issues with him.

"I have a real bad stomach ache." Mama Jo complained while constantly coughing.

"You haven't stopped coughing since we were at the hospital. I thought it was a cold but when I seen you weren't getting any better I wondered about that." Janelle replied.

"I'm way past having stomach cramps. I haven't had a period in years."

"I'm taking you to the hospital mama." Janelle announced.

"We just came back from the hospital Janelle. I'll be alright, I'll take some tea and my stomach will stop hurting."

"No mama you are going to the hospital. I never thought these words would ever come out my mouth but you and I are going to fight if you don't come with me to the hospital." Janelle demanded.

"Alright Janelle damn. You gone have to bring Janette since Monique done moved back in with her mama." Mama Jo surrendered.

"That's fine but lets get you to the hospital."

They packed up everything they could carry for the baby and jumped into the El Camino. Janelle decided to drive since Mama Jo was feeling so sick. She made a quick left on Rosecrans Boulevard and headed straight to Wilmington. She made that quick right and pushed on the gas as Mama Jo sat on the passenger side balled up cringing in pain. Mama Jo was scared to tell Janelle that she had been feeling this way on and off for weeks. It bothered her more that she would have to admit it when she went to see the doctor.

At home the phone rang and rang. No one was there to pick up so the phone continued to ring. Felicia was on the other end frantic after finding the dead body of her boyfriend. She cried begging someone to pick up the phone but no one did. She finally hung up and reluctantly accepted her other option to call the police.

17
IF I COULD DO IT AGAIN

Death got to be easy because life is hard!
50 Cent

"Look, I don't think we should tell mama that Jordan killed himself. She is dealing with stress about her condition. Last thing she needs is to be grief stricken. So we keep this shit to ourselves until she gets better."

Janelle said this to both twins out in the hallway of Mama Jo's hospital room.

"It's crazy because he told me he was talking about doing it but I didn't want to believe him. We at least got to tell Joseph. I'll let Sheila know and when he calls she can tell him then." Twin Deuce replied.

"So the doctors are saying that moms got lung cancer?" Twin Ace asked.

"Yeah, he diagnosed her yesterday. I ain't going to lie, I'm scared for mama. I have never seen her, this sick before. The doctors were saying it was all those cigarettes she smoked over the years." Janelle explained.

"So how can they stop it?" Twin Deuce asked.

"She has to go through something called chemotherapy. They were saying that she might lose all her hair. They were also saying that they detected it late. Whatever that means." Janelle lowered her head in grief.

"Well come on so we can see what's up with mama." Twin Ace walked into the room.

Janelle and Twin Deuce followed close behind him. He walked up to the foot of Mama Jo's bed and she was sound asleep. They all stared at her and within moments she opened her eyes. It was as if she could sense she was being watched.

199

"Three of my babies staring right at me. That's a real good experience. I wish ya'll would have found Jordan. To tell the truth I wish Joseph was out for a moment." Mama Jo smiled.

It was still surprising to see Mama Jo smile even though the twins were young adults.

"My two last babies are all grown up. Well I got ya'll this far so you are probably going to have to carry yourself after I'm gone." Mama Jo sighed.

"Mama don't talk like that. You will be fine; you just need to get some kind of therapy." Janelle protested.

"Who are you lying to because you sure ain't lying to me? I can feel it Janelle; I'll be meeting my maker real soon. If there is one. I ain't too afraid of that I'm just worried about ya'll."

"You don't have to worry about us mama we gone be alright." Twin Ace emotionally replied.

"I don't have to worry about you Jamil. But don't speak for everyone else." Mama Jo recommended.

"What's that supposed to mean?" Janelle cut in.

"Oh never mind. Just know that I love ya'll even though I might not have said it as much as I should. If I could do it again I would have said I love ya'll everyday."

"We love you too mama." Everyone said simultaneously.

"You ain't saying too much Jalil, what's wrong with you."

"I don't know mama; I ain't ever seen you like this. I think it's a trip to see you weak. It's just not you." Twin Deuce honestly replied.

Janelle smacked him on his shoulder. Mama Jo sat up in her bed so that she could look at him directly.

"No Janelle I'm glad that Jalil is being honest. I've always had to be strong because I had six children that were always watching. But believe that I've had many of times that I was weak. But I made sure I looked strong so you all would always be strong. If you all got anything from me it was strength but now I'm weaker than usual because of this cancer. But my love for all of you is strong, very strong." She replied.

"So why are you talking about dying? You are talking about leaving us and that ain't being strong." Twin Deuce persisted.

"Some battles you can't win baby. It isn't like I'm quitting it is just a battle I don't see myself winning. It has already got the best of me." Mama Jo calmly explained.

"But ain't that quitting by already saying you've been beat. You didn't teach us that way." Twin Deuce continued.

His eyes were watering because the thought of his mother dying was surmounted on him knowing Gangster was dead. It was too much for him to bear. He felt like exploding.

"I will fight the best I can Jalil but I'm preparing ya'll for whatever happens. Sometimes you have to know when your time is up. Of course I don't want to die but we don't decide when we are dying. Do you think Jason wanted to die when he did? If your number comes you have to take it, that's all I'm saying." Mama Jo explained.

By now tears had fallen from Twin Deuce's face. He walked over to his mother with a look of pure heartbreak. She smiled as he approached. He leaned down and hugged Mama Jo letting the tears fall on her shoulder. She embraced him while steadily rubbing his back. Janelle and Twin Ace quickly followed suit. They lightened up the conversation shortly after the long embrace. Mama Jo wanted her last days to be joyous.

After visiting hours both twins hit the block to holler at the homies. When they made it outside Meechie, Face, Dino, Tricky and a new booty named Nate was hanging out. Both twins had somber looks on their faces as they walked up. Liquor was being passed around to all the homies. Meechie had some Buddha Tybudd weed.

"This is some good shit cuz." Meechie said after seeing their facial expressions.

Twin Deuce puffed on the joint first and held it in for a few moments. After he exhaled he passed it to his brother.

"Look cuz, we gone have to put in work against them slob ass Mayo Lane niggas. I saw that nigga Dizzy roll through the set in his Cadillac. We got to show them slob niggas they can't roll through the hood and get away with it." Twin Deuce said.

"I seen that nigga too cuz. I think he might be fucking with some bitch that stay right outside the hood. But he still drives through the hood to get there." Meechie replied.

"And you," Twin Deuce pointed at Nate. "It's about time you put in some work to show if you are down."

Nate nodded his head in agreement. No one said a word as Twin Deuce took the floor as the commander.

"Just because my brother got a stretch and Snake got a stretch don't mean us baby gangsters can't hold it down. This is Alondra Block on mine cuz. We don't die we…"

The sirens went off as a squad car rolled up on the pack.

"Assume the position fellas."

All six were told to put there hands on the police car. The car was hot so everyone was naturally irritated.

"Why the fuck ya'll sweating us for?" Twin Deuce snapped.

"What your name?"

"Jalil Laney."

"Are you related to Joseph and Jordan Laney? One of your brothers hit a cop and the other just committed suicide. Wait a minute you two must be twins."

"Yeah those are my brothers what about it cuz?" Twin Ace replied.

The uniformed Linwood Sheriff was a young white man with sandy brown hair. He had a thick mustache and he was stocky from working out and lifting weights. He walked around the six Alondra Block's with a bravado and arrogance that irritated everyone.

"First of all I'm not your cuz. So don't say that shit to me. Second of all I don't have any problem locking up any of Laney niggers. To me your one big problem and I can lock your fucking homeboys up with you. So I need you to know that I'm Officer Williamson and this is Officer McMahon. We've been assigned to this gang unit area and we have been briefed on all of you."

"We just chilling Officer Williamson so you got the wrong people." Meechie protested.

"I know who the fuck you are Demetrius Collins. You must have forgot but a partner and I sent you to Los Padrinos over bags of Marijuana."

Meechie pondered on it for a moment then nodded his head. Officer Williamson didn't acknowledge anyone else. He allowed his partner to finish the body search of everyone else then hopped into his police car.

"Just know that if you got some contraband I might be lurking." Officer Williamson said while poking out the passenger window.

They drove off and Twin Deuce gave them the middle finger. He was irritated because Officer Williamson made him nervous. He hated feeling nervous. He had gotten word what the police did to his brother J-Ridah who was now facing sixteen years. He was stubborn though because he still planned to ride on the Mayo Lane's.

"We just got to be more careful cuz. 'One Time' is rolling but we just got to watch out for them. All the OGs are either locked up or dead so we got to let them know that the new generation is down to put in work. Those Mayo Lane slob niggas think we're weak right now." Twin Deuce continued his tirade.

"That muthafuckin pig knew us by name though. We might want to chill out for a while cuz." Face replied.

"What you scared?" Twin Deuce asked.

"Why this nigga being smart means that he scared. We got a whole bunch of other shit going on and you talking about those Mayo Lane niggas. Felicia gone need help with Jordan's funeral and we still ain't told mama. We got other shit to worry about Jalil." Twin Ace cut in.

"I know that nigga but we still got to hold down the hood. You so caught up with Karen that you don't want to risk getting locked up. You can't stay a day away from that bitch." Twin Deuce fired back at his brother.

"Fuck you cuz. Just because I try to do shit with some sense you want to say I'm pussy whipped. Two of our brothers are dead and our mama is on her deathbed and you are talking about fucking with some slobs. Fuck you cuz." Twin Ace pushed his brother.

It was obvious that Twin Ace was ready to fight. Twin Deuce being more of a shooter didn't really want to go there. So he backed up after getting pushed. He was just as frustrated as his brother so he wanted to take it out on some Pirus.

"What's up cuz, we can handle this shit head up." Twin Ace sneered. He knew his brother didn't want to fight.

"Naw ya'll brothers. Ya'll don't need to fight. Let's squash this shit right now." Meechie got between the two.

Twin Deuce was somewhat relieved but he still had to pretend he didn't care. He snatched away from Meechie and walked off. Twin Ace wanted to follow him and settle the shit but he knew he would be wasting his time. Twin Deuce wasn't a punk but it was well established who could win a fair one between the two. Twin Deuce always knew how to throw the fist pretty well that was why he never felt like he had to prove himself.

"Pass me that joint cuz." Twin Ace said to Face.

"Ay Twin, I didn't know Mama Jo was sick. I'm sorry to hear about that for real cuz." Face replied while passing him the weed.

"It ain't shit we can do about it so don't sweat it. She's a soldier anyway so she facing that shit like a soldier."

"You tell OG J-Ridah about Mama Jo?" Face asked.

"Naw but Sheila told him about Jordan. She said he took that shit pretty hard. All of us took it hard but I seen it coming. My moms don't know about Jordan because we thought it would be best to keep that from her while she's sick." Twin Ace explained.

The rest of the homeboys sat and listened since the mood had grown somber.

Mama Jo woke up to find Janelle sound asleep in the chair next to her bed. She had been dreaming and realized what she had to do. Tears came down her face as she looked at her only daughter.

"Janelle baby wake up." She said in a loud whisper.

"Janelle!"

Janelle's eyes slowly opened her eyes to see her mother sitting up in bed. She rubbed her eyes so that she could see Mama Jo more clearly. She stood up smiling.

"You need something mama?"

"I need you to listen."

"Okay, what's up?"

"First before I begin I want you to answer something for me."

"Anything mama."

"Something bad has happened to Jordan huh?"

Janelle lowered her head afraid to make eye contact."

"What makes you think that?"

"You still ain't good at lying Janelle Laney. Just like when you thought I didn't know that you were going to see Patrick when you were supposed to be running track."

Janelle tried to hold in her smile. Her mother was always good at reading her. Her best bet when she had to conceal something from Mama Jo was to avoid her.

"I can handle it Janelle. Something bad has happened to Jordan?"

"I didn't want to tell you mama because you were sick and everything. I just didn't think you needed to hear more bad news...Jordan committed suicide while he was on Sherm." Janelle cried.

"Each and everyone of you bore something from either Michael or myself. Joseph bore the anger that was inside of Michael. Jordan bore my guilt and addictions. Jason bore the repercussions of both Michael and me. I see these things play out in my head and always wish I could do it better." Mama Jo sadly replied.

"What did I bear mama?"

205

"You bore the strength and determination of us both. You go after what you want." Mama Jo proudly replied.

"What about the twins?"

"Jamil bore the confidence of Michael that made me fall in love with him. Jalil sadly has bore the bitterness and resentment that I carried for many years. We can be bad when we let pain make us bitter. Pain is a part of life but your quality of life determines how you handle pain. My life is a trip because I finally understand that now and my days are numbered." Mama Jo lamented.

"Quit saying that mama. Even if it's true I don't want to keep hearing it." Janelle cried.

"You are going to have to hold us together Janelle. At least what's left of us. I thought that I was strong enough to do it but I now realize that you are much more stronger than I am." Mama Jo smiled.

"What do I need to do?"

"I will explain all the details but I have to school you first on a few things. This way you will know how to be better than me in the same type of situations.

Michael had come home drunk one evening about the normal time he usually arrived. I was pregnant with the twins and I didn't even know it. Jason was barely able to walk. Pat had dropped you off late that night because she was fucking with Marvin and Shawny's father, Marvin Sr. She was in love with that nigga so she would keep you until late because she didn't want to leave him to drop you off.

Right when Michael walked in the door he had started trouble. He talked about not being able to do anything anymore. He was trapped into having a family and he wasn't ready. I was naturally offended. I knew he felt that way because of the old saying 'A drunk man tells no lies'. So I took Joseph, Jordan and Jason into the room and got them dressed. I wanted to take them to my mother's house. That's when everything escalated.

"You think I signed up for all this shit Michael? You think that I wanted to be fucking broke with four children to feed? You think I wanted to greet a man that comes home drunk all the time? So fuck you and feed yo fish Mike. You ain't a man, you are a fucking bum." I screamed.

My words must have stunned him because he didn't move for a few seconds. We've had plenty of fights but this time for some reason this stung him. The facial expression he gave me made me want to take it back. But I also felt hurt and betrayed.

"You won't take my muthafuckin sons bitch." Michael yelled.

"I thought they trapped you nigga. I thought you were tricked into having a family. As though I forced you to stick yo dick into me. You just want to punk out that's all." I fired back.

"I ain't ever been a muthafuckin punk. And you ain't walking out that door with my boys."

Jason began to cry while Joseph and Jordan stared at us with stone faces. I became hysterical because I couldn't push your father out the way with three boys in the tow as well. I pushed all three of them into Michael and my bedroom and closed the door.

"Look muthafucka yo ass is in and out of jail, can't keep a job, drunk all the time and you want to claim your boys. Why don't you stay out long enough to see one of 'your boys' grow the fuck up? I don't know what the fuck I saw in you."

Suddenly his open hand crashed into my face. The pain was so intense that it left me dazed for a few moments. My lip was busted and his handprint was across my face. When I regained my composure I looked at him with venom in my heart.

"That's how bad you made me feel with yo fucked up words." He yelled.

I went on the offensive. Coming at him full speed I grabbed a lamp off the hallway table and swung it like a Louisville Slugger. He tried to catch it with his arm but it broke across his forearm. His arm began bleeding but at this point I didn't care what happened to him. I dug my nails into his face and hit him with my fist. He didn't have to time to retaliate because I was all

207

over him. It wasn't the first time we had fought but I wanted to make sure it was the last.

I finally let up when he stopped trying to defend himself. Climbing from on top of him he kept his usual stern look.

"It's not enough you beat me down with yo words?" He said.

"You the one coming into the house talking about you feel trapped and you were tricked into having a family. How the fuck you think that makes me feel Michael? Your words can cut too. It seems to me you are the first to hurt with words and fist." I sharply replied.

"I was just trying to stop you from leaving that's all." He said while getting up from off the floor.

"What about you being trapped?" I fired back.

He had hurt me because it was times I felt trapped. There were times that I resented him hanging out with his homeboys while I was watching children for most of the day. But I never let it on how I felt. So I resented that he felt free enough to do it. So I intended on making him pay for his honesty.

"I feel like I can't move backwards or forward so it's like I'm trapped. I was tricked into having a family and not being prepared. I can't give my babies what they want I can't give you what you want. I didn't mean it towards you." He replied.

"Fuck that Michael you did mean it towards me."

"No I didn't Jo."

"Well why didn't you say to who you meant it for? Why do I have to be the person to hear that shit? You must have wanted me to hear it. So since you don't want this, then why don't you just leave and Janelle, the boys and me will be just fine?" I replied.

He tried to reach over and hug me but I pushed him away. Usually our arguments led up to angry sex but I wasn't in the mood for any of that. He tried one last time then reached for his jacket. He grabbed his pack of cigarettes and barged out the door. That infuriated me even more because he was once again allowed to leave when he felt like it. Ten minutes later Pat pulled up with you. I told Pat what happened and she sided with me. We couldn't talk long though because her man was waiting on her. She promised to call me the next day so we could talk all about it. Michael never came home that night. I would never see him as a free man again. So I tell you this as a warning Janelle don't ever use your words to hurt a man. Use them to uplift. If I could do it again I would have kept my man at home. I say this with hurt and pain. But remember a man protects a woman from the violence of the world but a woman protects a man from himself. If only I could do it again.

18

WE ARE FAMILY

For a woman it ain't easy trying to raise a man!
Tupac Shakur

Janelle, Auntie Tricia and Felicia decided that it would be best to have the funeral for both Mama Jo and Gangster on the same day. They would both be buried next to Baby Gangster. The twins watched them lower their brother and mother into the grave on the same day. Shawny-Ru was able to attend but Big Bamm had caught a dope charge and was facing some time. A few of the young homies from Alondra Block attended the funeral out of respect for the Laney family but other than that it was mostly private. Janelle cried constantly from losing her mother. It appeared as though she was also crying for both the twins. They stood at the gravesite with somber faces without allowing a tear to fall from either of their faces. Auntie Tricia tried to comfort her best she could but it was futile. Auntie Jackie showed up with her daughters for the funeral but she didn't drive to the grave site. She and Mama Jo were on bad terms for good when Monique had gotten pregnant from the train Turtle had pulled on her. She felt like her sister had betrayed her. They didn't speak any more after that. Auntie Jackie didn't want to go to the gravesite because of the guilt she felt for not making amends with her sister. Monique was the only person that cried as much and as hard as Janelle. She hated that she didn't get to say goodbye to Auntie Jo. Monique and Janelle hugged each other tightly right after the church services.

Twin Ace and Karen both decided to go back to the Laney household to change into regular clothes after the funeral. Janelle arrived a few minutes after they did with Sheila and Joe Jr. Janelle called everyone into the living room so that she could talk. She had some things that she wanted to be known before everyone got into the rest of the day.

"I plan on selling the house and moving up to Marino Valley." She announced.

"Moreno Valley? Where is that at?" Twin Ace asked.

"It's out near Riverside by the mountains. You remember when we went to Santa's Village when we were little up in the San Bernardino Mountains?" Janelle asked.

Twin Ace nodded vaguely remembering the trip.

"Yeah well I'm going to try to buy a house out near there. I can't live in this house anymore with mama not here. I don't want to move anywhere in Compton so I'm moving up that way. I already talked to Patrick and he said when he gets out he's going to come my way."

"I also talked to Joseph and he told me it was cool because he would need a change of environment. He's up there reading books and everything now." Sheila cut in.

"Where is Jalil because he needs to hear this too?"

"I need to hear what?"

Twin Deuce walked into the door after only hearing the last statement made by Janelle.

"I'm selling the house and moving out to Moreno Valley. About a month from now I plan to do this." Janelle explained.

"Move out the hood? Why would we move out the hood? This is all we know." Twin Deuce dreadfully asked.

"Mama moved out of the East Side of South Central because she wanted us to have it better than she. That's why we are moving out of Compton so our children can have it better than us. There is nothing but problems with us over here because everybody knows the Laney family. Friends, enemies and the police all know us and where we live. And now that mama is gone I don't want to live over here anymore." Janelle replied.

"That's a damn shame Janelle. Because mama is gone you want to leave where we came from. Mama always taught us to be soldiers for what we believe in and now you giving all that up." Twin Deuce shook his head.

"The hood is in my heart wherever I go Jalil. I want something better so that's what I believe in. You need to grow the fuck up and realize that gangbanging done played out. You want to run around here being super Crip when the rest of us want to live our life without all that bullshit." Janelle fired back.

"I'm with you big sis." Twin Ace cut in. "Karen and me wanted to getaway from here also. I can't see myself living out here without mama either."

"Oh here goes this simping ass nigga talking about him and his wife again." Twin Deuce antagonized his brother.

"Yeah whatever nigga, you ain't down to handle this shit from the shoulders though cuz." Twin Ace fired back.

"We are family though. We should stay where we know everybody and everything around. Why do you want to move way out to…Moreno something?" Twin Deuce protested.

"Like I said before I can't live in this house any more without mama Jalil. Why can't you get that through yo thick ass head?" Janelle said in frustration.

"Besides, Mama Jo wanted us to move away from here. She and Janelle had a long talk right before she passed away. You should stop tripping and come move with us Jalil." Sheila commented.

"Aw Sheila you were down with the hood back when Do-Dirty was alive. Now you want to give up what you have represented all your life?" Twin Deuce asked sounding disappointed.

"He just doesn't get it. Well you got a month Jalil, it's up to you. I'm going to pick up a few things from the grocery store so the discussion is over." Janelle sighed.

Twin Deuce barged out the door angry and frustrated. Janelle felt bad that he didn't want to go but she had to live her life and he had to live his. She grabbed her purse then headed towards the door. Sheila had planned on watching Janette while she was at the store.

With her brother heavy on her mind she went up to the store and grabbed a basket. She rolled past some loud mouth teenagers cursing like sailors as she walked into the store. They were all females so Janelle looked at them shaking her head remembering when she was that wild.

"That bitch Latrice don't want to see me cuz." One girl loudly said to her friend.

Janelle chuckled to herself as she entered the grocery store. She was inside the grocery store for an hour by the time she was finished. When she walked outside the same little girls were outside talking loud. She put her basket away after loading her groceries into the car. As she put the basket back one of the little teenage girls got in her way while playing with her friend.

"Excuse me little girl."

"Little girl? Bitch I'm grown, I don't know who the fuck you think you are talking to." The teenage girl fired back.

"Who do you think you are calling a bitch? I'll whip your little young ass. You need to run off before I tell your mother you need yo ass whipped." Janelle snapped.

"I don't need my mama bitch. I ain't scared of you."

"You need to be scared of me little girl." Janelle replied.

Janelle was trying to control her anger. Please don't let me go to jail over this stupid ass girl, Janelle thought. Janelle seen fear rise up into the young girl but the obnoxious teenager controlled her fear and wouldn't back down.

"You better watch who you talking to before you get into some serious shit." The teenage girl screamed.

"Yeah I'll end up in jail that's the only serious shit you can get me into. Now move so I can put this basket where it belongs." Janelle dismissed her.

"I ain't doing shit. You keep on talking and I'm going to get my big cousin to come and whip yo ass."

Janelle chuckled for a moment. She couldn't think of the last time she was afraid of another woman. The only one she could recall ever really being scared of had just been buried earlier in the day. Janelle smiled and decided to leave the basket there where it was. Janelle knew when to pick her battles at this point and it was obvious the girl was selling wolf tickets. The teenager being ignored became more infuriated.

"You know what, I'm going to get my cousin to whip yo ass. You in trouble now bitch. My cousin Big Nell Laney gone fuck you up." The teenage girl yelled.

Janelle turned around in total astonishment. She paused for a moment not knowing what to really think. The teenage girl began nodding her head as though she had put Janelle in her place.

"What did you say little girl?" Janelle asked.

"I'm going to get my cousin Big Nell Laney to whip yo ass. That's what I said." The teenage girl sassily replied.

"I'm Big Nell Laney, little girl. You want me to show you my ID?" Janelle sneered.

The teenage girl stood in front of Janelle with her mouth wide open. The rest of her homegirls grabbed her while she stood in shock. Janelle gave them a look so piercing they walked away with their heads down. Janelle opened her car door and sighed.

"I really need to get the fuck out of here." She shook her head.

Twin Deuce went out to meet up with his homeboys on the block. When he got over there Meechie was leaning on his black Monte Carlo. Face, Tricky and Dino was with him. Also Flintstone who had just gotten out of Soledad State Prison was hanging out.

"Aw what's up cuz? You just got out today?" Twin Deuce's mood lightened up.

"Naw, I got out about three days ago but I had to find a way down here. My moms moved way out to Palm Springs so it took me some time to get back to the hood." Flintstone replied.

"Yeah a lot of people are moving away." Twin Deuce cynically replied.

"I was sorry to hear about yo peoples. Gangster and Baby Gangster were both some down ass niggas. That nigga Baby Gangster was the coldest hustler I ever knew. He would slang on that corner from can't see to can't see some days. And Mama Jo was the coolest mama a nigga could know. I was really hurt to hear about yo loss cuz." Flintstone replied.

"Good looking Flintstone we need to get drunk and high to celebrate yo welcome home." Twin Deuce smiled.

"We passing around this skunk weed right now." Meechie replied.

Twin Deuce puffed on the potent weed and blew the smoke out smoothly. He needed to puff on some weed the way he was feeling as of late. Now his family was moving away and he didn't know how to drop that on his homeboys. He knew he needed to do it before his brother got to talking.

"Yeah man, Janelle talking about selling the house and moving out to Moreno something." Twin Deuce said while passing the joint.

"Are you serious cuz?" Face asked.

"As a muthafuckin heart attack. My whole family down to do that punk shit. I'm the only one that has a problem with it and I don't understand that for the life of me. It's like they want to forget where they came from." Twin Deuce said despondently.

"That's yo family though cuz. You should be with yo family and just come to the hood every now and then. Shit I wish I could get away from all this stupid shit. I'm down for the set don't get me wrong but sometimes a nigga gets tired of always having to watch his back." Meechie replied.

"Not you too Meechie? Damn nigga you think about leaving the hood?" Twin Deuce shockingly asked.

"I ain't gone lie, sometimes I want to get away from all this shit. This Alondra Block until I die. But if you got a chance to start over the set is always in yo heart but you can maybe do bigger and better things." Meechie replied.

"Yeah that's real though cuz." Flintstone agreed.

Twin Deuce nodded his head while pondering on their words. He never thought about it like that. He always thought that he would always live in Compton.

Janelle made it home still laughing to herself about what happened at the grocery store. She walked in the door to tell

Sheryl but she was on the phone. She sat the groceries down after Twin Ace helped her carry them inside.

"I'm talking to Joseph on the phone, here Janelle he wants to talk to you." Sheila said.

Janelle picked up the phone eagerly to talk to her favorite brother. The cord to the phone was long enough for her to put thing away while still on the phone.

"How are you Joseph?"

"I'm good. So are you ready to make that move out to Moreno Valley?" He jovially asked.

"Yeah I guess. It's just a little difficult to convince Jalil that he should do the same."

"Yeah I know. He got that stubborn Laney gene in him. If I get a chance to holla at him I'll talk to him good. He always listened to me."

"Yeah I know. In fact he's trying so hard to be like you that it's driving me crazy. He's trying to get the little homies to ride on…"

"Whoa hold up Janelle, we on a state phone. You don't know whose listening."

"Oh yeah I'm tripping. So what's happening big brother?"

"I took the plea bargain for twelve years. If I'm straight I can get out this bitch in about eight to ten. It's different now than it was when I first got locked up. I'm cool with Crips and Damus."

"Damus?"

"That's Swahili for Bloods. I met a nigga from Five-Seven Gangsters on the West Side of L.A. named Dre-Bo. He and I have a lot in common. He lost two brothers just like I did."

"Is his mother still alive?" Janelle asked.

"Yeah from what he told me. He beat a case involving a police getting killed then he got caught up on a gun charge a little later on. That's what he's in here for now. They were trying to fry him for the police murder but when he decided to fight it they had to thrown it out. He gets out for about three or four months and catches a gun charge. That shit sounds familiar huh?" J-Ridah laughed.

"Yeah that does sound like some shit you went through except for the police murder shit. I know one thing; it's good to hear you laughing." Janelle replied.

"Yeah I'm looking at life a little better now. I wish I would have been out for Mama's funeral though. Cancer got her huh? I remember how she used to puff on cigarettes all the time. I never thought it would kill her though. She was strong all the time. I'm going to miss her and her stories about her and pops. What's going on with Jamil? I heard that he and Karen are getting married. He always had more sense than all of us."

"He does have a lot of sense. He and Karen are both moving up to Moreno Valley and when you get out we will have our family back together again. It hurt me hard to know I wasn't going to see Mama again. I'm telling you Joseph I don't think I've ever cried that hard."

"That shit is rough for everybody. It's crazy because I was on my way to holla at Jordan when the pigs bumped me up and planted that gun. At first I wanted to serve both those pigs for that shit but then I thought about it. If Gangster wanted to kill himself he was going to do it if I was there or not."

"Well big brother I'm going to let you talk to your son he's looking at me like he is ready to jump into the phone."

"Yeah let me talk to him. Oh yeah, before you get off the phone Janelle I need to let you know something. Get the word out that Turtle is snitching. I seen some paperwork with my own eyes. Pookie might do a stretch behind some shit this nigga doing." J-Ridah replied.

"Are you serious? Mama should have let Jason serve that nigga then."

"Let Jason serve Turtle for snitching? Mama knew Turtle was snitching before she died?" J-Ridah asked.

"Never mind, here is Joe Jr."

She handed her nephew the phone and finished cleaning up. She was saddened when she realized that she would have to wait a long time to see her man. If Turtle was snitching, Pookie had all kinds of problems because Turtle used to slang for him. Before

217

she moved she would have to make it a priority to let it be known that Turtle turned snitch. She wasn't with gangbanging anymore but she still felt like it was her duty to let the hood know when a snitch was walking around.

The sun had just gone down because it was getting darker earlier in the day this time of the year. Twin Deuce put on his brownie gloves with his black beanie snug over his head. They covered his braids that went down to his back. Meechie was walking side by side with him when they finally came across a vehicle. Twin Deuce pulled out the snatch bar so that they could break into the van. They had decided that they would be the only two to go out tonight. Once the van was started up Meechie was the one to drive. Twin Deuce rode shotgun with the sawed off twelve-gauge pump on the side. They were definitely on the hunt. Twin Deuce was hoping he would run into Dizzy. If he caught Dizzy slipping it would be over. They rolled around for about fifteen minutes before they came across a pack of Pirus hanging out in an alley by the side of a house. Meechie didn't think there was a way to get to them but Twin Deuce insisted. So Meechie decided to go around the block and creep around from the other side. They rolled up on the loud Pirus as slow as they could possibly go without being detected. It was a timing thing. If they were too fast it would raise suspicion and if they were too slow it would do the same. Meechie decided to keep his lights on so that it wouldn't be obvious that it was a drive-by.

"Fuck slobs' cuz."

Twin Deuce started blasting into the crowd of Pirus. The buck shots started spreading as they tried to duck and hide. A few were hit instantly as the rest were showered with the buck shots. After hearing the screams Meechie screeched off into the night. They made sure to drop the van off on Alondra Boulevard. They hugged each other then walked back to the neighborhood while Twin Deuce had the sawed off twelve-gauge at his side. Once they knew they were in safe territory Twin Deuce quickly hid the gun and got rid of the gloves.

"We didn't get that nigga Dizzy but they gotta know that our set is still active. You know what I'm saying cuz?" Twin Deuce said with enthusiasm.

"Yeah nigga I know what you saying. You was hurting them niggas with that pump. Too bad Snake is locked up because this would be a good time to hang out in his backyard to lay low."

"I know but it is what it is. It seems like things always got to change huh? The homies getting locked up or smoked. I thought my moms was gone live forever. I don't know why but I always thought that."

"I know she was a soldier."

"Well alright then comrade I'm going to head to the house so that we can lay low. I decided to go ahead and make that trip with my family. I know that's how my moms would have wanted it anyway." Twin Deuce said.

"I don't blame you homie. I mean we just put in work but a nigga don't want have to worry about doing that shit all the time." Meechie shrugged his shoulders.

"Not all the time. But that shit was fun serving them slob niggas though." Twin Deuce laughed.

"Alright then I'll see you tomorrow." Meechie laughed then jumped into his Monte Carlo.

Once Twin Deuce made it inside the house he headed straight for the kitchen. Janelle was inside cleaning up. Twin Deuce smiled at her as he prepared to fix him a plate of food.

"The rest of that shit is in the oven. I figured you might come home for some of that chicken." Janelle said in passing.

"Ay big sis I thought about what you said and I'll probably roll with ya'll out to Moreno whatever."

"So you going to Moreno Valley with us?" Janelle said with enthusiasm.

She hugged him while he was fixing his plate. He appreciated the hug but he still had to pretend like he didn't.

"Damn Janelle get off me."

"Yo punk ass is always talking shit. But I'm glad you are coming. It's going to be different Jalil watch and see. I got some money to open up my own hair salon and everything."

"Where you get money to do all that?" Twin Deuce asked.

"Don't worry about all of that. You just start getting ready to be with your family in a whole different environment. Oh by the way, Joseph called earlier today."

"For real? What that nigga say?" Twin Deuce asked with food in his mouth.

"That he wanted to talk to you about moving out there. He said he's cool with Bloods and Crips up there."

"Yeah from what I heard that shit is more about race than what set you from in the pen." Twin Deuce replied.

"Well he said he when he gets out he plans to come out there to live with us."

"That's cool."

Twin Deuce finished his food then went to watch television in the living room. Nowadays he found himself sleeping on the couch with his nephew Joe Jr. Twin Ace and Karen would usually be in the room he shared with his brother. He never wanted to be a third leg so he would sleep on the couch. Sheila would sleep in the room next to theirs and Janelle and her daughter Janette stayed in the room by the door. Twin Deuce would take the sofa while his nephew would take the love seat.

Twin Deuce had dozed off with the television on when he heard a bang on the door. He thought he was dreaming until he heard a bang again. The second knock woke him from his slumber. Before he could get to the door Janelle had already opened the door. His eyes half open he listened in on whoever was at the door.

"We would like to speak to Jamil or Jalil Laney." A police officer firmly said.

"What for?" Janelle asked.

"We have some questions we would like to ask him about a shooting that took place earlier tonight."

Twin Deuce walked to the door at this point. He rubbed the sleep from his eyes.

"Can you step outside Mr. Laney so that we can ask you a few questions?"

Janelle grabbed his arm to let him know he didn't have to step outside. After rubbing the sleep from his eyes he looked directly at the officer.

"Whatever you want to ask me you can ask me right here."

"Where were you earlier tonight?"

"I was at home."

"You've been home all night?"

"Pretty much."

"You have a twin brother don't you? Where was he all night?" The officer pried.

"He's been laid up with his girlfriend all night." Twin Deuce replied.

"So neither one of you has left the house all day."

"Pretty much."

"Do you have anyone that can corroborate your story? Because we have a shooting that took place earlier tonight and you are the number one suspect."

"That's too bad."

Both cops looked at each other and wasn't satisfied with the answers they were receiving.

"Could you step out on the porch so that we can finish this investigation Mr. Laney?"

"Do you have a warrant?" Janelle cut in.

"No we do not but we have reason to believe that he was involved in a drive-by shooting earlier tonight."

"He told you he was here all day and I can corrob... whatever you said, his story."

"So you are willing to testify that he was here all day?"

"Yes sir!" Janelle said with conviction.

The two officers were at a stand still. They stepped back away from the door to have a talk. After a few moments the officer asking the questions approached Janelle.

"You have a good night ma'am we are sorry to have disturbed you."

"You do the same." Janelle closed the door.

Twin Deuce sat down on the couch now fully awake. He glanced over at his nephew to see that he was still asleep. He smiled remembering when life was that innocent for him.

"Thank You Janelle that was good looking out." Twin Deuce sighed.

"Don't worry about it we family. It's bad enough one of my brothers is locked up. If I can stop the other from being locked up I'll do my best. But you better be careful because Joseph told me that Turtle is snitching and he seen the paperwork. So it ain't any telling who else might be snitching." Janelle replied.

"Damn Turtle turned snitch? I don't understand some muthafuckas. Some of the homies catch him slipping it's over."

"I know, but I'm going back to sleep so good night."

"Good night."

Twin Deuce sat in the dark with the television glaring at him. He couldn't sleep now that he had waked up. He had a lot on his mind.

19
TRIAL IN THE STREETS

If the elements don't murder you the Ridahs will!
Lil Wayne

Twin Ace woke up earlier than usual this morning. He reached over in his bed to see that Karen wasn't there tonight. He panicked for a brief moment. Then he realized Karen had to finish some things at home so they agreed that she didn't spend the night. That awkwardness made him rise from the bed and walk into the living room. He noticed that his nephew Joe Jr. was sound asleep. But when he looked over at his brother he realized that he was wide-awake. The television wasn't on and there was no music playing. This was somewhat bizarre so he decided to sit down with his younger twin.

"What's up with you cuz? You damn near sitting in the dark."

"I got a lot of shit on my mind. This move to Moreno Valley is different for me. Leaving everything behind is hard to swallow." Twin Deuce replied.

"You were thinking about backing out?"

"Naw I'm going. I just don't know what to expect and that bothers me more than anything. Even though the streets are wild out here I still know what to expect. I expect the police to trip. I expect to get blasted on by my enemies. I expect to go to jail or catch a case. But I don't know what to expect out that way." Twin Deuce glanced at his brother.

"Yeah but it has to be better than all those things you named."

"That's the whole thing about leaving. We got a name out here. Everybody knows and respects the Laney family. Out in

223

Marino Valley we are a bunch of nobodies trying to escape our past like everyone else."

Twin Deuce got up from off the couch not waiting for a response from his brother. He went into the kitchen grabbed a glass from out the cabinet and filled it with water. He walked back into the living room and sat back on the couch.

"That's our problem when you really look at it. Everybody knows the Laney's so they always expect drama. Living out here means we always have to live up to that Laney name. Karen was telling me how this nigga was scared to speak to her because he heard that she was about to marry a Laney." Twin Ace said.

"Yeah but you see the power that has. No nigga is going to disrespect you or your girl because of your name. That's why I always tripped when you didn't want to go blast on some slobs or those Greenleaf niggas. We can keep that reputation where niggas can respect us." Twin Deuce passionately replied.

"Yeah but I got three brothers that are clear examples of why I'm not trying to get caught up. Joseph was gangbanging 24/7 and he was in and out of jail behind it too. Jordan did so much dirt that he couldn't live with himself unless he was on that Sherm. I mean that's two brothers right there that I knew not to follow in their footsteps. Then Jason…"

Twin Ace paused for a moment. To bring up Jason hurt him the most. He was the one least expected to die but was the first to go. Twin Ace lowered his head while his brother gave him time to silently mourn. It was a hurtful situation for them both to swallow.

"Jason was a good nigga that just wanted to take care of his family. But a bullet doesn't have any name on it. When you out there you always got to know that it could be you that could catch one. They just let me know that carrying that Laney name is something that I wanted to do different with. You understand where I'm coming from cuz." Twin Ace said emotionally.

"I always looked up to them but I never looked at it as examples of how not to be. Shit our moms and pops were both

Crips. This is just how the world was given to us." Twin Deuce shrugged his shoulders.

"Yeah but now we got a chance to getaway from all that bullshit. I'm sick of having to worry about a nigga blasting on me or me blasting him because someone decided that he's an enemy. Fuck that dumb shit." Twin Ace waived his hand glumly.

"Even when those Greenleaf niggas killed Jason? You didn't look at them as enemies or want to go ride on them?" Twin Deuce asked surprisingly.

"At first I did. But after awhile I was like, it won't bring him back. And besides, those niggas didn't kill Jason because he was from our hood they killed him because they wanted his shit."

"Yeah that's real. But Joseph told me one day that even Mama wanted revenge on the niggas that killed Jason." Twin Deuce mentioned.

"Yeah but if she could have done it again she probably wouldn't have been on that page. That soldier came out of her that's all. But even soldiers retire or they will end up dead. I'm trying to live. I ain't afraid of dying but I want to live. But I'm getting sleepy again so I'm about to go back to bed." Twin Ace rubbed his eyes.

Twin Deuce got up from the couch to embrace his brother. It sort of caught Twin Ace off guard but they quickly hugged each other.

"I know I've been giving you a hard time about being with Karen but I hope ya'll are happy together."

"Good looking out."

Twin Ace went back into the room while Twin Deuce tried to go back to sleep. He had dozed off in about ten minutes. The talk had done him good but forty-five minutes into his sleep Janelle woke up with the baby. It disturbed him for a moment but then he went back to sleep.

Janelle had gotten up with Janette and decided to sit on the porch and enjoy the sun. These were her last days in Compton and she wanted to look at her neighborhood from her porch. There was a nice breeze but it was still warm. That was the beauty of

California weather. It would be snowing in most places but here you might get a sunny day in October. She had just fed Janette so her daughter was content for the moment. She looked down at her daughter and smiled at her innocence.

"I wish you would have really got to know your grandma."

She stepped down off the stairs and into the yard. She made faces at Janette and watched her daughter giggle. It was a peaceful serene moment that made her cherish her last days. She turned around and walking past her yard was Flintstone. His eyes red as though he had just woke up. She wanted to pretend she didn't see him but they had made eye contact. He walked into the yard as though he was invited.

"What's up Big Nell?"

"What it do Flintstone?"

"Nothing really, I had rented a motel room around the corner. I could have stayed until eleven but I'm still used to getting up early in the pen." He replied.

"Why didn't you just go home?"

"My moms' lives way out in Palm Springs now. I just came out here to hang out in the hood. It was hard getting down here so I decided to stay a couple of days before I head back out that way." He shrugged.

"Are you serious? You miss the hood that much that you stayed out here a few days just to hang out with the homies? Ain't you starting new out in Palm Springs?"

"It ain't shit out there for me. My moms got a new boyfriend and my sister is about to get married to some nigga she met out there. All I do is sit around the house all day. In the hood niggas know me and I'm respected but out that way it ain't shit for me." He bitterly replied.

"You ain't trying to get you a job or something?"

"I got a felony charge so it's hard to get a job in L.A. so it's really hard to get a job out in Palm Springs. It ain't shit out there."

Janelle thought about her brother Twin Deuce. He still had that criminal mentality that would make it difficult for him to adjust. She didn't have to worry about Twin Ace. He still had that

226

street in him but she thinks that he would be more willing to change his way of thinking to get a job. It's hard for black boys to become men she pondered. She glanced at her daughter thanking her lucky star that she had a daughter. Imagine Mama's pain of having to raise five boys with no help.

"What are you thinking about?" Flintstone interrupted her thoughts.

For a few seconds she forgot he was standing there. The morning was a time for her to reflect and he was interfering with that.

"Big Nell you alright?"

"Yeah I'm cool I was just thinking about my brothers."

"I was sorry to hear about yo brothers passing. I really had love for Baby Gangster. That nigga was all about his paper."

"Yeah I'm going to miss both of them." She said as if to remind him that two of her brothers were dead.

"Yeah may both of them rest in peace. I heard that Rachelle moved out of state. Remember when Pookie, Rachelle, you and me used to go on double dates?"

"Uh huh. Those were some crazy times." Janelle pacified him.

"I always thought you looked good. I knew you were Pookie's girl so I would never step. How much time is Pookie looking at?"

Janelle fought with all her might to not laugh in his face. Is he really trying to holla at me? Like I would really fuck with one of Pookie's homeboys.

"He hasn't been sentenced yet." She blankly replied.

"Oh so we should kick it sometime." He pried.

"Well you know I'm about to move to Marino Valley." Janelle replied.

"Yeah but you not moving tomorrow. Maybe we can kick it a few times before you move out that way." Flintstone continued.

Janelle turned around to look at him. She was playing with her daughter at first with her back to him. He had on a tank top

227

with a pair of old 501 Levis. His light brown face had scars and permanent bruises. He had two teeth missing in the front. His body had tattoos all over his upper body. He had on Pumas that looked relatively new. He tried to smile without showing his teeth but Janelle already seen the gap. Her stomach began to hurt from trying not to laugh in his face.

"Well I doubt it especially since Pookie and I are still together." She smiled.

"Aw not like that. Just hanging out for old time's sake before you move out that way." He replied.

"Maybe, I will have to see."

"Alright then Big Nell you stay up." Flintstone said while walking out the yard.

Twin Deuce didn't wake up until noon. He was groggy and drained for some reason. He went into the bathroom to wash his face and brush his teeth. When he finished he noticed that it was extremely quiet in the house. He opened up the bathroom door to see who was home.

"Janelle?"

No one answered his call. He walked around the entire house with the washcloth still in hand. Once he covered every inch of the house he went back into bathroom. His stomach started growling so he sat the washcloth down to see if Janelle left some food cooked in the kitchen. After tearing up the entire kitchen he realized he would have to cook some food if he planned on eating. By this time it was twelve-forty-five so he decided get out in the streets and get something to eat from one of the fast food spots on Rosecrans or Long Beach Boulevard.

After jumping in the shower he threw on his blue Levi corduroys creased with heavy starch. They had one-inch cuffs with a split in the middle. He threw on a fresh white Pro Club T-Shirt 2X Long with his blue Puma sneakers. He glanced at the long hallway mirror and smiled at how he put clothes together. He threw up Crip then he threw up Alondra Block gang signs while posing.

He stepped out on the porch and began mobbing down his block. The usual neighbors waived and paid their respects and he felt good. He was headed to his road dog Meechie's house so they could maybe hang out for a while and get something to eat. When Twin Deuce knocked on the door Meechie answered the door.

"What's up Twin cuz?" They embraced.

"Trying to see what's up with you cuz."

"I was about to go see what's up with some of the little homies about my money. They over there around the corner curb serving but they done sold out by now."

"Alright then let's roll over there then I want you to take me somewhere to get some grub. I thought my sister was gone cook something but when I woke it wasn't shit in the kitchen."

"That's cool cuz I haven't had shit to eat either. You haven't got into some of this hustling nigga? You could have been got you a ride if you anything like Baby Gangster." Meechie inquired.

"I was thinking about it but I heard that nigga Turtle is snitching and I don't really know if I want to fuck with that shit. Plus now that I'm about to move it doesn't really make a difference."

"Yeah you was telling me that yo brother seen some paperwork on that nigga. That's some way out shit when a nigga gets to snitching." Meechie replied.

They hopped into Meechie's Monte Carlo so that they could get into the streets. They went around to one of the new dope spots and it was buzzing a little bit even though it was broad daylight. The little homies that were a generation under Meechie and Twin were outside trying to show out in front of them. A few of the homegirls from the neighborhood were hanging outside so they really had to prove something. Twin Deuce and Meechie sat back and observed while talking shit to everyone. Then one of the homegirls that liked Twin Deuce for a while walked over to talk to him. He didn't claim her as his girl but they had messed around a few times. She walked over looking as good as she could be. Her dark brown complexion glowed with a beauty mark right above her lip. She complimented her face with her hair braided in cornrows down her back. She had an exotic look like she was from another country or something. She had a Coca-Cola shape that really looked good in jeans. She had on her matching skateboard Vans with blue pom-poms sticking out the back. She came over sucking on a lollipop and smiling.

"I'll give you something to suck on." Twin Deuce teased.

"I don't know what you waiting for. My mama not at home or anything and you act like you would rather watch these niggas slap box or something." She teased.

"Ay Meechie we gone have to get something to eat in a little bit cuz." Twin Deuce smiled.

"Alright then I'll stay posted until you get back." Meechie glanced at them while watching the slap box tournament.

He followed her back to her house, which was right up the street. She walked inside and sat her keys on the counter in the kitchen.

"You want me to fix you a sandwich?" She asked while in the kitchen.

"Yeah that will be cool." Twin Deuce replied.

He was hungry as hell but he didn't want to seem too eager. He gobbled the sandwich down within minutes of receiving it. She put her hand on his leg and leaned in towards him.

"Why you don't come to see me that much?"

"I don't think yo mean ass mama likes me."

"Naw she just acts like that with everybody. I see yo brother with Karen all the time. Why can't we Cee together like them? What you don't want to claim me or something?"

"Naw baby it ain't that. It's just this Crippin' shit is an everyday thing 24/7. Then I'm hanging with the homies and I don't want my lady around all the homies like that." He admitted.

"Oh so you jealous?" Michelle said feeling flattered.

"I just ain't trying to have a bunch niggas staring at you like that." He shrugged.

"Well you don't have to worry about whose looking at me because I'm all yours."

She got up from the couch and stood in front of him. He wrapped his hands around her tiny waist while she grabbed the back of his head. He unbuttoned her jeans as she squeezed out of them. He kissed her on her belly button as she lifted his T-Shirt over his head. He stood up with his shirt off showing his Alondra Block tattoo written out on his chest. She rubbed her hand across his broad arms and chest. He unbuttoned his corduroy pants and slipped out of his pants and his sneakers. Her beautiful body was completely naked except for the footsies she still had on. She took his hand and escorted him to her room.

They got into the bedroom and began kissing before they lied on the mattress. She sat down on the mattress then lied on her back. He climbed in between her legs and eagerly penetrated. She wrapped her arms around him and gently stroked his back with her hands and fingernails. They passionately kissed while he continued to go inside of her.

"That's it Jalil right there." She moaned.

They made love for a good thirty minutes then they lied in bed and talked. She kept touching his upper body with gentle strokes. He cared about her but he was careful not to let her know too much.

"You want me to redo your braids?" She asked. She was trying to get him to stay longer.

"Naw, you just done them a few days ago. You think they looked fucked up or something?"

"Naw not like that. I just didn't know if you wanted them done again. I'll cook you something to eat if want me to."

"I told Meechie we were going to go somewhere to grub. That nigga probably got tired of waiting on me."

"Then let him go and you stay here with me." She persisted.

"How about I bring you around the corner to my house so we can chill with my family?"

"Are you serious?"

"As a heart attack."

"What time you talking about? You know I can put on something real cute to meet your family."

"When I get back from getting something to eat I'll come by your house to come and get you. Even if yo mean ass mama is at home." Twin Deuce teased her.

She playfully hit him in the arm. She stared at him for a moment really studying his mannerisms.

"You promise Jalil?" She slightly whined.

"I promise! And stop calling me Jalil. They call me Twin Deuce from Alondra Block Compton Crip." He playfully banged on her.

"Whatever nigga. Just make sure you come back to get me once you and Meechie got something to eat."

"Okay."

Twin Deuce quickly got dressed and hit the block. To his surprise Meechie was still outside hanging with the young homies. He embraced everybody once again then turned toward Meechie.

"You still down to get something to eat?"

"Hell yeah, I thought Michelle was going to cook you something. Where you want to go?" Meechie eagerly replied.

"I don't know something different than the burrito truck. I'm hungry than a muthafucka. You can't think of anything?"

"You know I drove over to Louis's Burgers off of Rosecrans and they got some good ass grub." Meechie glared at Twin Deuce in a devious way.

"Over in slob territory across the street from the park?"

"Yeah."

"I'm down if you down. But we better go through the drive-thru." Twin Deuce shook his head.

"That's the only way I'll go over there."

They hopped into the Monte Carlo and rolled up to the fast food restaurant. When they made it to the parking lot it was totally empty in the drive–thru. They were looking around paranoid as they ordered their food. It seemed to take longer than it should for their food to come up.

"You think they're trying to set us up?" Twin Deuce asked.

"Aw nigga you tripping but they are taking a long ass time with the grub cuz." Meechie replied.

Finally the order came up. After checking the bag to make sure everything was straight they rolled out. Twin Deuce took his food out the bag and started eating on the way.

"Damn cuz, you gone eat right in my face?" Meechie complained while they were at a stop light.

"Aw nigga you don't know how to walk and chew gum. Eat yo pastrami sandwich while you drive nigga." Twin Deuce laughed with food in his mouth.

Meechie laughed also then noticed the light had turned green. He punched on the gas but the car suddenly shut off. He tried to start it back up but it wasn't turning over. He tried it several times but it wouldn't turn over.

"What's wrong with yo car?"

"I don't know but we gone have to get out and push." Meechie said irritably.

Meechie cut on the hazards then the pushed the car over to the side of the street. Once they were parked Meechie went under the hood to see what was going on. Whatever he tried didn't work because the car wouldn't start. Finally he just gave up.

"Look cuz we gone have to walk back to the hood." Meechie said.

"I figured that after the fifteenth try nigga." Twin Deuce laughed.

"Fuck you nigga. I paid two thousand for this muthafucka and it's already tripping."

"I wouldn't even worry about it. Get a tow truck and take it to the mechanic so he can fix that shit and we straight. The hood ain't that far so we can just walk from here. We just got to watch out for those Mayo Lane niggas." Twin nonchalantly replied.

"Yeah that's about it."

They finished eating and hopped out of the Monte Carlo and started walking down Rosecrans Boulevard. They were watching every angle they could; they were trying to make sure no one snuck up on them. As they were walking they happened to see Dizzy from Mayo Lane drive by.

"That nigga seen us cuz." Meechie said.

"No he didn't nigga, now you tripping." Twin Deuce replied.

"Alright my nigga, if he comes back with a whole squad of niggas then you won't think I'm tripping."

"Alright then fuck it let's cut down one of these side streets then cut off into the hood."

"How do you know those Mayonnaise niggas ain't hanging out around here? We'll fuck around and run into a whole pack of them fools." Meechie nervously replied.

"Naw they don't hang this close to Rosecrans. They further away than this. Come on cuz lets raise just in case that nigga Dizzy did see us."

They quickly hit the side street and were able to walk down the block with no problems. They turned the corner and the block was relatively empty. They were still nervous but they began to loosen up as they drew closer to the Block territory. The paranoia kept them both constantly turning around and walking fast. They only had to make it past two or three more blocks before they were in Alondra Block neighborhood. They cut down one more street to make the journey shorter.

"I know we don't have some crabs walking down the street in our hood Blood." A shadow said from a short distance.

"You bullshitting Blood get the muthafuckin strap."

Meechie and Twin Deuce looked at each other then they both took off running. The Pirus that spotted them was close behind with a pack following them. They didn't know if any of the homeboys were hanging out but they were hoping some of the homies with straps would surface once they made it to the hood. Meechie felt like crying while Twin Deuce looked at it as an adrenalin rush. They were gaining a distance on the group of Pirus until they heard a whistle.

Suddenly out of nowhere another pack of Pirus came from behind an alley way. They were trapped. They split up and ran into two different directions. One of the Pirus with a gun decided to shoot at Meechie while the others try to grab Twin Deuce. The bullets flew by Meechie but none were able to hit him. Tears ran down his face hoping the best for Twin Deuce while he continued to run toward the neighborhood.

Two of the Pirus were able to grab a hold of Twin Deuce. After punching him up for a while they dragged him back to the pack. He tried desperately to fight back but both Pirus were bigger and stronger. His efforts were futile as the two Pirus slammed him on the pavement.

"Aw snap Blood this is one of those Laney niggas. I went to school with his punk ass brothers Joseph and Jordan. You know one of them niggas smoked the homie Du-Rock?" A nameless Piru firmly stated.

Twin Deuce looked up at them helplessly knowing that he wasn't about to receive any mercy. The Piru that spoke was unfamiliar but it was obvious that he was a shot caller. The shot caller glanced at his homeboys as if to ask what they were waiting for. In a matter of seconds they began to stomp and beat him. After countless blows to his body he could no longer feel the pain. His body was broken and blood smothered his face. Finally the shot caller waived his hand for the homies to stop. He looked at one of his little homies and nodded his head.

"Ay B-Rock put this crab nigga out of his misery."

B-Rock walked up to Twin Deuce with his thirty-eight snub nose pistol and pointed it right at his head. He looked him in his eye and pulled the trigger. Two bullets shot through Twin Deuce's head and his corpse lied in the middle of the street bloody and broken. The Pirus quickly dispersed to leave his lifeless body to be picked up by the coroners.

20
ENVIRONMENTAL EXTENSIONS

How you lived so fast and died so young!
Melle Mel

"No!!!" Janelle screamed.

"Let me the fuck go Janelle." Twin Ace bitterly replied.

"I can't let you do this Jamil. He was my brother too. But we are going to have to handle it differently this time."

"Fuck that, those slob niggas can't get away with smoking my muthafuckin brother. I'm about to go handle this shit." Twin Ace fired back. He had a chrome long nose thirty-eight at his side.

"We got to live even though Jalil is dead. I can't let you walk out that door." Janelle cried out.

Janelle blocked the door. Karen was balled up in a corner crying her heart out. Sheila had already known to take the children into the bedroom.

"What the fuck are you doing Janelle? They didn't show any mercy to Jalil. Why in the fuck are you stopping me from handling my business." Twin Ace yelled.

"Because I have to protect you from yourself. We have tried it that way and it hasn't worked. Daddy, Joseph and Jordan has tried it that way and it didn't make things better. I just want you to think about what you're doing. Come on Jamil you are smarter than this." Janelle calmly but passionately explained.

"Move the fuck out my way cuz." Twin Ace snapped.

Janelle grabbed his arm and held tightly. It was the same arm that he carried the pistol. He glanced at her viciously trying to snatch away without shooting his only sister. As he easily snatched away from her she got on her knees and grabbed his leg.

"Please Jamil; you have to be the man of the house now. Somebody has to live in order to protect us." Janelle cried.

236

Those words stopped him in his tracks. He never considered it like that. Joseph was in prison; so he was the only Laney man that was able to protect his family. He shook his head wanting to not listen to his conscience. He wanted revenge. He wanted to serve each and every Piru that was involved in killing his brother. He turned around to face his sister and his fiancé. Karen got up from the corner with tears running down her face and walked over to him. Both Karen and Janelle hugged him tightly. Janelle reached for the pistol and slyly took it out of Twin Ace's hand. He never wanted to be like his brothers but he understood the anger. He understood wanting to take it to the streets.

They slowly backed away from the door. Janelle let go so that Karen could escort Twin Ace to the bedroom. Janelle waited for the door to close then she quickly threw on some clothes. She walked back into the room where Sheila was with the children and slightly opened the door.

"I'll be back in a little bit."

She took the thirty-eight and hid it so no one could get a hold of it. She took the bullets out and walked outside. The day was gloomy and there was a chill in the morning air. She wiped the tears from out of her eyes the best she could then looked up at the sky. Her soul was hurting and her bones were aching. She jumped into the El Camino and backed it out of the driveway. She went down three or four blocks searching. She couldn't find what she was looking for. Then as she turned on another block she noticed the pack of young Alondra Block homies hanging out. She pulled up to the curb while everyone was hanging next to a brick wall near an alleyway. She hopped out the car and walked towards the pack. She found the person she was looking for and stood right in front of him. With all her might she punched him in his mouth.

"What the fuck you hit me for Big Nell?" Meechie yelled.

He was hurt and embarrassed as he held his mouth.

"Why in the fuck you run out on my brother? Why in the fuck are you alive and he's dead?" She gritted her teeth.

237

"We were both running. He went in one direction and I went the other way. I didn't know he was caught until just now." Meechie lied.

"That's bullshit nigga because you could have got one of the homies to take you around to see what happened to him." She replied.

She fired on him again right in his mouth. She was squared up with him ready to fight but he didn't want to fight Janelle.

"Look Big Nell I respect Pookie too much to be trying to fight you. But I told you I didn't know he was dead until now. But you best believe that we are going to ride on those Mayo Lane niggas tonight." Meechie vowed.

"I'm not worried about you doing that punk shit. That's not going to bring him back. You supposed to be his road dog you should have manned up if you seen your homeboy in danger. Fuck it though; none of you niggas is his homeboys anyway." She dismissed them with a hand gesture.

She looked up and seen this very attractive chocolate beauty with long pretty hair. Janelle knew how to turn heads but she had to admit that this girl was gorgeous. When the young beauty approached, one of her homegirls whispered something in her ear.

"No!!! How in the fuck did that happen?" She cried.

Janelle was somewhat stunned by the young girl's emotion. She made her way through the crowd and walked in front of Meechie. She practically pushed Janelle to the side. Janelle's natural reaction was to fight but she was more curious than angry.

"Why did you let this happen to Jalil? How could you let this happen?" She screamed at Meechie.

"I didn't let it happen that was just how fucked up it played out. We all just found out today. This is his sister right here." Meechie lowered his head and pointed at Janelle.

Michelle turned towards Janelle and looked at her with tears in her eyes. She gently laid her head on Janelle's chest as if she knew her all her life. Janelle felt obliged to wrap her arms around her. Michelle wept in her arms while Janelle held her tightly.

After a long moment of their embrace she followed Janelle to the El Camino. She got close enough so that Janelle could only hear her.

"My name is Michelle and I was supposed to meet you and your family when Jalil got back from getting something to eat with Meechie. I hate to say this right now but I'm two months pregnant by him." Michelle sobbed.

"How old are you?" Janelle asked.

"Seventeen."

"And you were messing with my brother Jalil like that?"

Michelle nodded her head sadly. Janelle pointed towards the passenger side.

"Get inside so that you can meet everyone else."

Michelle glumly followed her instructions. Before Janelle could take off she gave Meechie one more harsh look.

"We gone ride on those Mayonnaise niggas Big Nell, I promise." Meechie yelled while still holding his mouth.

Janelle rolled her eyes at him and sped off. The ride around the corner to the Laney household was relatively quiet. The radio was on but it was turned down low. Michelle followed Janelle into the house with her head down. She stopped at the door with tears in her eyes.

"Come on in Michelle its okay." Janelle said.

"I was just expecting Jalil to be with me. I won't ever see him again." She began sobbing uncontrollably.

"Its okay baby come on in." Janelle replied.

She wrapped her arm around Michelle and walked her inside. Janelle called everyone into the living room. Everyone looked at the beautiful girl and awaited Janelle's words.

"This is Michelle. She was seeing Jalil before he died and she is now carrying his baby." Janelle announced.

"Hey Michelle, I've seen you around the neighborhood. You know Karen right?" Twin Ace replied.

Michelle shyly nodded and smiled.

239

"Welcome I wanted you to meet her so that you could welcome her to the family."

One week later after Janelle introduced Michelle to the family they were all packed up to move. Janelle made sure to have a private funeral for Twin Deuce. She only wanted family to attend so that she could break ties with the hood. She had a few more arrangements to make before they made the move. Michelle was underage but Janelle promised her once she became legal she was welcome to move out to Marino Valley. She wanted to make sure they kept ties with one another.

A few days after Jalil Laney was put to rest the family moved out of the house in Compton. Janelle had bought a beautiful four bedroom home in Marino Valley from the house she had sold in Compton. She also had some money that Baby Gangster had put away that Mama Jo kept hidden for the time Janelle would make that move. Janelle didn't know anything about it until a few days before Mama Jo passed away. She had never stopped going to school and now that she was finished she had plans of opening up her beauty salon. She had already found a building out that way and was preparing everything for her new business.

Twin Ace eventually found him a job as an auto-mechanic while still attending school for the same trade. He had picked up a love for cars from classes he had taken at Dominguez High School in Compton. He had a lot on his plate but he was ready to settle down with Karen. He had saved up and with the help of Janelle he bought her a nice ring. They wanted to get married outside at a park so he put his money together for their wedding. Sheila helped Janelle fix up the new shop and they worked together until other hair stylists started renting booths. Joe Jr. was beginning to get big and command the respect of the other kids in his neighborhood. Janelle happened to be home on a Sunday listening to him talk outside to some of his new found friends.

"I'm Little J-Ridah from Alondra Block Compton Crip. You better recognize cuz." He yelled out.

"Joe bring yo ass in the house right now." Janelle yelled outside.

Joe walked into the house with his head down knowing he was in trouble. He walked into the bedroom where Janelle overheard him and stood before her.

"You wanted me Auntie Nell?" He humbly asked.

"Yeah, don't let me ever hear you say you are from any gang again. You hear me?"

"Okay Auntie Nell but I just was letting that punk..."

"I don't care what you were letting him know. You are Joseph Laney Jr. a member of the Laney family and not the member of any gang." She sharply interrupted him.

He nodded and she pointed for him to go back outside. Janelle got up after that to fix dinner with the help of Sheila and Karen. Karen had taken a few classes at Riverside Community College so she would make it home a little bit before dinner during the week. Twin Ace would make it home shortly after her. Janelle tried to have everyone sit at the dinner table all together at least once a week and that was usually on Sunday. Twin Ace would usually go sit on his porch in the evening time which wasn't always safe to do while living in Compton. Shortly after cleaning up, Karen would join him so that they could talk.

"Ya'll want some Kool Aid while ya'll sitting on the porch." Janelle peaked out the door to offer.

They both nodded their head and Janelle came back outside with two full glasses of Tropical Punch Kool Aid.

"I got a letter from Daddy in the mail yesterday. I wanted to wait until everyone was settled so that I could read it." Janelle said.

"I only remember Mama only reading a letter from him maybe once or twice back in the day." Twin Ace commented.

"Mama used to read us his letters a lot more often back in the day but then one day she stopped. She stopped going to visit him and everything. When she went to visit him after Jason died she hadn't seen him for at least ten years or received a letter. But I got in touch with him when we were moving and made sure that I wrote him and he wrote me back. I told him the most I could tell him about Mama and our brothers." Janelle explained.

"Well go get the letter so we can hear what he has to say." Twin Ace eagerly replied.

"Yeah Janelle I want to hear it too." Karen smiled.

Janelle went into the bedroom to quickly retrieve the letter. By this time everyone was on the porch. Janette was walking by now while Joseph Jr. and Sheila sat next to each other on a swing bench that was on the porch. Karen and Twin Ace sat on the steps as usual.

"Alright ya'll ready? This is what he said." Janelle began.

Dear family I hope this letter finds you in the best of spirits. I was sincerely sad when I heard that Josephine passed away from cancer. I wish I could have been there for her at least once. She was a good woman that picked a man that didn't know how to be a man and she deserved better than that. Please believe that I loved her with all my heart and I regret that I didn't show it in a better way. I've lost three boys because of this game and it hurts my heart because they were attempting to follow in my footsteps. I was never a good example to follow because I never had any good examples to follow. I developed my ideals of manhood after many years of being incarcerated. When I no longer spoke or seen your mother I had to look within myself and address my own issues. I hadn't learned how to love or to be in love. I didn't know the responsibilities of a man and how to truly define manhood. I just recently began to educate myself after doing many years in prison. As for my sons, I should have shown them a better way. Joseph was my pride and joy when he was born but he carried much anger in him like me. Jordan was a child that had supreme courage and I was able to see that at a young age. My boy Jason was always the observant one. I remember him as a young boy looking around trying to study everyone and everything. He reminded me of my biological father. I never got to know my son Jalil and that hurts me even more because he was probably a leader in his own right. As for Jamil I want to say this to you son.

I love you with all my heart. But you have to be a better man than me and your brothers could ever be. Your wonderful sister who is my only beloved daughter told me everyone was moving to Marino Valley. I say this to you all. Don't be extensions of the environment you just left. Don't look at Marino Valley as a place to escape but a place you have arrived after changing your thinking and behavior. We don't want to carry what we had in Compton to another place and have the same problems we had before. I hope to hear from you and when I do I want to hear about you thriving and doing well. I talked to my sister Pat and she told me both her sons are incarcerated for long periods of time. I see many Black boys come into the penitentiary and are suddenly forced to adapt to a violent way of life. That was what happened to me. They are forced to be soldiers before they even can grasp what a man is. I'm glad to hear I have a grandson and a granddaughter; hopefully Joseph can get out and be a father to his son even though I wasn't one for him. Tell my grandbabies that I love them and I pray for them every night. I sincerely love each and every one of you with all my heart.
P.S. Congratulations Jamil on you getting married.

Your Father and Grand Father
Michael Marcus Laney

Janelle let a tear fall from her face while she folded the letter up and put it back inside the envelope. Twin Ace at that moment was no longer Twin Ace but Jamil Laney. Karen held him tightly as he made this silent resolve. Joe Jr. hugged his mother while Sheila nodded her head contemplating the words that were just read. For a moment everyone was lost in his or her own thoughts until Janette grabbed her mother by the leg and laughed out loud. It brought everyone back to the present and they all laughed with Janette who kept tugging on Janelle's leg.

THE END!!!

243

Coming soon
@ www.ensbooks.com

Coming soon
@ www.ensbooks.com

PaPa Sak is a voice for the streets and the Black community for those that are usually misrepresented and misunderstood. His goal is to bring humanity to these characters and to bring understanding to other unpopular perspectives. His characters come from people he has known or interacted with at one time or another. One of his main focuses is to shed spiritual insight on stories that should be told in the Black experience and abroad. He is also a profound orator and inspirational speaker ranging in poetry, gang & street lifestyle, male and female relationships, manhood training, spirituality, Hip Hop and history. He is definitely a literary force in the new Millennium. You can find him at: http://www.myspace.com/papasakkingpen, Facebook or **www.ensbooks.com**

CPSIA information can be obtained
at www.ICGtesting.com
Printed in the USA
LVHW051920130323
741526LV00007B/547

9 780970 449542